moon river

a novel

Amber D. Tran

Jan-Carol
Publishing, Inc

Moon River
Amber D. Tran

Published July 2016
Little Creek Books
Imprint of Jan-Carol Publishing, Inc.
Cover Design: Tara Sizemore
All rights reserved
Copyright © Amber D. Tran

ISBN: 978-1-945619-00-7
Library of Congress Control Number: 2016946903

You may contact the publisher:
Jan-Carol Publishing, Inc.
PO Box 701
Johnson City, TN 37605
publisher@jancarolpublishing.com
jancarolpublishing.com

For Marcus.

You are still the voice inside our heads.

One

It was the spring of 1999 when I first met Ryan Mills.

A dark-haired boy with coffee ring glasses and that morning's breakfast folded in the corners of his mouth, my first impression of him was nothing less than an insanely fragile kid with a penchant for the *Goosebumps* series. My little heart didn't know, at that moment, that fragility could strengthen into a sorrowful, enigmatic substance in a matter of five years.

The first time we met, I remembered everything.

He probably only knew of me as the new girl on the bus. I was fine with that.

After my family moved from Stream Ridge, West Virginia, to a back-country gravel road almost 12 miles west, I switched bus routes. I went from riding Bus #20 for five minutes to enduring Bus #35's rocky, nauseating route for at least 45 minutes. Twists and turns, dips and bends, potholes as many as caution signs, the Appalachian region was an unforgiving sort, the kind of natural beauty draped in shades of hazel and gold that never let you draw in its morning dew without something in return.

At least, my Meemaw once said something similar to that, perhaps a little less poetic and more hard-lipped, while she canned deer meat for the winter.

It happened the Friday before Memorial Day, the first time I made eye contact with Ryan.

I followed classmate, new neighbor, and freshly-attained best friend Audrey Springs down the bus aisle. Her shoulder-length white-blonde hair whipped side to side behind her, like a horse tail swatting flies, and she was cursing loud children in her Southern tongue as we made our way to our seat. "Now dang, you kids! Use your inside voices!" A halo of sunlight complemented her hair.

One kid snapped back, "Shut yer mouth!" He barely had four teeth in his rotting gums. The inside of his mouth was the color of tar. Stained saliva solidified in the corners of his mouth like dirt underneath fingernails. We called kids like him baby chewers.

Audrey was raised by her grandmother to never snap back, so I watched her bite her bottom lip and slide into our bus seat.

She came from a farming family where everyone was practically born and raised in Bear Run Road, West Virginia, the place where I now lived. Her house began as a small, flesh-colored trailer perched a few feet from the nearest creek. After a few years, the house transformed. Her father, Todd Springs, loved starting projects. What he loved more than starting projects was never finishing them. Just the week before, he gave up on finishing the two-story structure that jutted from the left side of the mobile home. It was currently nothing more than a wooden skeleton, with only some beams for a spine and one floorboard for a leg.

That was why I called her home the Lego house. It looked like it was patched together with discarded puzzle pieces from various Lego sets.

I caught the last of Audrey's statement as she readjusted her Minnie Mouse backpack. "—so we don't get in trouble."

"Okay." She must have been talking about the Springs Reunion coming up that Sunday. Audrey described it as a family reunion with lame country music, and a bunch of old people sunbathing in lawn chairs and drinking all of the lemonade. They had it every Memorial Day weekend.

Her favorite part was when all of the old people left, because that meant all of the adults brought out the beer and moonshine. It was just the spring before that her mother, Tracy Springs, shattered the body of a Bud Light bottle across a tree stump and chased Todd around with its brown, shimmering teeth. The only reason Tracy stopped chasing him was because she heard the song "What's Up?" by 4 Non Blondes on the nearby radio and immediately stopped to sing, "And I say, *hey, yeah yeah, hey, yeah yeah.*"

My life wasn't as interesting as Audrey's. My family was relatively normal: the kind of normal where my stepfather blamed everything on the Amish, and my older sister thought that hibernation only existed in fairy tales. The only real person in my family was my mother, who made a fresh pot of coffee every morning and named every single rose in the front yard. She liked to clean the house every Sunday while blasting her Bob Seger CD on the Gateway computer.

"Psst."

Audrey and I both folded over the back of our bus seat. Fourth grader Kimmie Henderson shook a coloring book. "What do you think? Purple or blue? Laney wants purple, but that's gay, so I said blue." She nodded next to her, pointing out the freckle-faced Laney Hanson, sitting with folded arms and her hip-length hair in static-driven knots all behind her. With their outdoor tans and sun-kissed hair, they were the epitomes of southern summer tomboys.

Laney and Kimmie grew up together. They had known each other since they were physically capable of knowing another human being. They had been sitting with one another on the bus since Laney was in 1st grade, Kimmie in 2nd. Laney was in the same grade as me and Audrey, the 3rd.

"Why not pink?" That was Audrey's favorite color.

Before I could say anything, Laney scoffed. "Pink's dumb. No."

That was when my eyes caught something shifting in the seat behind them. Someone was squeezing a backpack up against the window, a lazy engineered way to create a pillow.

Soon I was able to follow the length of a pale arm until it became swallowed in the shoulder of a blue t-shirt. A black-haired boy pressed his rosy cheek against the padded strap of his backpack, his coal-colored eyes closing as he blended between the bus window and the corner of his seat.

One side of his glasses propped up behind his ear, while the other smashed against the backpack's pencil pocket. I traced the shape of a Game Boy in the front pocket.

Everyone in Stream Ridge, West Virginia, knew each other. I practically knew the middle names of all 46 of my classmates, the biggest class in Stream Ridge since 1959. I came from a town that had two traffic lights, each always blinking yellow: one in front of the high school and the other near the Pennsylvania state line. We had to drive over 30 miles in any direction just to get to Walmart.

Glancing at him for less than a few seconds, I remembered who he was. His name was Ryan Mills. He was Kimmie's older cousin. The two of them were raised like brother and sister, having grown up as neighbors for most of their life. Ryan was also one of my cousin's best friends. My cousin, Scott, sometimes mentioned Ryan in small talk, but I didn't know more than Ryan's fascination with the PlayStation and his love for his horse, named Tadpole.

I stared at him long enough that my vision blurred, like splashing away a water reflection in a puddle of warm rain; then I had to blink myself out of my own strange, studious behavior. That was how I learned his blue t-shirt was ripped a little at the collar, and there was a penny-sized scab on the tip of his chin. Instead of studying him, I now gave him his own backstory. I made up a life for him, like where his scab came from and what blue t-shirt he would wear that weekend.

Kimmie kicked the seat on which I balanced. "Abigail? What the hell are you looking at?" She was a strong-willed, rebellious girl. Her vocabulary mostly consisted of the f-word and the word *dude*. She never used adjectives, just curse words.

"What?" came out of my mouth far louder than I anticipated, far more boisterous than I had intended.

That was when Ryan's eyes shot open, and he noticed me noticing him.

We didn't break eye contact for at least three seconds. The doughy surface of his cheeks baked darker red the longer we stared at one another. Ryan couldn't see my knees rocking left and right, skin stuck against the brown vinyl of the bus seat: the nervousness running straight out of me through my knee bones.

I didn't know what to do, so I threw myself into Audrey, jamming her between me and the window, and she cried out in pain. She dropped Jesus's name in vain. A handful of blonde hair snapped against the side of my neck. Even Laney and Kimmie gasped when I wedged my shoulder into my best friend's side. It was a surprise that Randy White, the bus driver, didn't immediately order us to knock it off.

At least half of the bus was now quiet and watching the commotion developing in our seat.

After slapping at Audrey, who was slapping at me, my eyes crawled up to see if Ryan was still looking.

He was.

But then his facial expression shifted. The skin underneath his eyes held firm, and just one side of his mouth turned up, but he didn't look like he was trying to smile. Instead, it looked like he was trying *not* to smile. Holding on to that look, Ryan slid back against the window, the backpack pillow squished between the warm Plexiglas and his cheeks, and his eyes closed behind his wide-framed glasses. The smile still lingered. I remembered that.

"What the heck was that for?" Audrey yanked on my long brown hair. "Gosh darn, Abigail, you got me good."

Absorbing the color of Ryan's t-shirt like watercolor on a blank canvas, I blurted, "Blue," and sat back down.

Kimmie and Laney packed away their purple markers.

After that first encounter, I didn't see Ryan for another few months.

During that time, Audrey and I embraced the oncoming summer, with all of its hot cruelties and unjust tests of our resilience. The day of the Springs Reunion, we met two boys from Pennsylvania. Their names were Jamie and Richie. Jamie dropped the f-bomb more times than Kimmie, and Richie only wore clothes with the Flintstones on them. They were staying with my other neighbors, the Rogers family: Aunt Judy, Eustace, and their middle-aged son, named Buck.

Aunt Judy wasn't my aunt, but that's what my step-father Patrick called her, so that's what I called her. She was in her mid-80s, with brittle-blue veiny hands, and she fed her 40 cats nothing but chunks of Wonder Bread. There were mornings where I had woken up to the screeching howls of wild cat fights, only to see small patches of blood and fur on her Welcome mat on the way to the bus stop. The bread was always all gone.

Summer seasoned us when Audrey and I discovered Buck in my swimming pool with Jamie and Richie clutched underneath his barreled shoulders. Through his winter white beard, Buck told me and Audrey, "It's boys only time to swim," so we fumed only on the inside and walked back to my house. Relaying that type of dialogue to my mother, she immediately called Patrick. Before we knew it, Jamie and Richie were gone and Buck was in jail.

At the age of nine, Audrey and I both learned the meaning of the word *molestation*, and that word lay across the films of our eyes for the first half of the summer.

We tried to endure the spite of the season together. During the driest of days, Audrey and I pulled the summer's spill of every-17-years-cicada shells from cracking tree bark and lay them on the gravel road in groups of five. Five was Audrey's ideal number. She believed it to be holy. It was her trinity. So we pretended those cicada exoskeletons were walnuts, and we brought down stone after stone until the insects' shells were nothing more than what looked like shredded cassette tape spit out of an old boom box.

We didn't have to tell each other that we actually pretended the cicada shells were Buck's face. We just knew. We knew by the hard tears in our eyes, and the road's gravel dirt sticking to our cheeks. But we kept screaming at one another, "We gotta break these walnuts!" while sniffing in the dry summer dust and the dead cicadas' ashes.

By that June, Patrick finally gave up trying to convince me and my sister, Diana, that the pool needed to be taken down in the backyard, because according to him, "It was filled with pedophile juices." My sister, who was four years older than me, was adamant about keeping the pool so she had an excuse to lay out in the sun and tan. Her goal was to start her freshman year of high school with golden, glittering skin. Lately, all she could tan was her face, and that was because so many freckles were coming to the surface that they looked like one solid sheet of freckle.

The first few weeks of summer, it didn't rain. The grass outside was sandy, and the trees were skeletal with holey, brittle leaves, and they broke instead of ripping. While Diana sunbathed on our pool deck, while Patrick mowed the grass without wearing a t-shirt or sunblock, and while my mother smoked her eighth cigarette of the day and flicked her ashes in her marble ashtray, I sat in my room and doodled in my journal with my blue pen.

The pen had to be blue. Ever since I noticed Ryan on the bus that Friday before Memorial Day weekend, everything I did, everything I owned, had to be blue. My mother was confused the first time I asked to play as the blue piece in Monopoly Junior instead of the green piece, since green had been my favorite color for as long as we could remember. My favorite Powerpuff Girl was now Bubbles instead of Buttercup, because she was the blue Powerpuff Girl. I even stopped wearing my emerald earrings, my birthstone, so I could slap on fake sapphire stickies from the gumball machine.

My journal became a hub for Ryan, a consecrated sanctuary where my personal thoughts for him and about him were protected by my 50-cent lock with a lion's mouth as the keyhole. I documented random facts—like how on the last day of school, he and Scott stole four extra bags of chocolate milk from the cafeteria, and they eventually brought the square-shaped packages outside during recess and stepped on them like they were roaches, and chocolate milk exploded like liquid fireworks all along the basketball court—and I drew a cartoon version of him for every year he grew up, and when he turned 18, he was perfect and handsome and symmetrical.

During one of our weekly phone calls, Audrey dared me to search for Ryan's number in the phonebook. The first step was actually finding the long-forgotten phonebook in my house. My mother rarely used it, and Patrick's memory, the same one that could never remember where his truck keys last were, somehow always remembered his friends' and coworkers' phone numbers after just one dial.

My chances of actually finding the right Mills phone number, however, were nearly impossible, especially after I opened it to the M section of Waver County and saw what seemed like hundreds of Mills typed along the columns.

My update to Audrey in our next phone call was, "I failed my mission. I don't know his parents' names." Fearfully, I rolled the coiled phone cord around my toes. I wasn't sure why I was nervous.

She smacked her lips together. She must have been chewing something, like gum or the dead ends of her white hair. "Why don't you just try from the top and call and ask for Ryan?"

"Are you stupid or somethin'? There were like, hundreds of Mills in the phonebook."

"Then's best you start now." She hung up after that.

Two

One weekend in June, Laney drove an ATV to my house wearing nothing but a bathing suit tank-top and boy's swimming trunks. She wasn't even wearing a helmet or shoes. Thankfully, my mother was asleep in her bedroom, with all of the windows open and two fans blowing down on her, the drone somehow either masking or mixing with the four-wheeler engine as it cracked on loose gravel at the base of our driveway.

"Get your suit and come on." Laney pronounced *get* as "git," and the word *come* barely stretched out in its entirety. She was more of a tomboy than a redneck: the older I got, the more difficult it was to tell the two apart. Her most defining features were her hip-length blonde hair, which was either always in a ponytail at the base of her neck or in a chain of braided gold down the hollow of her spine, and her freckles. She wore freckles like Marilyn Monroe wore her signature mole.

That day, her hair dangled like a braid of sticky honey. Her bangs curled around her temples.

I fetched my bathing suit from the bathroom and snuck out to the garage. My mother never would have approved of me riding a four-wheeler driven by my helmetless, shoeless, nine-year-old friend.

We traversed the gravel terrain of Red Cliff Hill and White Run Road, the road where Laney lived. We stopped only once to pick and eat some roadside raspberries, keeping the leftovers cradled in the bellies of our t-shirts as we got back on the four-wheeler. If Laney wanted a raspberry while driving, without saying a word, she would move her chin over her shoulder with an angler-fish gaping mouth, and I would plop a raspberry or two on the tip of her tongue.

It wasn't until we passed her house on White Run Road that I realized we were going to Kimmie's.

When we found Kimmie inside her house going through her mother's belongings in her mother's '50s style bedroom-bathroom suite, we immediately lost interest in swimming and instead were focused on the slew of naughty magazines and R-rated VHS tapes sprawled out on the bed. Even though Kimmie had two older sisters, they were never home. The oldest sister, Kaitlyn, was a high school junior just put on birth control, so she was constantly visiting her boyfriend and frolicking on every piece of furniture in his parents' house. The middle sister, Kylie, often stayed at a classmate's house during the summer, a sort of tradition she rarely broke.

As for Kimmie's mother, she worked as a bank teller at the People's Bank in New Martinsville. She didn't say anything about her father, who seemed not to exist.

I learned all of this in a matter of seconds after hearing Kimmie utter, under her breath, "This is why they shouldn't leave me here to fuckin' rot by myself," as she sorted the magazines in alphabetical order. She tossed her long hair over her shoulder as she continued to organize the pornographic items. Instead of wondering why her mother owned so many naughty things, I paid more attention to the dye style of Kimmie's hair: white-blonde tips and dark brown roots.

We gathered as many of the magazines as we could and ran for Kimmie's bedroom. Funneling onto the top bunk bed, we opened the first magazine to a centerfold of two middle-aged women touching each other's chests. I didn't think either of the women was attractive. It may have been their feathered hairstyle and their lavender eye shadow that turned me off from the idea. I imagined both of them as singers from Divinyls, singing the song, "I Touch Myself," while rolling around on purple silk sheets on a water bed framed in oak.

Emanating the wisest of auras, Kimmie pointed at the blonde-haired woman. "See her boobs? See how there are veins in her boobs?" We nodded. "That means she's a slut."

On point, Laney and I both glanced down at the flesh around our bathing suit tops. We didn't see any veins.

"It does not," Laney quipped. "How do veins say something like that?"

"If you have veins like that in your boobs, it means you're a slut. Trust me."

Then we looked at Kimmie's chest. Aside from tan lines from her bathing suit top, we didn't see any veins underneath her dark skin, either.

Instead of arguing, we did as she said and we trusted her. We didn't have a reason not to believe her.

On the way home, I asked Laney to make the loop at the end of Postlewaite Ridge so she would have to drive by Ryan's house. She didn't argue. When she took me home that evening, she was the good friend that I knew she was, and slowed down right as we passed the Mills house. The grin on her face pushed aside the lake of freckles swelling across the slope of her nose.

Ryan's family lived about a two-minute walk from Kimmie's house. Laney practically idled the four-wheeler as she drove past the cabin-like structure adorned with its fairy stone statues, dead garden beds, and cutesy yard decorations, like a garden flag of a Precious Angel and a stone slab layered in rings of various colors: red, yellow, white, and blue. The porch stretched across the entire front of the house. I could see dust bunnies dancing in the corners from the road. A single rocking chair trembled near the front door. A basket of fake flowers lay in its belly.

"Aunt Norma is different," Laney called out over the gentle hum of the four-wheeler. We were going so slow the crunching sounds of the tires rolling along the gravel were actually louder than the engine itself. "You'll like her, but yeah, she's different."

That meant Laney believed I would eventually meet Ryan's mother. At least, that was what I assumed when she referred to her Aunt Norma.

I went home that night documenting Ryan's mother's name in my journal. Norma Mills. Right before bed, I opened the phone book for the second time that summer. Unable to find a phone number for a Norma Mills, I determined that their phone number was listed under his father's name, or they didn't have it listed at all. My next goal was to find out Ryan's dad's name. I wasn't sure how to accomplish that, but that didn't stop me from fabricating ideas: Roger Mills, Lonny Mills, Sir Vincent Cyrus Mills, Ryan Mills, Sr.

Shortly after Independence Day, Kimmie called me and invited me to her house for a small sleepover. Taking advantage of the slim opportunity to see Ryan, I dressed in my best clothes: a white and blue striped spaghetti-strap shirt, my newest pair of beige shorts, my sister's hand-me-down leather sandals from Walmart, and my blue stone necklace from the Giant Eagle clearance rack. I even packed my favorite pair of pajamas, the ones with silky blue pants and a fleece top with clouds of fake fur at the shoulders, just in case he came over in the evening to watch *Dirty Dancing* with us.

When my mother dropped me off at Kimmie's house, she said good-bye in her usual farewell cadence. "Make good choices." I closed the rusted Chevy Blazer door before she finished saying "good." I already knew.

The moment I stepped through the kitchen door, I heard a high-pitched, nasally voice come from the living room. "Oh my God. Why is she here?"

The voice belonged to self-proclaimed most popular girl at Gunners Valley School, Angelle Rose. She was the kind of 3rd grader who stuffed her bra; she'd worn string bikinis since she was seven. She lay like a weed in the flowerbed of pillows stretched across Kimmie's living room floor, especially since Angelle's artificial strawberry blonde hair (if anyone referred to her hair as blonde or light red, she would correct them with a bitterness thick enough to taste) had a sort of fluorescent glow in the block of sunlight spilling from one of the living room windows.

Kimmie and Angelle were best friends. They fought worse than sisters, and spent more days hating one another than showing off their matching BFF necklaces from Dollar General. The fact that I saw Angelle wedged between Kimmie and Laney on the sea of pillows meant that they were currently on the mend.

"I invited her. Shut the fuck up." Swinging a cushion like a baseball bat, Kimmie brought a pillow straight across Angelle's face. The three of us spent the next few minutes laughing hysterically and guessing the shape of Angelle's orange foundation print on the pink pillow, while she feigned tears underneath her mascara-ringed eyes, all the while somehow finding enough energy to check her reflection in the television case at least four different times.

I knew something was up when Angelle looked at the grandfather clock and said to nobody in particular, "Nyla's gonna be home in an hour." She was talking about Kimmie's mother. Kimmie and Laney seemed to understand the honest phrase hidden underneath Angelle's statement, for they both wriggled from the mouth of pillows and started for the basement door. My ears didn't filter her voice the way Kimmie's and Laney's did.

The entire time they whispered amongst themselves, I stared at the slew of PlayStation games stacked in the television case. I saw one of my favorite games near the bottom of the stack: *Parasite Eve*.

Two voices called from the kitchen. "Abigail, c'mon." The only reason I went was because neither of the voices belonged to Angelle. I trusted them.

I should have known something was going on when we got into the basement and Laney sat at least four arms' length away from me. She was on the sofa, her long legs folded and clutched against her chest, and she wouldn't even look at me. Did I say something earlier that upset her? While we watched an episode of *Friends*, I had made the comment that Laney had the same hair style as Phoebe. Perhaps that had offended her, in some way.

Before I had time to ask her what was wrong, Kimmie came back from the adjoining computer room. She wanted to play some music from Napster. When we didn't hear anything, we knew that she couldn't get it to run. She, too, sat on the sofa next to Laney. I was sitting on the floor—had been since we walked into the basement—so it was strange that they didn't follow to sit next to me or at least invite me onto the couch.

They were still whispering to one another as if I wasn't right there. I pretended that I didn't hear my name two different times.

As for Angelle, she emerged from the back part of the basement, from behind all of the cardboard boxes of Christmas decorations. She held a dolphin plushie the shape of a middle-sized dog in her arms.

When Laney saw the dolphin, she rolled her eyes. "This again? Really?"

"Not for you." Angelle dropped the dolphin on the floor in front of me. "For her."

"What's the dolphin for?" I reached out and touched it. It was just a standard dolphin plushie, probably from Sea World, so I wasn't sure why Laney was looking at it with a heavy, calculated glare. She practically burned holes in its fabric, her grimace was so malicious. It was a baby blue color with a white belly. Its fins were the size of my hands. It smelled like basements smell: like it had been packed away in some discarded box for its entire life. Its perfume reminded me of mildew, and my Granny's old house in Pennsylvania. Neither smell was one I particularly enjoyed.

Angelle flashed a grin that was so bright she could light up a backyard—or so theatrical and feigned that she could bring down an entire room with a simple snap of her fingers. I couldn't tell which. "You can't just be a part of our group without an initiation."

I frowned at her remark. "What are you talking about?"

"Us," she added, esoterically pointing at herself, Laney, and Kimmie, without indicating me at all. She was referring to Kimmie, Laney, and herself. I guessed *their* group was different from *our* group. "You can't just come over and be in our group. You have to earn it."

Her statements didn't make any sense to me. Regardless of my uneasy friendship at that moment with Angelle, we had been friends before, since as early as kindergarten, but her desperation for popularity transformed her into an artificial beast: a pretty young thing with boxed hair color, Kleenex breasts, and drug store eye shadow. Halfway through 3rd grade, I stopped sitting with her at lunch, on account of I was fed up with hearing her make fun of me and Laney: me, because I was the poor girl still wearing last year's summer sandals; and Laney, because she preferred to wear boys' clothes with Hawaiian flowers and drawstrings, instead of dresses with roses and white lace.

Laney grabbed a pillow and pressed her mouth against it. "This is stupid." Her voice sounded like it came from underwater.

"Shh." Kimmie elbowed her in the side.

They didn't give me a lot of time to think about what was happening. In all honesty, I thought the dolphin was some sort of personal relic of Nyla's, and that I had to mutilate it in order to become part of their group. I only spent a few seconds considering that before I moved my attention elsewhere, focusing on the green N64 near me, and the pile of bathing suits from Kaitlyn and Kylie near the washing machine, waiting to be rinsed clean. The smell of chlorine occasionally brushed across my nose, only momentarily replacing the musty smell of the basement floor.

That was when Angelle pointed down at the dolphin and smiled eerily. "Make out with the dolphin."

"What?" Moments later, I couldn't help but to laugh. "Why would I make out with a dolphin?"

"You have to. You can't be a part of this group without making out with the dolphin." Then she sneered. "Have you never made out with anyone before? Is that it?"

I held my tongue. Instead of giving in to Angelle's game, I remained silent on the basement floor. My knees ached. I rubbed the pads of my fingers over the lingering sticky trails of Popsicle juice staining the length of my forearm. In just a look, I tried to inflict a fatal injection in the side of her thin, tanned neck. Nothing happened. Realizing the absurdity of my intention, I calmly massaged both of my pale eyes and took in a deep breath.

Finally, the silence broke. Angelle snorted in laughter. "Figures you haven't. If you don't do this, then you have to go home." She bounced from one hip to the other. Expectedly, the two round protrusions from her chest remained fixed and unmoved.

"She doesn't have to go home," Kimmie said. Then she looked right at me. "You don't have to go home."

Angelle snapped, her arms jolting straight at her sides, "Yes, she does! She does if she doesn't make out with the dolphin!" She even stomped. The whole time, I stared at her Kleenex boobs and waited for them to magically bounce. They never wriggled to life. "She has to do this! She has to!"

Terrified, I quickly looked over at Kimmie and Laney, waiting for one of them to tell me that it was all a joke—that they were just teasing me, testing me, an effort to determine how far I would go to fit in with their group. However, they didn't do anything other than stay in place on the couch and avoid eye contact. Laney was chewing on the inside of her mouth, and Kimmie was biting her nails.

Was this happening? Was that why Laney avoided me the moment we stepped into the basement, because she knew what was going to happen?

I must have taken too long to gather my options, for Angelle snickered into her sunburnt shoulder. "I changed my mind." She kicked the dolphin closer to me. "You have to have sex with it."

What?

Hearing her say that, the bottom of my stomach ripped open and all of my nerves spread out in an incarnadine puddle of guts and innards around me. The soothing, warm sensation that spread from the core of my body was so terrifyingly calm that I had to glance down to make sure I didn't pee myself, the feeling so familiar in the back of my memory. My palms grew clammy. I would be a liquefied puddle of my own organs and waste in minutes.

"Angelle, fuck that. No. Now you're just bein' weird." Kimmie didn't say anything more than that, however. She didn't even encourage me not to have sex with the dolphin. She just continued to sit there and chew her nails. For a brief moment, I didn't exist to them. There was nothing to my transparent composition anymore. They could see right through me.

Laney was looking at the top of her hand for so long, her eyes were drawing shapes in her skin wrinkles. A moment longer, her eyes would turn into lasers and she would burn herself, she was so fixated on the up-close scaly nature of her backhand.

Anything my two friends could do not to look at me, they did.

I exhaled through my nose. "Really? I have to do this?"

Kimmie, avoiding eye contact, shrugged her shoulders. Laney didn't do anything.

At that moment, they weren't my friends. They were just pawns in Angelle's sick game involving me and a dolphin plushie.

I didn't even consider having sex with the dolphin plushie as an option. It barely grazed the padded insides of my brain. The more I sat there in silence, however, my body found by the spotlight of glances from my so-called friends surrounding me, I worried. I turned my worriment into fabrication, and then that fabrication transformed into an intoxicating blend that seeped into my veins, solidified, and blocked all of my passages; then I couldn't stop worrying.

Angelle was the most popular girl in my class. She had power. She worked her authority over the less fortunate kids. She had ruled the 3rd grade. If she wanted to, she could ruin me.

The fear of that overwhelmed me. Eventually, the film over my eyes turned into a sheet of oil water, and I succumbed to Angelle's plan. Blinded, numb, just a young girl wanting to start 4th grade without any hindrances, without the rumor mill flooded with my name, I stood up and pulled my white and blue striped spaghetti strap shirt over my head. From my belly button up, I was pale and nude.

Next, I unbuckled my brown sandals, kicked them aside, and knelt down to the dolphin. When Kimmie saw me reach for the dolphin, she gasped, said something like, "Oh my God, she's gonna do it," and then she and Laney each huddled underneath a knitted blanket, shielding themselves from the R-rated scene about to take place on the floor.

"Naked," Angelle ordered.

Shameless, I stripped completely naked. My bare, tiny, pink body trembled in the basement light overhead.

"Make sex noises," she commanded.

Unabashed, I started fake-moaning and saying things like, "Yeah, baby." In the pit of my voice, I was begging for mercy, while also asking everyone to look away; but nobody heard me.

"Hump it," she decreed.

Brazen, I did everything that she asked of me and more.

I knew when Laney and Kimmie peeked over the blanket, for they would shriek together, a blend of high-pitched noises that belonged in some sort of

Disney movie. Meanwhile, Angelle monitored me like a teacher punishing a misbehaving student. The look of her arms folded underneath her chest, the tarnished flash in her brown eyes as she watched my every move, my every shared moment with the dolphin plushie...it was enough that my brain grew more green the longer I watched her.

I worried how much longer it would be before I lost my breakfast all over myself. Swallowing the bile rising in my throat, I continued.

I didn't know what real sex was. My only taste of it was peeking through my fingers during sex scenes in movies when my mother asked me not to look, because otherwise, I wouldn't know why I needed to close my eyes. I didn't know the anatomy, where to put what, or where and when and why. On the floor, holding the dolphin between my legs and pressing my face against its floppy fin, I rocked back and forth, rubbing myself against it, kissing its eyes and mimicking noises that women made when they were having sex with men. I made the noises they made in movies, because I didn't know what sex sounded like in real life.

After a few minutes, Angelle called out, "Okay, stop, that's enough." She sounded terrifyingly calm. For just an instant, she sounded like she cared.

When she gave me the order, I opened my eyes and glanced down at the dolphin plushie packed between my legs. It wouldn't look at me. One of its eyes was missing, and I wondered if the eye was missing before I thrust it underneath me.

Angelle laughed for a few seconds and then said in a motherly voice, "There you go. Now you're part of our group."

I fell back on my hands, legs stretched out in front of me, and I couldn't quite absorb what I had just done. Did I just...? With a dolphin?

Angry, I kicked the dolphin away and lunged at my pile of clothes and sandals. Tears formed in my eyes, and before I knew it, they spilled down my cheeks and onto my bare legs. I didn't practice any self-control as I clutched my clothes and sandals for dear life, crying into them like they were a pillow to sleep on at night.

It wasn't just tears flying out of me. Uncontrollable, deep-in-the-pit-of-my-stomach cries came out of me like wildfire, and I exhausted myself up and down. My cries were their loudest when I was sitting straight up, their softest when I was practically lying chest-first on the basement floor. The smell of chlorine returned to my memory each time my nose dove for the floor, and the musty aroma pushed its way back into my brain when I came up for air. No longer could I associate that smell with my Granny's basement. It would now and forever be related to the dolphin. I couldn't fathom seeing that image every time I went to a public pool.

Angelle went back upstairs right after it happened, proud of what she had made me do. When she took her first step on the stairs, she told Kimmie and Laney to follow her. Moments later, they did.

They didn't even apologize on their way out. They didn't say a word to me as they walked around my ignominious body and proceeded up the stairs.

I lay in the basement for a while. Even though I embraced a ball of my clothes in my lap, I didn't immediately attempt to dress myself. The embarrassment, the absolute shame, filled my body with cement, and all of that cement pushed what tears were left straight out of my eye sockets. Drool spilled over my chin. Snot caked my nostrils.

I knew I must have looked like a toddler, the kind of brat who fell on the sidewalk after running home, knees scraped, elbows bleeding–except my blood wasn't noticeable. Transparent along my pale skin, I didn't have to see anything to know that I was bleeding. My wound was supernatural and confusing.

The sun began to fade from the bunker style windows in the basement. The last of its orange glow stretched along the floor, finding just the tips of my toes in its final reach.

Footsteps echoed above me. Anticipating that it was either Kimmie or Laney coming to apologize, I refused to put my clothes back on, because I wanted them to see me at my worst. I wanted them to hurt for me.

The basement door opened, its loud screech mirroring the creak of old floor boards, and the footsteps spilled onto the stairs. They hopped, one-two, one-two, one-two.

Then I heard three sets of voices giggling directly above my head. They didn't come from the throat of the basement. That only meant one thing.

"Then who–" I wasn't able to finish my thought aloud, for the silhouette of a body appeared in the doorway of the cellar. Despite my attempt to shed my pain so that it lay on the surface of my skin, exposed for my friends to see, venomous with just a single look, it wasn't inflicted on either of them. Even though I was able to ignore the images of what I may have looked like naked and rocking with a dolphin plushie, there was one thing I wasn't able to ignore.

Standing in front of me, showing myself in the reflection of his glasses, was Kimmie's older cousin. Ryan.

Ryan stopped walking the moment he noticed me. It looked like he walked face-first into a glass wall; his nose and eyes smashed together and he squinted in place, falling back so much that he nearly tripped over his own feet. His pale face opened in red shock. It started at the base of his neck, like dropping a thermometer in boiling water, and he quickly turned around and screamed, "I'm sorry! I didn't know you were...didn't know...you're..."

Naked. That was the word for which he was looking.

There was so much wrong with me in that moment that I didn't even bother telling him to go away or not to look. The shock of just having had sex with a dolphin filled my veins with ice, and like a gelid statue, I just sat there with cold eyes on Ryan as he faced away from me. The tears were so fat that they didn't even roll down my cheeks anymore. They just built up in my eyes until I couldn't see anything, and then *slip*—they were splashing on my knees.

He must have been waiting for me to say or do something; it took him at least one minute before he turned his head over his shoulder, his dark eyes clenched shut. The pale wrinkle between his eyebrows was remarkably animated. "Hey, uhh, can I use the computer?"

So that was why he was here. Kimmie had mentioned before that Ryan spent a lot of time at her house, because she had internet and he did not. They liked watching videos on websites like Stickdeath and Joe Cartoon.

As I opened my mouth to tell him that I didn't care if he used the computer or not, a fraught whimper rolled out from the back of my throat. Fast, I covered my mouth with my spaghetti strap shirt and exhaled until my palms were warm with my filtered breath.

"Are you crying?" With eyes still forced closed, Ryan turned completely around, his body facing me. Then he wedged one eye open, just for a second, long enough to see tears flowing down my chin, and then he turned back around. "Hey, you're crying." I watched his shoulder blades roll around. He must have been rubbing his hands together, for the front of his body wriggled and writhed in sync with the dance of his back. It was a calming sight, for whatever reason, a fixture of his body that made me forget that I was still nude.

I was so maudlin that I was nearly unable to form words with my voice. "They didn't tell you?"

"Tell me what?"

I didn't respond. I just sat there hunched over, water gushing from my hard eyes like a broken red fire hydrant on a street corner.

Ryan stretched his hands behind his back. I watched his fingers squirm and twist and fidget and pluck each other. It was a hard read; I couldn't tell if he was nervous or if he was angry that I was still in the basement, preventing him from using the computer. Finally, he said, matter-of-factly, "I just want to use the computer."

So he was angry.

Literally, I was the only physical impediment preventing him from stepping into the attached computer room.

"Cover your eyes." I commanded him with an imperious manner, something a king or queen took years to perfect. Yet I had perfected it in a matter of seconds.

He groaned. "My eyes are closed."

"I don't care. Cover them."

Surprisingly, he did. Ryan pulled his arms back in front of him, and I saw his elbows bend and his hands spread over both his eyes. The arm of his glasses propped up on his left ear. He started humming a song by Vertical Horizon.

I struggled at putting my clothes back on. Even though the blue spaghetti-strap shirt was my favorite, I knew I couldn't ever wear it again after what happened. I wouldn't be able to without thinking about the dolphin. I decided that no matter what, I would throw it in the garbage when I got home. Favorite shirt or not, it was no longer a memento to me. It was now a symbol of desperation, and I didn't want to ever reach that low of a point in my life again.

My panties were inside-out. I tried so hard to work under pressure and against time that I turned them into an even bigger mound of wrinkles and folds before I unraveled them to their proper, floral-print way. My hands wouldn't stop shaking. I nearly dropped them four or five times. During one instance, Ryan stopped humming and asked me if I was okay. I grumpily told him to keep his eyes closed until I said so. He went back to humming.

Stepping into my beige shorts, I fastened my sandals and said aloud, "Okay, you can look." Before he could see me, I vigorously wiped away the tears around my eyes, as if he hadn't already seen me cry.

Ryan curiously looked over his shoulder before turning back around.

We stood in front of one another, our bodies rooted in place, without saying anything. Was I supposed to say something, or was he? Above us, hard footsteps and loud voices cascaded through all of the cracks and crevices of the house. It sounded like Kimmie was picking a fight with Angelle.

I looked at Ryan's tiny face. His brown eyes doubled in size behind his thick-framed glasses, and pieces of food clung to the folds of his mouth. It looked like he'd had toast or potato chips for dinner. There was a tiny mark on the tip of his chin, the same scab that I saw a few weeks earlier, but now it was a scar the shape of half a fishhook. For a moment, I made up a story of a time when he took his bicycle all over Red Cliff Hill and wrecked face-first in front of Laney's house. It seemed suitable.

I waited for it; I had been waiting since he walked into the basement and found me, naked and trembling in a puddle of my own tears and clothes and regret. I waited for him to ask me why in the world I was naked in Kimmie's basement, holding on to my clothes, staring quite blankly and irritably at a conspicuous dolphin plushie nearby.

When Ryan continued to just stand there, offering no words, I did it for him. "Don't you wanna know why I was down here?"

He shrugged his shoulders. "If you wanted to, you'd tell me." He licked the side of his mouth. "But you haven't said anything. So I just wanna use the computer."

I sighed as if I was angry he didn't ask me to tell him what happened.

It was then that I realized we were wearing matching colors. My shirt was blue, and his shirt was blue. My shorts were beige, and his shorts were beige. Had he been wearing shoes, I bet they would have been brown sandals, just like mine. Glancing closer at his t-shirt, I saw a pack of wolves running through a bright white river. Behind them, a slew of Chinese symbols lit up in blues and whites and grays.

I nodded at his t-shirt. "What does that say?" For some reason, as I said it, the bottom of my neck started to heat up. Then the heat rose to my chin, to my cheeks, to the top of my forehead. I knew the blanket of blush was so heavy that it would hide the river of freckles running across my cheeks and nose. My armpits grew hot. The folds behind my knees were clammy and moist. To settle the heat, I scratched at it. The sensation multiplied.

Like we were each other's mirror reflections, his face changed from pale to red. Ryan even reached underneath one of his arms and scratched his armpit. "My shirt?" He glanced down and ran his fingers across the calligraphy print. "It, uhh... It says, 'powerful blue wolf.'"

I blinked in shock. "Really? You can read Chinese?"

He didn't even falter. "Uhh, yeah. Duh." He said it with the kind of inflection that implied everyone should know how to read Chinese calligraphy.

I didn't even care that he was lying, because I knew there was no way that Ryan could read the language on his t-shirt. What I cared about most was that he continued to talk about his shirt in grave detail. He gave each wolf its own name, and he told me that they were crossing the Moon River, a place that he said, "Is where all wolves go when they die."

He stepped closer to me, and I smelled his breath he was so near. His voice smelled like sour apples. At one point, he reached out, grabbed my hand, and forced the pad of my finger to touch one of the foreign symbols. "Blue," he told me. "That means blue." I closed my eyes and pretended the faint texture of his shirt was written in Braille, and that I, too, could read blue with just a single touch.

Ryan pushed my hand away. "Wolves are my favorite. I have them all over my bedroom."

I asked him to teach me more about Chinese and wolves and the Moon River, but he said he wanted to use the computer before it got too late.

As I watched him step around me and go into the computer room, after hearing the computer chair cough as it cradled his tiny body, I turned on my heels and walked up the stairs. Ryan never even asked me why I was naked or why I was crying. I was too young to know that I should have thanked him for that.

I called my mother that evening to come pick me up. I didn't waste any time walking out of the basement and finding the cordless phone. Kimmie and Angelle were both sitting on the couch, facing away from one another, while Laney was on the floor in the living room playing the PlayStation. Still, not a word from anyone. Not even a "Hi," or a "Sorry."

My mother didn't ask me any questions, like why I suddenly changed my mind about spending the night with Laney at Kimmie's house. She showed up a few minutes after I made the phone call, and as I walked into the garage, Kimmie yelled out, "I'll call you later." I acted as if I didn't hear her and walked straight for my mother's car.

Kimmie did call later. She practically called me as soon as I got home. It was only then that she apologized at least one hundred times. After about the tenth or twentieth time that she said she was sorry, she was crying, pain-in-my-ears-just-listening-to-her crying, so I told myself that I needed to forgive her, and Laney. Kimmie even said that Angelle was a bitch and that she was weird and mean, and that they called Angelle's mom right after I left to come pick her up because Angelle was misbehaving.

I forgave her a little bit more after hearing that part.

Honestly, I was running out of real reasons to stop being friends with Laney and Kimmie. At first, when everything happened, I hated them. I never wanted to see them again. I didn't even want to look at them. After talking on the phone with Kimmie for over an hour, things settled back into the place they were before the dolphin incident. She even admitted that Angelle made Laney do something similar in order to be part of their group, but that it wasn't anything close to what I did. That didn't help me feel better, but it made me feel less alone.

Kimmie invited me to come back next weekend to swim.

I told her that I would ask my mother.

Right before we hung up, Kimmie quickly added, "Oh, hey, listen. Ryan thinks you're cute."

I laughed in flattery. "No way. What? No." Then I wrapped the phone cord around my toes. It was my new habit. "Did he, uhh, say anything? Like, about me bein' in the basement?"

"Nah. He doesn't know. He's dense." That made us both laugh. Then she scoffed. "But I know my cousin. He's like, fuckin' in love with you. He came up after you left and asked me where you went. He said, 'Hey, where's that one girl,' and I said, 'She went home. You want her number?' And he got all red and went back downstairs."

"What? What?"

Click. She didn't even say bye.

My mother sat behind me on the couch. She lowered her puzzle book. "Everything okay? You sounded scared."

I hid my reddening face from her. "Yeah. Just Kimmie. She wants me to stay with her next weekend."

I excused myself from the living room and threw myself onto my bed. Reaching underneath my pillow, I found my journal still locked and secure. Opening it with my secret key, hidden underneath my Eevee figurine, I began to document my rather awkward, but somehow perfect, first evening with Ryan Mills.

The only reason I found the evening perfect was because Ryan looked for me after I was gone. That, to me, seemed like a moment straight out of a movie: the image of him stepping out of the basement, brown eyes searching left and right, little mouth asking Kimmie where I went. My brain was determined to give his facial expression the most attention, the defeated cups underneath his eyes when he didn't see me sitting next to Laney on the couch.

In that particular journal entry about Ryan, I wrote down, "He likes wolves, and I like him. He will teach me Chinese one day. He wears glasses and a lot of blue, and he is small just like me."

Then I drew one of the Chinese symbols from memory in the bottom corner of the page. It was horrific and rambunctious, with some lines wobbly and others too long, but I didn't erase it. I doodled a heart next to it, and then I closed my journal, locked it, and stuffed it back underneath my pillow.

Three

The drought of 1999 consumed the rest of the summer.

At the Lego house, the air conditioner was turned off for good shortly before August.

My friendship with Audrey, my love for her family, and spending the night with her 16 days in a row... It showed the more I stayed with her during those rough, dry, bleak days.

We tested one another by sleeping in the same bed every night, completely naked, covered in puddles of our own sweat, trying to fall asleep but not being able to because Audrey's baby sister in the next room wouldn't stop crying, and her little, severely dehydrated brother TJ writhing in pain on the couch because he can't keep down any food or water. We were practically bathing in the house's dense film of air that smelled like rotting vegetables and salt.

It wasn't like the drought came on without any warning. The grass had been losing its color for weeks. It looked more like beach sand than green blades by the time July came. It was impossible to take a walk on Bear Run Road without feeling sandpaper in the back of our throats, from either the dryness of the air or the lingering road dust still trying to float back down to the gravel.

It hadn't rained in weeks. By the end of July, Stream Ridge was ordered on a reserve water policy. The rest of West Virginia ordered residents to conserve water a few days after that.

Eventually, the entire East Coast and some of the South were under a water conservation regime. Audrey's family and my family were unaffected by Stream Ridge's water conservation policy because we used well water, but that didn't mean we didn't obey the policy. If we didn't obey, the wells would dry up.

One morning, Todd was watching the local news as we stumbled from the bedroom, and Audrey and I came face to face with images of our Appalachian wilderness crumbling to ash as the wildfires took over our entire state. On the television, aerial segments captured the southern counties as if they were sheeted with a sepia tone. The depictions were haunting. My brain refused to draw in the reality that my state was dying, thirsty, withering away. Back and forth, dry death and fire death. I almost started crying.

Audrey grabbed my hand, our palms slipping and sliding with our night sweat, and she cried out, "Mom, are we gonna burn to death?"

Tracy, slaving over the morning breakfast, snapped back, "Now, Auddy, damn it, we're not gonna burn. We're far too north."

Todd sipped on his coffee. "We better go check on Aunt Judy. Make sure she has enough water."

"Take her that there fan there," Tracy ordered, "the one with the busted blade."

After eating our breakfast, Tracy ordered Audrey and me to drink two glasses of water before playing outside. TJ had been in the bathroom the entire morning, fighting cramps. He was practically glued to the toilet, so Audrey and I had to pee behind the house.

The moment we stepped outside, the cement walkway burned the soles of our feet. My shoulders singed as the sun ruthlessly beat down on my pale, bony body. Audrey shrieked that we were walking on lava, and by the time we settled into our sandals, we had to take them off because the straps burned our feet.

Everything burned. Everything was dry and dead.

I called my mother and asked her what was going on with the weather. As she spoke, I could hear our old-fashioned air conditioner humming behind her. In between her exhausted breaths, an electric fan also blew into the phone. Not even the gift of dancing in cool air was enough to bring me back home. I valued Audrey far more than a working fan and an air conditioner. "Abigail, we're experiencin' a drought. A heat wave. Drink water every chance you get."

"What if I don't drink any water?"

My mother exhaled. I didn't need to see the cigarette smoke coil around her face to know that she was stress-smoking. She was raw in her life lesson. "If you don't drink water, you will die. Hundreds of people have died. Our state is on fire right now. Do you want to be on fire?"

I quickly hung up.

We couldn't even jump on the trampoline, the elastic mat was so hot. Instead, Audrey and I walked a ways down the trail behind the house, and dipped our feet in the shallow creek bed. Looking around, I noticed the discrepancy of depth in the creek compared to what it was before the drought. The embankments alone, with their natural water lines drawn in the grass beds, were at least three or four inches above the surface of the water. The creeks were dying, too.

Eventually, we rolled around in the creek water until our clothes were dripping wet so we could stay as cool as possible. We had to re-dip every few minutes.

The only solace during the drought that summer was waking up, if I had fallen asleep at all the night before, to the symphony of cicadas outside. They somehow managed to survive the blistering heat. Audrey was worried that they were melting on all of the trees, leaving behind black goo similar to road tar. Their incessant hums, still as strong as they were when they first started singing back in May, told me otherwise.

In the midst of all of the chaos and heat and sweat, they greeted me every morning when I opened my eyes. Sometimes, they even helped me fall back asleep. I felt bad having spent most of my summer hating the cicadas; now that they were dying out and crawling back into the ground, only to come out again in another 17 years, I was going to lose them soon. It felt like I was letting go of a pet. I didn't want to let go of a pet.

Audrey started liking them too, so we held on to their blankets of buzzing for as long as we could, every morning, before we were ordered out of bed and back to work.

We spent one entire morning around a circle of rocks, hands pressed together, heads bowed, praying for forgiveness. We still hadn't shed the moment where we once sabotaged a mass amount of cicadas with our rocks because we wished they were Buck's face.

Hopefully we had been forgiven.

The last time I went to Kimmie's that summer, I noticed the back of her bedroom door was covered in angsty preteen graffiti, executed in Sharpie (of course). We had already spent the day swimming until the pads of our fingers were transparent and wrinkled. Locking the knob, I was able to step back a bit and absorb the vast, historic document sprawled along the back of her door.

Most of the graffiti phrases were names, like **Lane & Kimmz BFF**, ~~**Angelle**~~ **& Kimmz BFF** (her name was literally crossed out), **Kait Rox!** and so forth.

There were some images, like of the bubbly word **SMILE** that always starts off with six vertical lines to make the S, and there were some hearts, cats, bathing suits, sandals, and beach balls.

There was even a cheerleader pompom with the name Kimmie on it, and right next to it, a basketball with the name Laney on it. Had I been initiated on the graffiti door, I guessed that my sport of choice would be marked by an N64 or PlayStation controller.

But then I did see my name, right there towards the bottom-right corner of the door. My name wasn't alone, though.

Abigail + Ryan.

I reacted out loud, pacing back and forth. "What the heck? What the *heck?*"

My heart stopped pounding long enough for me to turn on my heels and notice Laney and Kimmie had managed to climb the ladder to the top bunk bed as quietly as humanly possible: like they flew right up there and landed with the force of a piece of paper. I stepped back far enough so I could see them. Nervous, I cried out, "Who wrote that?"

Kimmie and Laney were too busy holding on to each other's arms and giggling to hear me. Impatient, I clenched my hands into fists. I raised my voice loud enough to scare them both to death. "Who wrote that?"

They literally jumped back, and the bunk bed skeleton trembled against their bouncing bodies. Kimmie said the f-word, and Laney said something that sounded like "Holy cheese and rice."

"Jesus, Abigail. What? Wrote what?" As Kimmie leaned over the wooden banister, I pointed at the green text in the bottom right-hand corner. Surprisingly, she shrugged her shoulders and replied in a soft, cool voice, "Oh. I wrote it."

"Why would you write that?" I stared up at her from the bedroom floor, and she stared back down at me from the highest bunk bed. She blinked a few times, and then she cracked a friendly smile. At least, I thought it was friendly. It looked friendly enough. Her hair broke over her burnt marshmallow shoulder, the ends white-blonde, her roots dark brown.

She was waiting for me to say something else. I swallowed hard. "He's going to see it and think I'm some kind of crazy person."

Kimmie rolled her eyes. "He was here when I wrote it. He knows."

That changed everything.

Slowly, my swollen shoulders softened. "He knew about it? Did he try to stop you?"

She kept rolling her eyes. "No, he watched me do it—because you two love each other. That's why I wrote it." She groaned while falling back on the bed. "You two are gonna bone and get married and love each other, okay? I know it; he knows it, too. Deal with it."

I stood in the middle of the bedroom in intense thought, in a metamorphic state as I developed from little girl to just girl. Struggling to put all of the pieces together, I held out my hands and imagined all of my options right there in my tiny palms. My arms balanced back and forth as my brain unloaded all of its choices into my palms.

Admit to Ryan that I liked him? Act like I hated him, so it wouldn't be so obvious? Beg Kimmie to invite him over to her house when I was there? Tell Scott that I wanted to date him, so he could tell Ryan?

"Abigail, what the heck are you doing?" Laney's voice brought me out of my balance beam trance of decisions. I looked up and saw both her and Kimmie hanging over the wooden banister, their chins perched atop the boards like a parrot on a pirate's shoulder.

Embarrassed, I dropped my hands. "Nothing."

We spent our last summer day together gossiping about Kimmie's new boy-friend, the one she met at 4-H Camp a week earlier. She held on to an imaginary head and showed Laney and me how to tilt our faces in order to kiss a boy properly. Then a pink slimy thing extruded itself from Kimmie's mouth, and she proceeded to mentor us on the technique for French kissing.

At first, we tested our French kissing skills on the backs of our hands.

That wasn't enough, so Kimmie dared us each to French kiss her.

We did.

I didn't pay particular attention to Kimmie and Laney when they French kissed. Their mouths made fishy noises, like gills or fins under water, and that was enough for me to look away. Glancing out the open window, I saw Ryan skipping down the length of Kimmie's gravel driveway.

A part of me went into override with assumptions: he was coming over because Kimmie told him I would be there; he felt my presence at her house and just had to see; he watched us swim in Kimmie's pool from his back porch just a few meters away; or he called earlier and asked for me to come over himself.

"Okay, your turn." I glanced over at Kimmie, whose lips were now dark and wet. Laney's were, too.

It wasn't as strange as I had imagined. French kissing Kimmie was like rolling the end of a lollipop all over my tongue, of course without its stick or the taste of something fruity, like blueberry or cherry. She made noises when she breathed, so I made noises when I breathed. At one point, I felt the shape of her tooth behind the stretched blanket of her upper lip, and it was strange to me that I was able to feel that sort of detail with the tip of my tongue alone.

By the time Kimmie pulled away, her bedroom door shook. "Hey, let me in." Ryan's voice sounded so fragile from the top bunk bed. It was like he was half his age. Laney thought so, too; she leaned closer to me and giggled into my neck. Eventually we let him in, and he joined us on the top of the bunk bed as if he'd been a girl his entire life. The fact that his knee touched my knee while we gossiped was enough for me to forget that the last time I saw him, I was naked, trembling and defeated on Kimmie's basement floor. The song "Torn" came to me as I realized that.

"Hey, you wanna go shoot some squirrels?" Ryan jumped down from the bunk bed and ran straight for a cedar chest near Kimmie's closet. Laney and I remained on the bunk bed, uninterested, while Kimmie and Ryan sprinted outside with a BB gun.

The sound of shattering glass filtered through the open window.

A few minutes later, while Kimmie and Ryan hid in her closet, a neighbor knocked on the front door. We ignored him. We also ignored the series of unanswered phone calls as they came in every ten minutes.

Nyla was greeted at the end of her driveway by the neighbor, who apparently no longer had a living room window. My mother picked me and Laney up that evening. We were spared from punishment by Ryan, who cleared our names when Nyla confronted him.

Had Kimmie and Ryan not shot out a window, we could have had more summer days together; but that was the last time Laney and I were allowed at Kimmie's that year. Kimmie and Ryan were grounded until after football season. They were ordered to work off the cost of a new window for the neighbor by doing extra housework, mowing the grass, and cleaning their parents' cars every weekend.

I called Audrey the moment I got home and told her, "Me and Ryan touched knees at Kimmie's today."

Again, she was smacking her lips together. She was always chewing. "Yeah, but did you touch his hand or face? You gotta touch more than a stupid knee for it to mean something."

I thought about it. "I may have touched the back of his leg when he jumped down from the bunk bed?"

"What did it feel like?"

I didn't have to think about it. "A bat wing."

"Don't go comparin' boys' legs to bat wings. You're ruinin' boys' legs."

Audrey told me to think of something more romantic than a bat wing to compare to the back of Ryan's leg.

The summer of 1999 ended with me sweeping out thousands of dead cicadas and their crispy, dry exoskeleton shells from our gutters.

My mother only trusted me to stand on our dilapidating roof with a broom and fish out the carcasses from the gutters, because she was too afraid that Patrick's hefty size would cause him to fall straight through our roof, and Diana was too afraid to stand on the roof because she was afraid of heights and didn't want to get dirty.

As I used the bottom of the broom like a shovel and flung the carcasses out from the gutters, Patrick and Diana waited below with a blue tarp to collect all of the cicadas' broken, brown cadavers. He didn't want the shells to just linger and lay waste in our yard, so he was going to take all of the bodies to a remote place in the woods and burn them. He mentioned he would need to leave the tarp and locusts in the garage until at least September. The drought was mostly over, but he didn't want to risk the fire spreading. Our grass was still brown, and the dirt still bone-dry, but it had rained at least three times the last few days.

Any time that my sister threatened to drop the blue tarp loaded with dead bugs, Patrick threatened to take away her telephone and television privileges. That always got her to straighten up fast. She needed the telephone to talk to all of her popular friends, and she needed the television to watch MTV.

It took almost four days to flush our gutters completely clean.

While Audrey, Laney, and Kimmie were at the county fair called Town and Country Days in New Martinsville, I stayed home and helped my mother with housework: sweeping locusts, vacuuming lady bugs, and de-cobwebbing the corners of the house.

My favorite part was planting flowers in my mother's garden bed, outside of my sister's window. Now that the drought was over, the flowers could actually survive. The state of West Virginia was still under a declaration of emergency, on account of the fields that were still burning, and elders were still being found dead in their homes; but other than that, the state was on its way to recovery.

Tracy brought Aunt Judy at least three jugs of water every day that summer.

As my mother dug out soil and dropped the sets of flowers in the bed, I tiptoed across our front yard, avoiding any greening patches because I didn't want to hinder the grass's recovery. I didn't show any sympathy to the yellow patches of grass, or the brown spots of dirt.

My mother was handing me scores of housework jobs in her effort to mask the fact that we couldn't afford fair tickets that year. My three friends had all-week passes. All Diana had to do was ask her grandmother for a ticket, and she could go. I didn't have that. We had different dads, and her dad's side of the family was far wealthier than mine.

The day before I started 4th grade, my mother cooked an especially large dinner with deer steak, mashed potatoes, corn, and gravy. We didn't delve into the deer steak unless it was a special occasion. The last time we fetched it from the cellar freezer was when Patrick got a promotion as an electrician.

We found out the next morning that the dinner was my mother and Patrick's way of celebrating. After my mother felt just how sad it was that she couldn't spare me $5 for the Town and Country Days entry fee, she went out and got a part-time job working at the convenience store in Oldestown, called The Country Cupboard.

My mother and Patrick didn't say it like that, though. They didn't expose the truth in any form. Instead, Patrick said, in perhaps the most cheerful tone he had ever used up to that point, "Your mom is working so you kids can have some new clothes and toys, and," he looked right at me, "video games." When in reality, he should have said, "Your mom is working so we don't have to live paycheck to paycheck, so we don't lose the house, so we can afford electricity and cable and water."

Diana immediately asked for a new pair of shoes.

My mother told her to wait a few weeks. Shockingly, Diana didn't throw a fit. She was too proud of our mother to ruin such a perfect weekend. She even screamed in joy, "Thank you, Mom!" and ran down the hall into her bedroom, probably to call one of her friends to tell them the great news.

"What do you want, Abigail?" My mother clutched at her blue coffee mug. It was half-full.

I shrugged my shoulders. "I don't need anything, but thank you."

Patrick was stepping into a pair of work boots. He was going outside to mow the yard. "C'mon now, Abigail, you gotta want something."

I thought about it. "I want to learn Chinese."

That made Patrick laugh. He asked me again, and I said it again.

"You know Chinese. Ching-chong. There ya go."

My mother, however, told him to knock it off and asked me what kind of Chinese I wanted to learn. "The symbols. Calligraphy. That kind."

The next day, my mother drove all the way to Morgantown to buy me a book of China's history. I taught myself how to write *wolf* in Chinese calligraphy. Ryan's shirt was wrong.

Four

I spent most of my time as a 4ᵗʰ grader sneaking peeks of Ryan on the bus, every morning when I stepped up into the aisle, and when I threw my backpack over my shoulders to step off the bus at the Bear Run Road stop. Audrey, best friend that she was, let me know when I was transparent: her way of looking out for me so I didn't appear as desperate and transfixed as I appeared.

One time, I had stared at him for so long she had to tug on my long brown hair to physically pull me out of my dreamy spell. If Ryan hadn't seen me staring at him that day, he definitely heard me as I howled, turned in my seat, and yanked back on Audrey's white-blonde hair. She had rejected my abuse with such stubbornness that her glasses fell into her lap. Our bus driver looked up at us in his hot dog-shaped mirror and yelled, "Girls, ya best behave!"

We automatically replied, "Yes, sir," before hiding in our bus seats.

During the school day, however, I wasn't so apt to stare at Ryan, mostly because he was two grades ahead of me; we didn't see each other often. The only time I did manage to find him in the crowd of kids in Gunners Valley School was during the Annual Spelling Bee.

As a 4ᵗʰ grader, I made it to the semi-final round with just five other students, most of them upperclassmen. Laney would have been sitting next to me, but she purposely misspelled *cafeteria* because she hated spelling bees. I flunked out on the word *ukulele* because I made the reckless decision of assuming eye contact with Ryan, his little pale face a mere smudge in the array of kids in the bleachers. The rafter lights in the gymnasium flashed like stars in his glasses as he moved his head about.

The teacher conducting the spelling bee, Ms. Kendall, asked me if I needed her to repeat the word.

I shook myself back to reality, and after asking her to repeat ukulele by itself and in a sentence, I made eye contact with him again. Gripping the wooden podium, I dreamily said into the microphone, "I have no idea," and I took the Walk of Shame back to my 4th grade class sitting in the bleachers.

A series of chuckles came from the 6th grade class. Glancing up, I watched Scott nudge Ryan with his shoulder, and the two of them pointed at me and laughed with squinty, sneering eyes. I was less upset by being laughed at than excited about Ryan even noticing me.

There were times that Kimmie dared me to sit with him on the bus, but I passed on every chance. She didn't pass on her chance to call me a pussy every time I refused.

Audrey suggested that I write him an anonymous love letter and leave it in his locker. That I passed on as well, because I didn't want to walk the dangerous route to the junior high school ward of Gunners Valley School, risking my chances of either being caught my him, slipping the note in the wrong locker, or being seen by my sister—giving her the golden opportunity to make fun of me with her posse of 8th grade friends.

My 4th grade year wasn't all about Ryan, however. I tried out for the unisex basketball team, which wasn't much of a tryout, because if anyone showed up they were automatically given a spot on the team. I was undeniably the worst player on the entire team, and that included junior varsity players.

While I played basketball, Audrey and Kimmie cheered for me on Gunners Valley School's cheerleading squad. On one occasion, Kimmie warned me that her family was coming to see her perform her latest gymnastic stunt, which meant that Ryan would be there.

I begged my mother to take me to my Aunt Darla's to get my hair done for the basketball game. My Aunt Darla was one of two beauticians in Stream Ridge; my stepmother, my father's new wife, was the other. At first, my mother was reluctant to ask her sister to spend over an hour on my hair, when it was just going to get thrown up into a ponytail and doused in sweat (if I even got to play).

My Aunt Darla, however, shooed her away with a hot iron in her hand. She snapped, "Let me fix her up, Grace. Get out of here. Find Dan. I don't even know where he is." She was talking about my Uncle Dan.

We left the salon ten minutes before warm-up, and I bounced out of the spinning chair with a head full of curls and an aura of hairspray following my every move.

I managed to run inside Gunners Valley School just in time, right before the basketball teams were unleashed for warm-ups on the gymnasium floor. A class-mate, Zane, headed straight for me as if magnetized. He sniffed only once and asked, "Why do you smell like a tramp?" I hit him on the side of the face with a basketball. Our coach, Willy Sine, immediately ordered me to run two suicides.

I only got to play the last two minutes of the basketball game. Gunners Valley School's team was currently undefeated, and they were up on Elk Grove by 15 points. As Zane and I substituted in, I hobbled backwards on the court to look into the thinning crowd. Kimmie's mother, Nyla, stood out like a sore thumb. She was far too beautiful to be secluded in such a small town. Her red hair, with its blonde highlights and natural curl, contrasted with the boring browns and blacks around her.

She saw me look at her, and she waved. I knew she called me Six Pack Abbs under her breath. She loved calling me that. I hated it.

Next to her, I saw a black-haired woman wearing a feathered necklace wrapped twice around her neck. The way she looked at me, it was almost as if she knew who I was, for she smiled a bit, and her dark eyes twinkled. That was when I noticed the familiar form of her face, the oily texture of her short black hair...all of it nearly identical to the boy sitting to her left—Ryan. He was at the basketball game with his mother, Kimmie's Aunt Norma.

I missed all of my shots. Coach Willy threw his arms down against his knees every time I missed. He and the entire team were trying to give me my first points as a basketball player. Zane, already having a few points underneath his history belt, passed me the ball for a layup at least four times; I missed all four times. I threw too hard, too soft, way off, or got fouled.

The only good thing about that night was winning the game. Nothing else seemed to pan out as I expected.

Kimmie promised to bring me over to her Aunt Norma, but after the game, she peeled away from the cheerleading squad and immediately snuck to the playground to make out with a 6th grader named Brent King.

After I changed out of my uniform, I found Audrey and asked her if I played as horribly as I felt like I did. She bit her bottom lip. "Well," she started, as we walked slowly for the parking lot, "at least your hair looked great?" We rode home in the back of her grandfather Bob's black Chevy, stargazing all across Route 2 until we pulled into Bear Run Road.

Shortly after Gunners Valley School finished final exams, most classes spent the last few days of school either outside on the playground, or inside the gymnasium for award ceremonies. Audrey and I took advantage of this opportunity, and clung to one another. We were in different 4th grade classes, so we only saw one another on bus rides or during lunch. With linked arms, we skipped along the creek embankment and gossiped about what we wanted to do together that summer.

She automatically sang, "I wanna meet my future boyfriend and play with his hair."

My response wasn't as ambitious as hers. "Yeah, well, I wanna go swimming at night and drink as much pop as I want."

She kicked at a rock. I heard her toenail scrape the edge, and she howled out. "Ouch! Now, dang it." It took her a moment to right herself. "You have to do somethin' that involves a boy. You gotta like, call Ryan, or something."

"I tried doing that, remember? I couldn't find him."

"Try harder. Ask Kimmie or somethin'."

At that moment, I glanced around the playground to find him. After a few tries, my eyes discovered his black hair, complemented with a sun halo, bouncing up and down. Two circles flashed on his face, the sun multiplying in his frames. He was running away from Scott. His short, thin legs were half the size of Scott's, yet he managed to stay at least four feet ahead of him. As he stepped in an unseen pot hole, he buckled on impact, his glasses nearly falling off his face. Scott slammed into him, and the two boys toppled to the ground overcome with laughter.

I tugged on Audrey's arm so she knew to follow my move as I turned away from the two boys. "I'll talk to Kimmz, okay?"

Audrey grinned. Her teeth were stained red from the after-exam Fruit-Roll-Ups our homeroom teachers passed out to the entire class. "There ya go. Dreams, Abigail, you gotta have some dreams."

All of the students had to clean out their desks on the last day of school. That meant no more pencils, crayons, markers, or pencil boxes. After I cleaned out my desk, packing away my markers and notebooks and sticker sets, I squeezed my pink and yellow Pokémon backpack to give the zipper more room to zip, but then there was a snapping noise, and even though the zipper was still going along its trail of metal teeth, the metal teeth were not connected. They split.

I gasped so loud that Jimmy Curl glanced over at me through his long, straight blonde hair. "You cut yourself?" He looked like a young Link from *The Legend of Zelda*.

My eyes watered. My voice tripled in size as it escaped me. "No, I broke my fucking *backpack!*"

Now my entire class gasped.

My homeroom teacher, Mrs. Gentt, immediately stopped writing on the chalkboard and ran straight for me. Her good-bye message lay half-finished on the green base: *Have a nice su–* Kids pointed and laughed, chanting the chalkboard message in a musical tone, "Have a nice *soooo!* You have a nice *soooo*, I'll have a nice *soooo!*"

I tried over and over again to fix it. I tried pulling the zipper back to the beginning of the teeth so I could push it back up, but that didn't work. Tears overwhelmed my eyes now, so much that I could barely see. I started cursing under my breath, saying the f-word because I was so angry, and I tried so hard to fix my backpack, but the teeth kept busting apart. Nothing could fix it.

My backpack's mouth wouldn't stay closed. I started treating it as a disobedient patient in a dentist's office, and me the most professional of professionals, I started punching my backpack in succession with every f-bomb.

Mrs. Gentt pulled me aside and gave me a strong lecture on not using bad language. Then she tried to ease the situation by taping up my backpack with duct tape. When she was finished, she sent me out of the 4th grade classroom to one of the most dismally starting summers of my young life.

Her efforts didn't ease anything. Instead, they pretty much shined a bright spotlight on my broken backpack, like I was asking the entire school to "Look at me, and my stupid Pokémon backpack that's now broken!" I wasn't in the hallway for one full minute before four different kids asked me what happened to my backpack. The beacon was painfully bright on me.

As I hobbled on to the bus for my last route home as a 4th grader, I carried my backpack instead of wearing it. If I carried it, I could hide some of the duct tape with my little arms. I didn't want anyone to see that I ruined my backpack on the last day of school. It was so embarrassing, like I had just peed my pants on a class field trip.

That was the first time I didn't try to find Ryan's little head in the near-back of the bus. The only reason I knew he was somewhere behind me was because Kaitlyn, Kimmie's oldest sister, sang out, "Man of a man of a man mankind!" She always greeted Ryan with that phrase, and it always brought a clean-cut smile across his face.

Instead, my focus traced my seat with Audrey, and I kept my eyes there until I could sit.

She was the only person who noticed that something was wrong with my backpack. That was probably because I sat with her on the bus, so she felt the weight of my disappointment as I plopped down next to her and huddled into my own little ball of anger and regret. Her body lifted off the seat and was midair for half a second upon my impact.

Audrey was growing up much faster than I was. At least, that's what both my mother and Tracy said. While I was still under-developed, frail, and the shortest kid in my entire class, Audrey was growing taller, her hair was getting bigger, and there was shape to her hips. Her white-blonde hair was permed now, so it was always bouncing and floating with curls. She called it a spiral perm.

During Phys Ed that year, Audrey got slammed in the face with a basketball, so her glasses broke right across her nose. It left behind a little scar between her eyes. Her new glasses were smaller, with purple frames, so even her glasses made her look older.

It wasn't just her body, though. Her face was longer now, and there was definition to her cheeks and lips. I pinched my mouth some mornings, trying to swell my lips to the size of Audrey's, but nothing ever happened. My only solace of growing up was growing into my front teeth. They didn't seem so invasive or troublesome anymore.

Aware of her surroundings, and aware of the tears clouding my large blue eyes, Audrey immediately questioned the blanket of duct tape all around my backpack. She gasped with the gravity of an elderly woman, "Oh my goodness gracious, what happened?" At least that hadn't changed. For whatever reason, she still acted like an adult. Her tone was archaic, her choice of words seemed to come straight from some historic novel, and she constantly complemented her voice with a sort of ancient hand-dancing gesture, like she was a princess greeting a peasant or something.

"The zipper broke," I choked out. The world seemed to fall on my shoulders right then as I acknowledged the fate of my Pokémon backpack: that it was probably unsalvageable.

Bus #35 roared with cheers, chants, excitement, sing-along songs, and balloons. Kids were blowing up balloons to full capacity and launching them off into the air, saliva and fart noises filling the aisles as the late students raced for their seats. One balloon dropped into our bus seat, and Audrey quickly cried out, to nobody in particular, "This is disgusting! This is so gross, you heathens!" I never told her, but with each day, she sounded more and more like her grandmother, Mam.

The bus idled for a few more minutes before driving off, giving students enough time to say good-bye to classmates they never saw during the summer. Glancing around, I noticed that Kimmie wasn't in her assigned seat with Laney. When I moved my eyes down to the gymnasium doors, a whip of blonde hair and tan skin zipped by at the speed of light. The bus didn't even topple to one side as Kimmie glided up the steps, cheerfully greeting our bus driver Randy with her standard, "What up, Rand-O?" and she sauntered down the aisle.

Like Audrey—pretty much like all of my friends but me—Kimmie was growing up, too. She still didn't look a year older than me or Laney or Audrey, but she acted like it. She made friends with the 6th and 7th graders with relative ease, and she was still making out with Brent in between classes and after baseball games. They weren't officially dating yet, but they held hands when nobody was looking, and they wrote each other notes on Tuesdays and Thursdays.

She told me and Laney that she didn't want to have a boyfriend right now, in case her boyfriend from 4-H Camp wanted to date again that summer. His name was Tanner Short. He still called her once a month, but they hadn't seen each other since the summer before.

As the bus kicked out of idling, it didn't take too long for the farting balloons to zip back and forth across seats again. Even worse, kids were purposely filling some with spit and sending them off like saliva bombs. My broken backpack came in handy, with its extra padding and armor of duct tape. I propped it up above my head, so Audrey and I could use it like an umbrella and sit underneath it.

The bus ride home that day was super long. Audrey rattled off my right ear with a slew of stories, mostly ones I was there for—like things that happened during the Springs Reunion that year.

The bus lurched over Junk Hill. Audrey was wearing her favorite outfit. She saved it for the last day of school, even though she liked wearing it every Friday: a solid black, stretchy skirt and a pearly button-up shirt. She wore the outfit as many times as I wore my favorite pair of bell-bottom jeans. The knees were so worn out on my jeans that they were pale blue, almost white, while the legs and pockets were a dark blue. I wasn't wearing them that last day of school. Instead, I wore a pair of beige shorts, the same ones I wore when Angelle made me have sex with the dolphin plushie.

The dolphin incident was a bit easier to talk about now, considering that a few days after 4th grade started, Kimmie called me one night and confessed. She confessed that she felt so bad for what Angelle made me do with the dolphin that she turned it into an everybody-has-to-do-it thing, including herself. I was right when I thought that Laney had sex with the dolphin (she actually only had to French kiss it, but still), but apparently Kimmie and Angelle had never done anything with the dolphin.

After Kimmie told me that, she went on and on about how she made Angelle have sex with the dolphin. She didn't even sound embarrassed when she told me, "And then I fucked it, because you're my friend."

Right after that, of course I begged her to just throw the poor dolphin away to put it out of its misery. She laughed and told me, "Already did. That dolphin was a whore."

The bus doors opened for me, Audrey, and TJ to hop off on Bear Run Road. As the doors squeezed shut behind us, I looked over my left shoulder. I was filled with liquid joy when I noticed a pair of dark eyes peeking at me from behind two layers of glass: glasses and Plexiglas. Ryan was looking at me.

On cue, Kimmie quickly leaned out of her open bus seat window and yelled, "Ryan wants to know if you'll be his girlfriend?"

Immediately a voice echoed behind her. "I did not! Shut the fuck up, Kimmz!"

A series of laughs blasted from the belly of Bus #35. Kids came together to chuckle at Ryan's torture. He eventually cowered in his seat, using his backpack as a shield, and refused to look back out the window. Randy kicked the bus out of idle, his calm voice coming over the flood of kids' excitement, "All right, all right, settle down, kids. Last day of school, y'hear?"

The exhaust farts spit down the length of Red Cliff Hill until I couldn't hear anything at all. Audrey, while holding her little brother's hand, tugged on my arm, guiding me down the 15-minute walk home we had down Bear Run Road.

Todd got laid off that summer. The first few days of June told the tale of why Audrey wasn't fond of her father staying home. It didn't matter that Todd was home. I still vowed to repeat my routine from last summer, staying at Audrey's until I was nauseous with homesickness. It wasn't long before my homesickness turned into desperation to leave, but I just couldn't abandon Audrey like that.

In the mornings, if we were still in bed around 8 o'clock, Todd would burst into Audrey's room screaming and yelling and hollering, "Get up, kids! You're not gonna sleep all day! We got work to do!" On his way out, he always cursed under his breath, uttered things about us being lazy kids and that we didn't appreciate anyone or anything, and expected everyone to give us anything we wanted.

It became so bad that we forced ourselves awake as soon as it became daylight, just so we wouldn't have to hear his lecture on how ungrateful and spoiled and languid we were.

By noon, Tim, Bob, and family-friend Ray would pack up some sandwiches, bottles of water, and plastic bags of potato chips and journey off to the hay fields with rusted sickles and two tractors that *put-put-putted* in unison. Every evening, all of them would come back with red shoulders, exhausted faces, sweat and dirt lining their hairlines, and growling stomachs. Ray was the only grown-up not affected by the heat and labor required when working in the hayfields. He always came back with a tobacco-chewing smile, teeth rotted straight out of his swollen, bleeding gums, and he always gave me and Audrey a flower or a weed from the fields.

Ray was in his mid-30s, but he had the mentality of a ten year old. Audrey's family let him stay in a little camper in the backyard. As long as he helped out with the farm work and took a shower every night, he got fed breakfast, lunch, and dinner.

One time, Audrey told me that Ray had For-At-Ya.

When I asked her what that meant, she said, "You can't tell if he's lookin' for ya or at ya."

I shouldn't have laughed, but I did.

That went on for most of June. For the second summer in a row, I practically lived at the Lego house with Audrey and her family. As long as I cleaned up after myself and helped Tracy with housework and cleaning, my presence was always appreciated.

On July 1st, Kimmie called the house. Miraculously, I was actually home when she called and not at Audrey's making stromboli from scratch or spraying down the patch of carpet for the living room. I hadn't spoken to her since the last day of school a few weeks prior. She didn't even wait for me to say, "Hello?" when I picked up the phone before she rambled off.

"Hey, put your mom on the phone."

I blinked in confusion. Not wanting to anger Kimmie, I handed my mother the phone. She, too, flashed an expression that said, "What?" As she pressed the phone to her ear, I watched her nod in thought. A few seconds into the conversation, she snapped in a gentle mother tone, "Kimmie, language." Kimmie must have said the f-word. My mother didn't like that. Then a smile broke her pale face and she said, "Yes, she can go. Thanks for inviting her."

My mother asked me to put the phone back on the hook. Then she said, rather flatly, "You're invited to a friend's birthday party tomorrow. Ryan?"

My heart slid off track, its vessels grinding against the structure of my rib cage. "What?" It sounded like my voice was drifting through coffee grinds, it was so hoarse. I tried again. "What?" It didn't help.

"Was that not his name?" She pinched the bridge of her nose. "Well, you can go."

Instead of saying thanks, I sprinted for my bedroom and slammed the door behind me. I spent the next fifteen minutes perusing the small inventory that was my wardrobe, looking for the perfect outfit for his birthday party. After selecting a baby-blue tank top to wear with matching dark blue cotton shorts, both pieces strewn with glittery stars and flowers, I left the outfit draped across my bedroom floor as I sprayed four puffs of vanilla-scented body spray directly above them.

It took me much less time to figure out what to give Ryan for a birthday present. After once overhearing one of his conversations with Scott, I knew that he liked Digimon, and I had a large selection of Digimon figurines and trading cards on display on three of my bedroom shelves.

Snagging one of my pristine duplicate cards of Matt Ishida, Ryan's favorite character, I set aside the trading card and forced myself to go to bed. It was only 6:30 PM.

Five

"See? I told you she would come."

That was the first thing my cousin Scott said when Kimmie and I stepped into Ryan's house.

My face instantly boiled in red. So did Ryan's. He tried to hide the rosy glow by cowering behind his small, bony shoulder. Without anything to hide behind, I leaned down and started to peel back the straps on my sandals. Maybe if I pretended it took me over five minutes to take off my sandals, my blush would be gone by the time I was finished.

Because I was familiar with Scott's group of friends, I knew all of Ryan's friends who were there: Scott, Jace Cross, and Cameron Hill.

A short, affable woman with black hair approached me before I could even slip my feet out of my sandals. She was soft on the eyes. When she smiled at me, it reminded me of an anime character. Her face was creepily cartoon-like.

The woman's voice carried over me. "You must be little Abigail, from up the road."

The grin forming on Kimmie's face warned me that she was about to say something that would either embarrass me or upset me. I tried reaching out to stop her, but my balance would have toppled and I would have fallen straight on my face, so I pulled my hand back and braced myself for the damage she was about to cause.

Right before I clenched my eyes shut, I noticed Ryan taking one step into the kitchen. He, too, was ready to intercept his cousin and her naturally majestic, yet problematic, personality. But just like me, he was too far away: too late to save us both.

Kimmie snickered, but she spoke with a proud roar. "No, Aunt Norma. She's Ryan's girlfriend."

Oh, God.

Moving my eyes back and forth between Kimmie and Ryan's mom, I couldn't read a single expression on either's face. Still grinning, Kimmie was flaunting her pearly white smile, her tan cheeks cupping the bottoms of her eyes, chin up, ears perked. Her strong smile didn't show any form, however, so I wasn't sure if she was proud or if she was looking for trouble. She looked ready for flight, regardless. Norma, on the other hand, didn't move an inch. Initially, she was leaning down a bit when she approached me. She was still leaning down, as if she completely forgot how to move back up into rightful posture.

Her eyes traveled the length of my body at least four times. I barely moved against the feeling of her studying me with a layer of judgment. Why was she so interested in a dorky ten year old wearing vanilla extract behind her ears?

To break the silence, as I stepped out of one of my sandals, I let it fall straight to the tiled floor. It snapped like a firecracker.

Immediately, Kimmie shook herself out of scallywag mode, and Norma stepped away, brushing back her short, black hair. "Well, Abigail, it is nice to meet you." She moved her chin over her plump shoulder, her beady eyes outlining her son's near-trembling body in the kitchen. "Ryan having a girlfriend is news to me, but if he likes you, I am sure you are a sweet girl." Her voice carried at least two types of definition: genuine shock and a tone that screamed *We'll discuss this later.*

Ryan's face drained. Behind his glasses, I saw his eyes revert a bit back into his skull.

Desperate, I shot a glance over at Kimmie, my eyes ordering her to fix what she just broke. She coughed a bit. "Well, uhh, they're not dating yet, Aunt Norma, but I'm tryin' my best here to play matchmaker." In between words, she kept looking at me, as if I was capable of invisibly handing her all of the right words to say. I wanted to hand her a bathtub plug for her mouth, so she would stop talking.

Even Scott joined in the mission to save Ryan. He spoke with a mouth full of potato chips. "Yeah, Mama Norm, that's my little cousin over there. She has a huge crush on Ryan."

I scoffed. "Scott. What the heck?"

Norma pinched the bridge of her nose. "Scott, please, don't call me Mama Norm." As she released her vice grip of frustration, Ryan's mother gave me a flat, yet genuine, smile. "My son is a little shy, but he does have an old spirit."

Ryan dropped a can of pop on the kitchen counter. "Mom!"

She ignored him. "You just have to learn to appreciate his wisdom."

He tried again. "Mom, God, just stop."

"Okay, okay." Now she was smiling with the fire of maternal pride. It was so eerie, though, I couldn't tell if that was a good sign or a bad sign. "So glad you girls could come." She reached out and took my overnight bag. "I'll hold on to these until it's time to swim. The boys were just taking a break from video games." That was probably why they were all huddled together in the kitchen, reaching around each other for cans of Coca-Cola and jamming cookies and potato chips into their mouths.

None of them looked alike. Maybe Ryan and Jace, a little, because they both were pale with black hair and striking eyes hidden behind round-framed glasses. They all looked so animated, however, fishing for food and speaking to each other with full mouths. Jace's voice was already deep and dripping with maturity, while Ryan's still squeaked a bit when he spoke, lingering youth hanging on as long as it could.

I saw pieces of food flying from Scott's mouth as he spoke. Behind him, Cameron pretended to bench-press two boxes of cheese crackers, the veins in his neck pumping from forced muscular exertion.

Seconds later, Kimmie uttered, "Eww, gross." She must have seen it, too.

The only two who didn't seem to be boys at all were Ryan and Jace; they were vigilantly methodical in the way they drank their pop and ate their snack food. A few crumbs broke off and fell onto the counter. Jace, mid-conversation, reached for a napkin and scooped the crumbs inside. Meanwhile, Ryan ran around his three friends with a wet napkin and soaked up any Coca-Cola splashes on the counter and near the sink. He didn't show any facial expression as he did it.

The playful shoves in the kitchen stopped after Scott, who was considerably bulkier than Ryan, shoved him against the wall; the screen door to the back porch deck nearly snapped off the track. Norma immediately ordered the boys to calm down. She used plain-as-day words, "Boys, now behave," but her tone was lethal.

All four of them snapped upright like soldiers in the military. Cameron dropped a cookie. He pretended to cry before straightening, the cookie exceeding the five-second rule. He wasn't built like the rest of his friends, nor did he demonstrate the physical features that boys his age should. I watched his broad shoulders tense and the red patches of skin above his cheeks push up against his small, hard eyes. If I didn't know any better, I would have guessed him to be at least 15, not 12.

Norma glanced over at me and Kimmie. She was giving us a victorious grin, almost like she was saying with her expression alone, "Let's see how long I can keep these boys tame."

Kimmie nudged me. Her whisper tickled my ear. "Think Jace's gorgeous?"

I looked over at him again. The corners of his mouth twitched as he did his best to suppress a building smirk. Next to him, Ryan barely held it together. Now the boys seemed to be playing each other, testing one another at who could hold still the longest. "I guess, in that vampire kind of hot." Jace's black hair and pale skin automatically defined him as a vampire; at least, that was what I thought. The fact that he almost always wore black was another vampire-defining feature.

Jace caught me looking. One of his dark eyebrows arched. Terrified, I pretended to be suddenly interested in the kitchen ceiling.

Kimmie nudged me again. "He's gorgeous."

I rolled my eyes. "You think everyone is hot."

With a tug on my hair, she corrected me. "Gorgeous. I don't think he's hot. I think he's gorgeous." She paused a moment. "He's quiet. He probably thinks I'm a bitch. I'm pretty sure of it. I don't blame him."

I massaged the roots near my temple. She had pulled harder than I thought.

Norma stepped around the line of boys still in formation. She wiped a few excess crumbs from her kitchen island. She even tapped Ryan on his shoulder, a clean smile cutting her face in half at the bottom, an indication that he was being a good boy and not misbehaving. Still, nobody moved. The boys were quiescent little beings, nothing moving around them except dust particles floating through the block of light from the kitchen window.

The moment that she walked out of the kitchen and disappeared into the hallway, the four boys relaxed. Shoulders slouched, groans escaped their ravenous mouths, and every single one of them grabbed another can of pop. They argued about who the winner was for at least ten seconds.

At an impasse, they asked Kimmie who won. She looked directly at Scott without any hesitation. "Him."

His face grew hot. Instead of disagreeing with her choice, the boys absorbed Scott's facial expression for what it was worth. Cameron opened and closed his mouth like a fish out of water; his every attempt at mocking the situation blundered, and nobody seemed interested in bringing it up again.

It wasn't often that a pretty, popular girl like Kimmie singled out my cousin like that.

"C'mon, let's go to my room." Ryan waved his little hand in the air and everyone followed. The entire time we walked down the hallway, I noticed Kimmie tracing the white-blonde streaks and the feathered, fraying ends of the hair curling along the base of Scott's neck.

There wasn't a lot of room for everyone in Ryan's bedroom. It was of a decent size, but definitely not for a group of six people. The first thing I noticed was the poster of a tiger running through water in the winter. I had the same exact poster in my bedroom, but I didn't say anything. His walls were blue, one with wolf wallpaper, and his bedframe screamed old-style country cabin with its polished wood and petrified branches stacked on the headboard.

The boys cramped together on Ryan's bed while Kimmie and I wove together a few throw pillows on the floor. I eavesdropped on their conversations, about how they spent most of the morning playing *Final Fantasy VII* and *Worms*, and that they were ready to play a new game on the PlayStation. One of Ryan's birthday presents was a GameShark, so they were also discussing options on how to appropriately use it to its best advantage.

For a while, it seemed that Kimmie and I didn't exist to them. Instead of sitting on his bed, Ryan stood directly in front of his small television, remote control in hand, colorful PlayStation images reflecting off his wide-framed glasses. When he turned to ask what game he should play next, Kimmie held up a hand and yelled rather loudly, "*Ehrgeiz!*"

Scott countered her. "Fuck that game. Play F-F-seven again."

Ryan reached for the *Final Fantasy VII* case. Next to me, Kimmie deflated. We both sank back against one of the bed posts, Kimmie's shoulder underneath mine, both of her feet stacked atop my right ankle, and we acted like the hebetudinous, unentertaining dolls that the boys pretended we were.

At least an hour passed, and nothing linked us to the boys aside from a few glances. There was an occasional question or two from one of the boys, usually

Ryan, who seemed the only one trying to keep us all together for the sake of his birthday party. At one point, Cameron dropped his legs over the front of the bed, and he must have forgotten that Kimmie and I were even there; his steel heel cracked the soft center of my skull. Shocked that I screamed, he threw his leg aside just to kick Kimmie square in the nose.

Eventually Kimmie excused herself from the bedroom and, reaching down to grab me by my shirt strap, pulled me with her.

The boys didn't even flinch. They didn't even react as we left.

I caught a glimpse of a timeline of Ryan's school portraits adorning the narrow hallway's walls. I recognized the background and theme for the first one. I had the same one when I was in 1st grade, so that meant his timeline started when he was in the 3rd grade. Ryan's smile was timeless, in that his sweet young face was the only changing feature across the photographic evidence surrounding me.

There was something inherently intimate about seeing chronological portraits of Ryan in his own home. It was unusual, almost indescribable, what I felt as I skipped along with Kimmie. Had any other girls, aside from his family, seen his life documented like that? Butterflies stirred in my stomach each time I made eye contact with a different Ryan. It got to the point that I fought back a little bit, tugging Kimmie to slow her down, just so I could have a few more seconds to observe and memorize the contours of his smile dimples.

Waiting at the mouth of the hallway were Norma and a man who I guessed was Ryan's dad, holding a platter of freshly grilled hamburgers and hot dogs balanced in his tanned, oily arms. While his mother stacked cans of pop on top of one another to carry outside, his father balanced plates atop the tips of his fingers like a waiter while stepping outside, all the while carefully keeping the sliding door open with just the tip of his boot. He had to spin on his toes to avoid Norma as she ran back inside for a bowl of ice.

Strangely enough, they didn't say a word to one another while they worked. That was why I didn't dislodge myself from Kimmie to offer them assistance. A part of me, the part my mother raised me to be, saw myself peeling away and at least holding the sliding door open, but another part of me, the part that enjoyed studying from afar, refrained.

The understanding between Ryan's parents, how Norma did this and his father did that, was as remarkable as watching lightning bugs illuminate a hayfield. Every few moments, I noticed a flicker of realization between his parents.

The flicker could light up the entire house without a sound. I didn't want to interrupt that kind of silence.

As we stopped in the open dining room, Kimmie's hold on my arm now felt like the cow bite trick kids in my class pulled on each other. The top of my skin burned while the hairs on my arms jolted and folded right out of their follicles. "I can't believe they're just ignoring us like that. For fuck's sake, that's my cousin. Yours, too." She swallowed hard. I watched her face wrinkle as she contemplated for a moment. "Maybe it's because you're here."

Something snapped in the pit of my stomach. Perhaps snapped wasn't quite the way to describe it. It felt more like nausea on an empty stomach, my organs shifting around in empty space, and the little air pockets pushing against my skin.

I couldn't help but to gasp. "But I thought you said I was invited?"

Near us, Norma cursed underneath her breath. I quickly glanced over and saw an overturned bowl of potato chips on the floor.

"You were invited." Kimmie didn't say anything else after that.

Guiding me around like a dog on a leash, she brought me towards the dining room table, where Norma had packed away our overnight bags with our bathing suits and towels. All the while, I obeyed without any backtalk and trusted one of my best friends. Kimmie's controlling nature overwhelmed that of Audrey's or Laney's, but I didn't mind it so much. She knew what she was doing. After all, we were in her aunt and uncle's house. I trusted her to do what was best for me, and I understood that, regardless of being invited or not, the boys were just acting like boys.

As much as I wanted her to let go of my arm so I could get a hot dog and some potato chips, I bit my tongue while she pulled me into a different room in the hallway and locked the door behind us. "We'll go swimming without them. Screw them. *Fuck* them." She blinked at me. "You okay?"

I rubbed my hands together. "If they don't want me here, I don't want to be here."

Kimmie's eyes took the shapes of almonds. She didn't like hearing me say that.

Approaching the situation at a different angle, I tried, "And you've been dragging me around."

She laughed. "Yeah, well, I'm pretty pissed. Sorry."

We weren't in a guest bathroom, or anything like that. It looked like a guest room undergoing a slow transition into a computer room. One large window acted as the heart of the room, with red beams of light filtering through maroon curtains. As I held my leg out, I watched my knee change from flesh-colored to blood red. Kimmie did the same after watching my skin pickle in the sunlight.

A red canopy protruded from the center of the room. I had to shove part of the gauze-like apparatus away just so I could reach for my bag and not get tangled in its artificial cobweb.

To the left, there was a small bookshelf snugly packed away in the corner; to the right, a computer monitor flickered in and out of focus. The screensaver must have been busted. It looked like a desk for a busy mind, full of stacked papers, books, folders, and coffee rings. If I turned my head a certain way, I could use the sunlight to uncover real cobwebs streaming down from a plant hanging from a hook a few feet above my head.

Kimmie must have noticed me looking around, for she gently slapped my bare shoulder. "C'mon, don't stall. Put your bathing suit on."

Oh. She thought I was wasting time so that I didn't have to change into my bathing suit.

There was that ominous feeling that, somewhere, there was a little tiny hole that the boys could look through and see me and Kimmie, naked and all exposed. Like they were all huddled together, shoulders touching shoulders, hands on knees, eyes searching the red room for just a glimpse of skin. I had to bite my tongue at imagining something like that, because the thought alone grabbed my stomach with its ice-cold hands and dropped it in a cauldron of boiling water.

It could have been worse. There could have been a camera recording our every move. Quickly, I stole a glance at the computer for a webcam. When I didn't see a red eye blinking back at me, I deemed the room as safe as possible.

Reluctant, yet determined, I reached into my overnight bag for my bathing suit. Kimmie had already draped hers across the back of the computer chair.

She snorted. Her eyes pointed at the lock turned in the doorknob. "It's not like they can get in here."

"Yeah, but..." and I stopped right there.

As soon as she said that, right after I tried to reason with her, just as I had slipped my blue tank top over my head, when she had nearly stepped completely out of her panties, the boys stormed from Ryan's bedroom, slapping and touching every single wall and door on their way out.

As they stampeded for the kitchen, I bunched my bathing suit up in front of my mouth and yelped into it, suffocating the harsh rawness of my scream. Kimmie froze, however, which was much unlike her. I saw the color of her tan skin flush. The base of her neck was now skirted with a red glow. She haphazardly shot me a look dripping with fear. We made sure to keep our eyes together until it was over.

By the particular attention the boys showed the door hiding a half-naked me and an almost-naked Kimmie, the fact that every single one of them pounded away at the door and yodeled like a pack of wolves on the hunt, they were definitely aware that we were on the other side.

Someone's hand brushed the doorknob. Both Kimmie and I lunged forward, dropping pieces of our bathing suits, making sure the door never so much as cracked. It was just a fluke, perhaps an accidental touch as the four boys migrated in an unorganized fashion down the thin hallway.

The wildlife calls dissipated. The last noise to brush the door, a set of fingers clawing at the wood, echoed into nothingness. Kimmie and I pinned our ears in the direction of the kitchen. The sounds of cans of pop hissing and the sliding door screeching across its track let us know that the boys were back in the kitchen: away from us, away from the door.

We both exhaled in relief.

We decided to swap bathing suits. I wore hers, which had a frilly pink top with red and pink bottoms, and she wore mine, teal boy shorts and a tank top covered in purple and blue flowers.

As I finished adjusting the layers of pink frills in the top, Kimmie glanced over at me. Her hazel eyes were curious. "Abigail?"

I didn't look up. "What's up?"

"Oh my God, you have tits."

"What?!"

She ran over to me and cradled both of her hands underneath my chest. It wasn't until I glanced down to see her pink palms that I noticed two small lumps jutting right above the creases of her fingers. I couldn't help but to step back and shield my chest with my arms, as if she suddenly had X-Ray vision and could see my most personal features.

My comment flew out of me in a roar of mortified thunder. "Holy crap, when did I get boobs?" Kimmie reflexively waved her palms in my face, a gesture ordering me to quiet down.

As she settled, she shrugged her shoulders. "Don't know. I don't stare at your chest all day, Abigail."

I glared.

Snickering, Kimmie finished dressing in the bathing suit. She fixed the twist in one of the bathing suit straps. "Shake 'em."

I blinked a few times. Curious, I jumped up and down in less-than-eager efforts, but they didn't shake. They were far too small. In succession with my jumping, Kimmie made sound effects. "Bunka-dunka, bunka-dunka."

I buried my face into both of my hands and moaned. I wasn't supposed to have boobs yet. I wasn't even supposed to have the beginnings of boobs yet, but they were right there, right where Kimmie pointed. My older sister still didn't have so much as mosquito bites on her chest; yet here I was, four years younger than her, already too far developed for a training bra.

Using the pink frills of the bathing suit top as a complementary accessory, my eyes studied the small, quarter-sized curves tucked underneath the stretchy swimming fabric. Now that I knew they were there, I couldn't stop staring at myself. I was so distracted with my body's newest assets that I couldn't feel the slightest bit affronted at having discovered these two new pieces of myself at an older boy's birthday party.

Aptly inquisitive, I touched one of the lumps. It moved like the flesh between my index finger and thumb. "Does that mean I'm supposed to wear a bra now?"

"Probably." Both of Kimmie's hands fanned out from her chest until they dangled at her knees. "If not, they'll sway like old lady's boobs."

We took a moment to compare each other's bodies. Kimmie's legs were longer than mine. She made the comment that she was all legs and I was all torso. We even used our imagination and traced each other's bodies with our eyes. Kimmie told me that girls' bodies were compared to fruit. She told me I was a pear, and I told her that she was an apple. The only reason I called her an apple was because I knew she liked eating apples. I honestly had no idea what fruit she looked like.

When she asked me why I called her an apple, I lied and likened her skin color to that of a red apple: colorful, bright, tight and shiny and juicy. She laughed through her nose. "Ha. Juicy."

Suddenly, Kimmie asked me how old I was.

Frowning, I answered, "I just turned ten in May."

She looked me over, up and down, left and right, before raising her eyebrows. "I'm not tryin' to be mean, but you're gonna have back problems by the time you're in high school."

"Why is that?"

She cupped at her imaginary boobs and, leaning over, she arched her back like a humpback and stiffly marched back and forth without hardly making any progress forward.

I understood what she meant. I cowered in fear. "Oh, God." She straightened up in laughter.

Together, we emerged from the computer room in our bathing suits, skin glistening with sunblock and smelling like warm coconuts, only to see that somehow, the boys had managed to beat us outside and were already creating a whirlpool in the pool in the backyard. The remnants of grilled food littered the back porch. Paper plates weighed down with condiment bottles showed signs of wear, bun crumbs and half-eaten potato chips stuck on streaks of excess ketchup. Crushed pop cans teetered in the breeze.

I made it a rule that Kimmie was not allowed to talk about my chest for the rest of the day. As we stepped from the kitchen entryway onto the back deck, she promised that she wouldn't bring it up again. I wasn't sure if I could believe her or not.

We descended the wooden steps and approached the shaking pool walls. The best sign of the day was when Scott threw his arms in the air and proclaimed, "Yeah, the girls are here! Help us with this whirlpool!"

That meant we were now wanted. For the first time that day, we felt welcome. Kimmie pushed me up the ladder, and while I waded in the chin-high water, she dove and went straight for Scott's ankles.

Jace did so many bellyflops on purpose that his entire chest and stomach were lobster-colored within just ten minutes. There were even oddly shaped welts streaked across his chest, like someone took a branch of poison ivy and brushed it all over him. Nobody was quite sure what motivated him to drop onto the water belly first over and over again. Nobody was quite sure how many times he had flopped, either: at least eight times, maybe nine. Scott tried counting, but he lost track after six or seven, and that was at least four or five flops ago.

The entire time it happened, everyone cheered for Jace. Scott hooted and hollered, throwing his balled first into the air and barking like a dog. Kimmie and I eventually performed cheerleading moves we'd learned when we were cheerleaders together, back in 3rd grade. We were afraid that not participating would further segregate us from the group, more so than we already were, even though we both shared the concern that cheering Jace on would further heighten his risk of getting injured.

We stood on the pool walls. Our feet clawed at the metal covers. As she and I made big Vs with our arms and clapped in sync, Cameron joined in and mocked us. He was too big for the pool walls, so he crawled out of the water and ran up to the back porch deck. He snapped his hips back and forth, and said in a high-pitched, lisp, "Yeah! Go team! Go Jace! You look *so good*, let's go!"

Kimmie and I tested his flexibility by doing herkies in the air, followed by kicking our right legs, toes pointed, straight up towards the sky. Surprisingly, and so effectively we were amazed, Cameron matched us move for move. We nearly doubled over in laughter.

Everyone seemed to find their place: me and Kimmie cheering, Jace in a rhythm of slithering out of the water just to slap belly first on the surface once more, Cameron winking and spinning around like he was Serena from *Sailor Moon*, and Ryan and Scott wading in the water in front of us, arms out just in case we slipped and fell in the water. It was a comforting gesture.

Eventually, Scott readied a sponge ball and threatened me and Kimmie with it unless we got back in the water. I threw in the white flag without a fight and slid back into the tumultuous chlorine waves. Kimmie, on the other hand, tested Scott's warning, and her lissome body danced along the edge of the pool on just her tippy-toes, the muscles in her thin legs flexing every time she was midair. He screamed out the f-word and launched the multicolored ball right at Kimmie. She slid on the wall trying to stop herself, the sponge clipping her side, and she tumbled face first into the water.

Something hard smacked the wall before Kimmie was completely underwater. Immediately I assumed she broke her ankle. Scott uttered the f-word again as he swam for the dark figure sinking to the bottom.

It was no surprise that Kimmie torpedoed from the water completely swollen with laughter. The paleness of Scott's face, however, wasn't humorous. He gritted his teeth and splashed water in her face. "You're a bitch."

She smirked. "So?"

The tension fizzled out a bit when the water rippled shortly after a quick, sharp snap. Another one of Jace's bellyflops.

I was the first to get out of the water for a break. Even with sunblock, my pale skin couldn't withstand the harsh July sunlight. I'd unintentionally started a trend; one by one, everyone else emerged from the pool to towel off and regenerate with pop and potato chips.

The only two who actually went back in the water were Jace and Cameron. While Jace readied himself for a new round of bellyflops, Cameron danced around the edge of the pool doing his best to create a solo whirlpool. Every now and then, he called out a number. I guessed the number was associated with Jace's bellyflops.

As we reached around each other for napkins, my face grew hot noticing Ryan next to me. His wet hair was blindingly shiny. In the sunlight, it looked like his black hair was streaked in whites and yellows. Speckles of water peppered his bony shoulders and parts of his chest. His pale skin pretty much glittered if he moved at the right angle. I saw the beginnings of a sunburn encompassing his nose and the top of his forehead.

He popped a cookie into his mouth. It hung between his lips. "You guys wanna get in the hot tub?" We didn't need to answer. The excitement in my and Scott's eyes was enough for Ryan to grin, a gesture that nearly let go of his cookie. He bit it in half and chewed.

Ryan didn't even ask for parental permission to use the hot tub. Instead, he asked Scott to help him lift the lids from the tub. Seconds later, he pressed a few buttons and the jets were gushing. The smells of hot dogs and hamburgers were wafted away by the powers of the chlorinated water and fresh, churning steam.

Norma's voice called from somewhere above us, "You boys make sure no food gets in that tub!" I looked up. She was staring down at us from a kitchen window. All I could see of her was her eyes and black hair. She studied us for a few more seconds before she stepped away. I was relieved to have seen a faint smile on her face before she vanished. I wanted her to like me enough that I could come back whenever I wanted.

The three of us could barely get ankle deep in hot tub water before Kimmie ascended the wooden steps. She sprinted on her purple-painted toes, like an elegant dancer leaping in the air, towards the hot tub. She managed to also snag her own can of Coca-Cola on the way. Snapping her can open, she exclaimed, "Make room for me!" I stepped away from Ryan a bit, giving Kimmie enough room to stand between us. I figured the way we were standing was how we were going to sit.

At first I thought she would squeeze into the seat next to me, the place I purposely left room, but shockingly, she sat across from me, putting Scott and Ryan at my sides. We were now the four corners of a square in the hot tub.

Another splash snapped behind us. We didn't even have to look. We knew. Seconds later, Cameron cried out, "Twenty-three!"

We extended our legs out so that our feet met in the middle. Scott went first so that his legs would be on the bottom, since they were the longest and the biggest. Ryan was next and then Kimmie, even though they were both pretty much the same size. They made me go last because I was the shortest.

As I dropped my legs on top of Kimmie's, I wondered for a moment if any part of my skin was touching Ryan's. Thinking about it gave me goosebumps again. Nervous, I expected someone to ask who had the goosebumps—but thankfully, nobody seemed to notice. My legs were the only ones that didn't stretch out into the other person's seat. Ryan's feet were kind of in Scott's corner, and vice-versa, and the heels of Kimmie's feet were barely touching my corner.

Her purple toenails were like noticeable pebbles underwater. My anklet, a beaded thing my sister made me at her last slumber party, matched Ryan's swimming trunks.

Scott giggled. "Poor Abigail, too short and tiny."

"Shut up." I splashed him directly in the eye. He hissed and shielded his face. "That's what you get, jerk."

Reaching underwater, Scott attempted to cup a gallon of water and throw it in my face. Ryan shoved his foot into Scott's side, "Hey, don't. Don't be mean."

"Fine, birthday boy." My cousin dropped his weapon.

It was quiet for a few seconds, like we all were afraid to talk or something after that. Nobody mentioned anything about our feet in the middle anymore, or our legs still touching each other. We stayed like that the whole time. Sometimes, someone would move, and Kimmie would shriek, "Eww, it feels like snakes!" and we all would laugh and writhe our legs around like serpents in the water, but we never pulled back.

The most that happened was Kimmie tried plucking her big toe underneath the side of my bathing suit bottoms, but I shoved her away in time before she yanked it down far enough to reveal anything. Naturally, she grinned at me. The boys didn't even notice. I rolled my eyes. Of course she was trying to pull down my bathing suit bottoms in a hot tub with two boys. Of course she wasn't going to tone down her natural crazy self at my expense. I even mouthed it to her, "Of course you would." Her pride shone like a beacon.

Ryan eventually looked up, the tips of his black hair pointed and wet, and he asked, "Are you guys having fun?" The bottoms of his glasses had started to fog up in the steam.

"Heck yeah!" Scott splashed the water ceremoniously.

"We're also going to see a movie." Ryan looked at Kimmie, then at me. "Are you guys coming?"

I frowned. Kimmie never warned me that we were also going to see a movie. I thought that we were just going to Ryan's house to swim and play video games for his birthday. Even if I had known that we were seeing a movie, I probably wouldn't have been able to go. My mother gave me options when that summer began. Most importantly, if I wanted to go to Town and Country Days with Kimmie and Laney in August, I wasn't allowed to do anything else so I could have enough money for one of the night passes.

My response lifted from my lips like a thin cloud of gauze. The steam rolled all around us in swirls of cigarette smoke. "I can't. I didn't bring any money."

It was doubtful, even if I did know about the movie and asked my mother for the money, that I would be prepared to go. We didn't have a lot of money to spare when it came to things like shopping or going to the movies. My mother and Patrick did their best to keep me and Diana happy, even if that meant having to walk by a new pair of sandals or miss out on the latest Hollywood hit.

Most of my friends were aware that my family didn't have a lot of money. There were some topics between us that we knew better than to ever bring up.

"I can pay for you."

My heart dissolved and dripped down my rib cage in a hot, molten film.

I moved my eyes up. Next to me, Ryan smiled like an innocent little boy. Now the peaches of his cheeks were kissed red by the sun. "I can pay. Mom said everyone can come." He even pushed up at his slipping glasses. Everything about him at that moment was mellifluous, dear, something I wanted to bottle up and keep on a shelf in my bedroom.

In the water, I clenched my hands together. Could they see just how nervous I was? My toes were even curling without my control. Across from me, Kimmie saw my feet move around underneath the water. Understanding me, she leaned over and purposely pulled her hair out from the back of her neck. Her hair moved atop the water, blocking at least Ryan from seeing the nervousness wave of my little toes.

Quickly, she looked up, flashed a wink, and I pretty much thawed in relief. Voiceless, I told her, "Thank you," with just my lips. She winked again.

"So, you gonna come?" Ryan leaned closer to me. The corners of his mouth still stained in pink, I looked for my answer there. His fingers grazed my elbows. "Please?"

My feet slithered even more. Kimmie now used her entire body to hide them.

"Umm." I bit my bottom lip. "Are you sure you're okay paying for me?"

Ryan nodded. "Yeah. It's my birthday. That's what I want."

Scott even interjected. "Dude, Abigail, just go."

Finally, I caved. "Okay. I'll go."

The sliding doors flew open. "Boys, dry off. We're leaving soon!" Bringing her hand down from her megaphone mouth, Norma glanced over the banister to see only red-stomach Jace and Cameron in the pool. Realizing she was four kids short, she immediately looked over at the hot tub. She must not have expected us to still be in the hot tub.

Instead of saying anything, Norma nodded at Kimmie, and then she did the same to me. "You girls coming with us to the movies?"

"Yup!" Kimmie trapped Scott in a headlock. He rolled around in the hot tub water.

Dodging a random foot in the air, I squeaked, "Yes, ma'am."

She wiped sweat out of her forehead wrinkles. "Ryan will be happ—" Another slap ricocheted from the backyard. Norma walked over to the banister, fingers clenched around the top like claws. She yelled, "I said get out of the water!"

She gasped. She must have just seen Jace's chest.

Her voice took on a motherly tone. "Jace, what on earth did you do?"

I swore I heard the number thirty-five before she dropped both fists down on the banister and ordered the boys out of the water. That was our cue to get out of the hot tub as well, the four of us struggling in biased methods of teamwork to help each other out. Kimmie helped me, but I didn't help Scott or Ryan, and she and I darted straight for the sliding door.

We spared the two boys our assistance to get out of Norma's maternal yet strict clutches. I heard the verbal lashing from the computer room as Kimmie and I changed out of our swim clothes and into our day clothes. In sync, four boys' voices repeated the phrases, "Yes, ma'am. No, ma'am. Sorry, ma'am."

As we stepped outside to head to New Martinsville, I wasn't expecting to see a black luxury sedan idling in the gravel driveway. It practically glittered of money when I approached the back door. Ryan opened the door for me. "Mom's new car. She's wanted one for years."

The moment the door swung open, new car smell oozed into my nose. It was only the second time in my life that I'd smelled new car smell. The first was when Angelle's mother bought a new mini-van equipped with a television set in the center console. We had always watched *Titanic*.

Kimmie called shotgun and slid into the front seat without anyone batting an eye. As I slid into the back, Scott pushed me halfway onto the center cushion. On my other side, Jace and Ryan crawled into the backseat and tried to situate everyone so that we weren't packed in shoulder to shoulder. Eventually, Cameron unbuckled his seatbelt and pushed everyone into the back seat.

Somehow, we managed to fit all of five of us in the back seat; Scott and Ryan shared one seat, I shared the center cushion with everyone's knees, and Jace and Cameron shared the other.

As Norma sat in the driver's seat, she readjusted her rearview mirror with a harrowing glimmer in her eyes. "Now remember, kids—if anyone makes a mess in my brand new car, I *will* kick you out, and you *will* have to walk home."

Everyone got silent.

I glanced over at Ryan for some sort of signal, perhaps a wink that indicated his mother was merely joking. Unfortunately, he appeared just as dazed and horrified as anyone else.

We went to the Cinema 3 theaters in New Martinsville to see the movie *Chicken Run*. Norma bought everyone's tickets and shooed us into the theater like a line of baby ducks. We were all allowed to share three small bags of popcorn and one box of candy.

The movie itself wasn't as interesting as watching Kimmie struggle to get Scott's attention. The group realized shortly after the movie started that Kimmie had a crush on Scott, which didn't seem to fit the standard mold of popular girl liking unpopular nerdy boy. She reached for his hand in between scenes. When he wasn't looking, Kimmie touched the tip of his scabbed knee, a butterfly kiss in the end of her finger, and Scott's entire body rippled with shock.

At one point, he yelled out, "Kimmie, knock it off!"

She fought back: "Stop bein' such a pussy!"

Norma ended the fight for both of them by tossing kernels of popcorn onto the crowns of their skulls. She sat behind our row full of kids, a hawk in human form, night vision eyes singling out every little mishap we contemplated committing.

My favorite part of *Chicken Run* was sitting next to Ryan. We even shared a bag of popcorn, our buttery hands at times grazing one another, knuckles on fingernails, palms over hand tops. He invited me to share with him the most humorous parts of the movie by reaching over and tapping my knees, usually wheezing through buttery lips, "Ha-ha, that was so funny! Don't you think? Don't you?"

"It was!"

Rains of popcorn drizzled over us. "*Shh!* Kids, watch the movie." Norma was on point with her kernel bullets. That went on every fifteen minutes or so, for the duration of the movie.

After the movie, Norma treated everyone to McFlurries from McDonald's.

As we idled in the drive-thru, Scott handed me my McFlurry, an Oreo one. Everyone else either got M&M's or Reese's Cup. We continued to use our hands like a conveyor belt, passing off McFlurries to their rightful destination.

Norma reminded us to be careful, with the same cold stare as before the movie. "Remember, if anyone makes a mess in my new car, I will pull over and kick you out, and you will walk home." The luxury sedan rolled out of the parking lot.

Ryan breathed out through his nose. "Mom, we get it."

"Scott," Kimmie looked over her shoulder, "that means don't fuck up."

"*Kimmie!*" Norma brake-checked everyone. We all lurched forward, miraculously holding our McFlurries in place. We waited until the car was moving smoothly on Route 2 before continuing to dig into our ice cream.

We were a little more than halfway home when Scott pushed his knee against mine. "Abigail, lift your leg, I don't have room." He was a drama king who liked attention; he purposely stretched out his legs when we first got into the car at Valley Cinema 3 so he could have an entire seat to himself.

Ryan and I squeezed into the center cushion while Cameron and Jace wedged their ever-growing, preteen bodies into the seat behind Kimmie. She was quiet while scooping mouthfuls of ice cream and Reese's Cup chunks into her mouth without saying a word. The only thing not quiet about her was her lips, smacking together after she swallowed every bite. It reminded me of Audrey and her dreadful hair-chewing habit.

I fought back when I noticed Scott was purposely pushing me closer and closer to Ryan, whom I was already essentially sitting on top. Ryan couldn't help but to push back, so the two of them were making an Abigail sandwich. By the time I was able to hold my ground, using the bottom of Norma's seat as leverage to keep my legs in place, Scott buckled his shoulder and pressed it against mine. I didn't stand a chance against my cousin. He was literally twice my size.

Limbs moved. Hands gripped. In between shoves, I glanced down to see that part of Ryan's leg was wrapped around mine. My other leg propped up against Scott's violent knee as he continued to push underneath me, tipping me over until I lost control.

Ryan's left knee was now under my right leg completely. He started making noises, like he was in pain, so I tried wedging my leg to keep it from weighing on his. Where our skin met it left behind a little patch of sweat, and it cooled as our bodies continued to fight against one another. I growled through clenched teeth, "Scott, stop it. You have more room than anyone. Cut it out."

From the other side of the back seat, a voice called out, "Hey, guys, stop moving so much. We're gonna spill." Cameron's voice sounded miles away, like the backseat of Norma's luxury sedan was a private island, and he was stuck on one side while the rest of us were on the other. My eyes caught a glimpse of Cameron and Jace each holding their McFlurries in the air. As long as their ice cream was above their heads, it seemed safe, untouchable. Mine continued to slip and slide around in my tiny hand.

Another shove brought me back to the other side. "You're in my space." His space? Since when was the seat behind Norma Scott's space? "Sit closer to Ryan."

Any closer to Ryan would mean I would have to sit on top of him, and I wasn't ready for something like that. Nervous, my voice unhinged from my throat like a battle cry. "I already am!"

Ryan chimed, "Scott, leave her alone. *You* scoot over." He tried reaching over to slap Scott on the leg, but his arms were too short, and his elbow was dangerously close to my McFlurry.

"Guys, guys, guys," Jace sang.

Yet Scott fought back. "No, dude, my legs are—"

Whoosh.

In slow motion, all five of us in the backseat watched as my Oreo McFlurry leaped from my frail little hands, tumbling ever-so-elegantly midair. During our altercation, Scott's knee bumped up into my hands, launching my container of ice cream straight from my fingers. Even if I had prepared myself for something like that to happen, which I should have by copying what Jace and Cameron did, it wouldn't have helped. Scott thrashed against me in one last desperate effort to catapult me out of his so-called space.

Instead of sending me packing, he sent my McFlurry on a non-stop flight to the back of Norma's polished leather seat.

The McFlurry seemed to stay airborne long enough that we all stared at it, at the beauty of it, at the rawness that something so insignificant was about to label me a luxury sedan ruiner.

We watched in awe with growing, horrified eyes.

Hovering inflight, spinning majestically, we didn't have enough time to act. In a matter of milliseconds, Ryan quickly reached over into the back pocket of Kimmie's seat for a napkin. I tried to defy the odds of gravity by reaching out and trying to catch my blue and white container. The slipperiness of it caused it to slide up and out of my grasp, causing the ice cream to turn upside down and head straight for the floor.

Seconds to impact, Cameron jumped out of his seat, gasping, reaching over Ryan's lap with his long, strong arms. The tips of his fingers barely grazed the plastic lid.

Our efforts were too late.

The McFlurry splattered upside down, in a head-on collision with the floor behind Norma's seat.

I said the only word that came to mind.

"*Fuck.*"

Astonishingly, Norma didn't look up from the road. Both she and Kimmie seemed to be swaying in unison. They didn't hear the fatal weight of my f-word as it climbed from my lips.

It was dark outside. The black swallowed the sedan as we continued on Route 2 to Red Cliff Hill. Scott and I both tried to lean up and see the damage melting at our feet, but we bumped heads. Cursing, we retreated back against the seat, rubbing the soft spots near our temples. All I wanted to do was see the damage. I wanted to see just how much trouble I'd caused before being kicked out of the car to walk the last seven or eight miles home.

Maybe the ice cream was still in the container. Maybe it didn't spill anywhere. Maybe there was still a chance for me to live.

Up ahead, a large streetlight hovered above a one-lane bridge. The orange glow got closer and closer; the anticipation nearly overwhelmed us all as we jerked left, right, up, down, any which way we could to see. Jace whispered across our bunched bare knees, "A light's coming up. We'll check then."

My mind sucked in all of my creative energy, spooling my imagination into a paranoia that constricted around my entire body. Closing my eyes, I saw nothing but black. Opening my eyes, I saw nothing but black. Images swept across that dark blanket: strange images, like the ice cream transforming into a liquefied monster that leeched its cold hands around my ankles, yanking, pulling, roaring in bubbly, hot breaths.

The whole time this creature attempted to pull me under, Ryan stood nearby, his eyes overflowing with tears, a look of disappointment bleeding across his pale, innocent face.

At that, I started panicking. My body lurched forward. I didn't know why. Coming back to reality, I pressed my spine against the leather seat and started grinding my bones like a saw against a tree. "Oh my God, I'm gonna die. I'm gonna die, I'm gonna die. She's gonna—"

"*Shh*, just wait for the light." Cameron was leaning so far over that he was in Jace's lap.

We all waited impatiently for it to get closer, closer, just a little bit more...

Cameron hit Jace, who hit Ryan, who hit me, who hit Scott, and he whispered hard, "*Now!*"

As soon as the orange light broke into the backseat, we all leaned over, using the few seconds we had, and studied the black and white mess sprayed all over the floor. My heart didn't have any more room to sink when my eyes recognized the melting, shiny splatter sprayed at mine and Scott's feet.

Even though most of the McFlurry smashed all over Scott's foot, it wasn't enough to save me. There had to be more ice cream hiding somewhere else.

Reaching down, I picked up my McFlurry container and looked inside, only to find just a few spoonfuls left.

The rest of it, at least half of the quantity that had remained, already started to congeal all over the backdoor handle, the back of Norma's seat, and the seat Scott had hogged. I couldn't even find my plastic spoon. Knowing my luck, it was probably underneath Norma's seat, a bat in a cave.

Scott flicked his foot. "It's on my shoe? It's on my shoe!" Immediately I weighed down his uncontrollable legs by dropping both of my hands over his knees. He struggled against me, but I wasn't about to let my cousin kick up McFlurry ice cream everywhere like we were dancing around in rain puddles.

"Stop kicking!" Ryan reached over and brought his palm to the back of Scott's head. The snap ricocheted in the backseat like a firecracker.

Scott screeched through clenched teeth, his voice a few decibels below a whisper, "Abigail, it's all over my shoe!" He tried smothering a ticklish giggle. "It's so cold!"

I hissed back, "That's because you kicked it everywhere, you fuckin' dumbass!" The f-bomb from earlier left the gates open for all other rebellious words to slip through them. I was taking advantage of my curse word inventory, the one I had been building up for years, before Norma could kick me out of her car and order me to walk home with some coyotes, bears, and whatever else decided to roam the Appalachian hillsides.

"*Shh!* Scott! Don't say anything!" Ryan handed me a napkin, which I handed to Scott reluctantly, who leaned over and started to dab away at the ice cream melting across his ankle. Ryan quickly chastised him. "Don't clean your shoes, you idiot! Clean the seat! Hurry! Clean the door!" Another firecracker snap. "Anything else *but* you!"

Cameron plucked at the fabric between his shoulders. In the dark, his arms and elbows looked like skeletal structures of wings. "You guys want my shirt?" He waited for a response. "No? You don't want my shirt?"

Jace lowered his head. "It's too late." His voice burrowed deep in the backseat, the bass vibrating against my rib cage with a gentle yet forceful drum. It danced across our knees, over the tops of our feet. Looking over at him, at the outline of his head against the house lights zipping by in the backseat window, Jace looked like he sat next to a camp fire. He was about to tell a story.

Eyes flickering, hazel bursts pulsating, he whispered, "She's going to die."

I gasped.

The radio's white noise dissipated from around us. "What's going on back there?" Norma's voice rang through our bodies like a wave of dry ice, and we all froze in place. She reached up and started to adjust her rearview mirror. "Is everything okay?"

We all heard her fingers and rings clanging against the dashboard. Thankfully, she was struggling finding the light switch in her brand new car. That meant I had a least a few more seconds to say my goodbyes, tell Scott that I hated him, tell Kimmie that she was one of my best friends, tell Ryan that I thought he was cute, and that I liked it when he wore blue.

I closed my eyes and lowered my head, trying my best not to cry. My dark hair slipped across my bare shoulders. At least my body knew of its oncoming demise, its last caring effort to shield my glassy eyes from everyone around me.

Ryan wouldn't ever get the Matt Ishida Digimon trading card for his birthday, which still laid unnoticed back at his house in the birthday card from me and Kimmie and her family that he hadn't opened yet. Norma wanted to wait until after going to the movies for him to open presents.

The dashboard light came on. Norma's eyes peered over her right shoulder. "Boys?"

Scott arched his neck and opened his mouth.

Oh, God, this is it.

Next to him, Ryan reached over and tugged at his arm, trying to prevent the nuclear war that was about to start, but it wasn't enough. I reached out, grabbing anything and everything possible. My fingers clenched around the leather compartment between the driver seat and the passenger seat. Sneakers wedged between seat tracks, I willed an invisible shield around my entire body for whatever was about to happen next. An arm locked with mine. Ryan formed a link with me and him. The butterflies living inside of my stomach were far too terrified to even flutter.

I listened to Ryan order Jace and Cameron to lock arms, as well.

Moments later, Scott sang in the tone of a tattle tale. "Abigail dropped her McFlurry!"

Instantly, the car whipped across the oncoming lane of traffic. Everyone screamed. My fingernails ripped away from the compartment, my body soaring into Scott's lap. Scott's head slammed against the back window. The underwater noise of the *bop* upon impact harmonized with the shreds of gravel rolling underneath the vehicle.

Cursing, both Ryan and Jace fell into my lap. I tried to keep them there, to hold them in place while the car continued to bounce and spin, but my arm was too frail, my grip not tight enough; one of them dropped to the floor in front of us. I felt fingers climbing my legs. Meanwhile, Cameron squealed like he was on a roller coaster as he held on to the back of Kimmie's seat for dear life.

The whole time, Norma grinned in the driver's seat. She was an avid entertainer, a practiced showoff, and a liberally creative mother.

The car dropped from the cement road and eased into an abandoned parking lot for what used to be a gas station. Ryan cursed next to me—over and over again, he uttered the word *fuck*—which meant if he was next to me, Jace was the one draped across our feet. Fingers clutched my knee, and moments later, his powerful hazel eyes came up for air. His black hair was knotted, out of place, and pushed up on one side. They each helped the other, Ryan easing Jace back in place and Jace pulling Ryan out of my lap.

In the last few seconds of silence, as brown clouds of dirt knocked on all of the windows surrounding us, Scott reached over and touched my knee to apologize, but I slapped his hand away. Cameron and Jace were confused and asking aloud why we had stopped, even though the question itself was rhetorical. All the while, I clenched my fingers together and braced myself for Norma to yank me from the backseat by my hair and drop me into a puddle of mud outside.

When the car stopped, Norma casually forced the car into Park and she opened her door. Even the way she moved was horrific, the kind of scary that seemed too calm, too serene, to even be remotely dangerous, but you knew there was something wrong. She tapped the back of her headrest. "Little Abigail, get out of the car." I didn't move. The only part of my body still alive was my knees, and they were knocking together like a pair of drumsticks.

She sang, "Little Abigail, c'mon." Then she opened the backdoor herself, reaching in, her flashy, ring-covered fingers dancing right in front of Scott's stone-cold face.

Hurriedly, I glanced up at Kimmie, who was just as shocked as I was that I was about to get kicked out of the vehicle. She was sitting on top of her feet, like a bird perched on a ledge, her eyes the size of oranges. As best I could, I forced words into my eyes, a last second plea, and pushed them into Kimmie's, words like *Help me*, and *Do something*, and *Goodbye*.

Resignation flickered in her face.

Fingers snapped in front of Scott. Panicking, I somehow managed to throw one foot around Scott's leg. I felt three hands press against my back. Jace, Cameron, Ryan. They were touching me one last time before I disappeared forever.

The instant the tip of my sneaker touched ground outside, Kimmie made a noise. It sounded like she was choking on food, it was so muffled and smothered. She wasn't choking, however, I saw as I quickly looked over my shoulder. My heart found life again as I watched her lift her McFlurry from her lap. Determined, she snapped the plastic lid off. Sucking the spoon inside of her mouth and keeping it there, Kimmie did what any best friend would do. She made sure to show me her characteristic smirk before making her move.

As if it was nothing, Kimmie purposely overturned her McFlurry and placed it down on the floor in front of her. The backseat erupted in gasps. The boys definitely weren't expecting that. For good measure, she even rubbed it back and forth, moving the container like a marker across a coloring book page, making sure that ice cream spread like butter across the paper mats and the fuzzy floor.

Proud, she extended her chest, a loud, mature voice bellowing from her lungs. "Aunt Norma, I dropped mine, too." My heart now melted at her effort. I wasn't going to die alone anymore. Kimmie was coming with me.

An abandoned gas station nozzle swaying behind her, Norma smiled at us, her lips forming a straight line across her face. It was impossible to determine if she was smiling at her niece's friendly creativity or at the bonus that she was now exiling two little girls into the West Virginian outback. "Kimmie, get out of the car, too." She exited the vehicle. The boldness pumping in her veins, filling her to the brim, she even pushed her aunt away so she could reach for me. Norma's eyebrows rose at that.

While I climbed from the depths of the luxury sedan, I made sure to kick Scott a few times on my way out. Kimmie even pinched his knee. He called us brats.

We stood like prisoners waiting for our public executions. Kimmie leaned over and whispered in my ear, "How did that happen?"

"Scott," was all I said. Then I gave her a questionable look. "How did you not hear us? We were loud."

She nodded at the driver's door. "Aunt Norma had the radio full-blast up front. I couldn't hear a thing."

"Girls, what did I say from the very beginning?" Pacing around us, Norma was using the motherly tone on us. My mother did that to me all the time. First, she would ask a harmless question in a misleading comforting, sing-song tone. And then, out of nowhere, she would start yelling at me, saying that I was a wild child, that I didn't ever listen or behave well, and that I was being difficult and childish. I didn't expect Norma to give me that kind of treatment, but I did expect her to deliver our method of punishment right after securing our trust.

That's what all mothers did when scolding, whether they were disciplining their own kids or not.

Kimmie looked down between her toes. She appeared a lot calmer now. "You said not to make a mess in the car."

"And what happened?" Norma looked at me for an answer.

I sighed. "We made a mess."

She stopped pacing. "And how do you fix a mess?"

Cameron yelled from the backseat. I hadn't realized she left the backdoor open, allowing the boys to become an audience to our execution. "You clean it up!" Both Ryan and Scott elbowed him in the gut. He cowered back into the dark.

Norma rolled her eyes. "This isn't for you, Cameron."

He choked, "Sorry, ma'am." Jace called him an imbecile, but he was smiling about it.

Norma folded her arms. I looked up at her and thought it was strange how her hair was so dark, I couldn't find it against the black sky. In that moment, I probably spent at least ten seconds trying to find the outline of her short black hair, but it was impossible. It was just so dark. The only light came from the vehicle, and the dashboard lights weren't enough. She sighed, which meant she was about to deliver the final blow. "Okay, girls, this is what's going to happen."

In the end, Norma didn't make us walk home.

Instead of being sent off like a pair of wild orphans, Kimmie and I were ordered to clean out the vehicle as best we could. It took about twenty minutes to scrub at the ice cream, which had already embedded itself across the carpeted floor. The leather made it easy to wipe up any excess ice cream on the seats themselves. The boys didn't give any lip if we asked them to move, which was nice.

At least Kimmie spilled most of her McFlurry on a paper mat, which we just ripped into pieces and stored in a Walmart bag in the trunk until we got home.

Her mess took only a few minutes to clean up. Mine, on the other hand, took significantly longer.

The whole time I leaned over and scrubbed at the floor with a ratty, nearly useless napkin from McDonald's, Ryan talked to me. Just me, nobody else. Jace and Cameron talked to one another. Everyone gave Scott the silent treatment.

We talked about various things, like video games and movies. Ryan talked more than I did, but that was because I tried to focus on cleaning the ice cream out of his mother's backseat. Even if I scrubbed at it for the rest of the night, she would still need to get it washed. The milk would sour and permeate the new car smell right out of the vehicle.

He swung his feet back and forth. "I really liked the Digimon card."

Mid-scrub, I arched my neck up so fast, I gave myself a headache. There was even a pinch in the back of my neck. "You opened the card? I thought you hadn't opened anything yet!"

"I opened Kimmie's card. She pretty much made me." That sounded like Kimmie.

"What about the cards from, like, Scott and Jace and Cameron?"

"I guess I'll open them when I get home." His smile was sideways now. "The card you got me is awesome. Matt is my favorite. He's so cool." Ryan reached up and held a block of air in front of his mouth. "The way he plays the harmonica is like, *berr-beh-berr-berr*. I wanna learn how to play one." He started blowing wet puffs between his fingers. The sounds coming from his skin were the total opposite of any harmonica sound I was familiar with, but I smiled and rubbed in sync with his slobbery song.

I wanted to say, "I know Matt Ishida is your favorite," but I didn't want to sound obsessed. So instead, I said, "Mimi is my favorite." My napkin crumbled. Ryan handed me another one.

"I'll start calling you Mimi if you call me Matt."

I blushed. "Okay. And Scott can be Tai, and Kimmie can be Sora."

Ryan blushed, too. "Okay, awesome." He moved between the two front seats and tapped Kimmie's shoulder. "Hey, we're gonna start calling you Sora and calling Scott Tai."

"Sora from Digimon?"

"Yeah, from Digimon."

Scott tried to speak with us, but we kept interrupting him.

69

My knees were red and sore by the time I was finished. The only reason Norma asked me to stop cleaning was because I went through her entire stock of McDonald's napkins and used up most of the water in her spray bottle. Ryan made a joke that his mother carried a spray bottle in her car since he could remember, and that day was the first time it actually came in handy. I didn't know whether to feel good about that or bad.

Packing the used napkins in the same Walmart bag with the paper floor mat, I hopped into the backseat and wriggled my way between Scott and Ryan.

The car ride home was soft and quiet. Even though we were allowed to talk, we felt like we needed to whisper, just in case we said something that upset Norma. She still hadn't shown any signs of life. She drove with a blank expression on her face. At least she allowed Kimmie to turn completely around in her seat so she could talk with us, unbuckled from her seatbelt and everything.

Jace pointed out his window and said he saw a werewolf jumping across trees, keeping up with us, flying like a super force in the air. Then we all gave each other werewolf names and personalities. Ryan wanted to be a black wolf, but I told him to be white so his eyes could be blue. He agreed.

Norma dropped me and Kimmie off at her house. The boys threw themselves out of one of the back windows, hands waving, voices yelling, ululating that reverberated off Kimmie's big house, while Norma backed out of the driveway.

Kimmie whistled, gave someone the middle finger, and then she pushed me inside.

My mother wanted me to call her when we got back. As she answered with her standard "Hello?" and bombarded me with questions about how the party was, how much fun I had, and what movie we saw, Kimmie was rummaging through her cabinets for tall beer mugs. She mentioned that all of the McFlurry cleaning earlier made her crave a root beer float. I didn't notice I was pacing in the dining room until Kimmie told me to stop shuffling my feet. I pressed the cordless phone closer to my ear. "So you're staying with Kimmie tonight?"

"Yeah. I'll call you tomorrow," I told her.

Kimmie opened the refrigerator. I watched her eyes count the cans of root beer chilling near the eggs. She asked me over her shoulder, "Hey, Mimi, do you want one or two cans of root beer?"

I felt obligated to call her Sora, so I did. "Just one is fine, Sora."

"Okay!" She grabbed three cans. One for me, two for her.

My mother was at my ear again. "Who is Mimi? Who are you talking to?" "Nothing, Mom. It's nothing."

After Ryan's birthday party, the four of us were inseparable. Almost every afternoon, if Scott wasn't already at my house unpacking his overnight bag, he was calling the house to see if he could come over again. Even if he was at my house, we didn't stay there for long. Either Kimmie or Ryan would drive the four-wheeler to my house to pick us up.

Naturally, Scott rode with Kimmie, and I rode with Ryan. He was nervous about wrecking and getting hurt, so he had to tell me over and over again to hang on to him and not the bars on the back. Always careful, I barely pressed my fingers to his sides. Ryan was so frail, I feared breaking him in half.

Usually we ran straight from the four-wheelers and jumped into Kimmie's pool, sometimes even with all of our clothes on. If it was a cool summer day, we would throw the top off Kimmie's hot tub and jump right in. We got so out of hand with each other that, one time, Scott carried me right off Ryan's four-wheeler and dropped me in the hot tub, clothes and shoes still on. I ended up spraining my ankle, but I bit back the pain and laughed.

It took only a few days of spending time with Kimmie for Scott to hold her hand. They liked swinging their arms back and forth in the water, fingers linked, and hearts beating in sync. She tried kissing him a few times, but he always pulled away.

I never tempted Ryan to hold my hand. As much as I wanted for him and me to look just as adorable and girlfriend-boyfriend as Scott and Kimmie, I couldn't find it in me to sabotage his innocent, sweet complexion. The heat on his face the first time he saw me step out of the hot tub was a big enough sign that he still hadn't had his first kiss.

The last weekend before Town and Country Days was the last weekend that we could all spend time with each other.

Scott and I waited for Ryan and Kimmie to pick us up at my house. The two of them sped into my gravel driveway before noon. We made it back to Kimmie's house in record time, not even taking off our shoes before jumping into the water.

The excitement mixed with the desperation to keep the summer alive, to stretch it out just a little bit more, was a troublesome blend. Inhibitions smothered blind, Kimmie took off her t-shirt, shorts, and socks. All that was left was her panties. Her excuse was that she was too lazy to go back inside and change.

My cousin nearly fainted seeing Kimmie shirtless. Ryan looked away. Then he looked at me.

"Well," was all I said at first.

Before long, sets of shoes and shirts lay soaked across the pool deck. My hair was long enough that it covered most of my naked chest. I owed Kimmie for smothering her McFlurry in her aunt's new luxury sedan. My debt was paid when I threw off my Pokémon t-shirt and unbuckled my training bra.

Kimmie admitted that she wanted the sun to kiss her in new places, so she was free in her somersaults, allowing her lighter skin to blend in with the golden skin. I was more nervous of an adult catching us swimming without tops than of Ryan seeing me naked.

Scott and Ryan didn't get as naked as Kimmie and I did, but they did take off everything but their underwear. After a while, Scott put his t-shirt back on. He was probably self-conscious compared to the smaller, frailer Ryan swimming next to him.

That day, we referred to each other only by our Digimon names. Tossing Ryan's wet shirt back and forth like it was a hot potato, we screamed out our new identities.

"Mimi!" Ryan chucked me his wet t-shirt.

I underhanded it to Kimmie. "Sora!" She always caught it, arms straight over her head, blonde hair shimmering like chains of liquid gold all around her. She had no regard for the sleek naked nature of her young body.

Then, of course, she kissed the wet shirt before throwing it over at Scott. "Tai, catch!" Her intentions contrasted. The kiss fooled Scott enough that he didn't expect the t-shirt to fly at his face at 100 MPH. Kimmie was trying to impress him. The shirt dropped in the water before Scott could catch it, and he blamed everything but his lack of athleticism.

"The sun was in my eyes," he said.

"I wasn't ready," he said the next try.

A few tries later, out of nowhere, he blamed me. "Mimi was distracting me!"

I scoffed in disbelief before throwing it back to Ryan. "Matt!"

The cycle continued.

We managed to entertain ourselves for hours. Doing the same thing, over and over again, calling each other the Digidestined, laughing together, sharing sunburns on our noses, getting close underwater but pretending to be so far away. That was how I tried touching Ryan's stomach, by accident of course, but he wriggled away just in time, like a sea eel, before I could.

When it was time for us to get out of the water, Kimmie went first. Her stride was methodical, salacious, hair whipping side to side. It was almost as if she knew the exact angle of the sun for it to cast on the pool water, bounce back up at her, and illuminate her entire body in patches of water mirrors. She was giving Scott one last look at her, one honest-to-goodness last look, before the summer was over. He practically ate her with his eyes, his mouth hung wide open, eyelids pulled apart and nailed to the bottoms of his eyebrows and the tops of his cheeks. My cousin aged a bit ahead of schedule when that happened.

Ryan looked over at me. The water slapped against the bottom of my neck. "Are you, umm, gonna do that?"

I shook my head. "Nah."

The corners of his mouth turned up. "Good."

Kimmie draped a towel around her neck like a feathered boa. She still hadn't put on a shirt. "Abigail should. She's got the boobies."

Rolling my eyes, I sunk a little bit further in the water.

The summer ended in Kimmie's pool that year, with the sounds of her stepping in rhythm across her small pool deck, noises matching her extended neck as she danced. "Bunka-dunka bunka-dunka." It was hard to ignore the sudden protrusion of her lungs as she inhaled without exhaling, her ribs stretching her pale skin, her dark nipples flat across her chest.

I pretended that I didn't notice Ryan's heavy, brown eyes searching underwater for something.

Near us, Scott still hadn't cranked his mouth back shut.

We slithered out of the water right as Nyla pulled in the driveway. She didn't double-check our expressions when she stepped in the kitchen and found us reaching around one another, bottles of whipped cream and chocolate syrup dangling between our fingers, bowls of melting ice cream lining the counter. She couldn't see beyond the liquefying vanilla cream, where our eyes were doubled in size, studying one another, making sure there was no proof that we were just swimming inappropriately a few minutes earlier.

Before we went our separate ways, we documented the epitome of our summer on Kimmie's graffiti door.

Tai + Sora, Matt + Mimi.

Six

When I started 5th grade, I was nothing more than skin and bone, a little girl with '70s bangs and a blanket of summer's freckles fading across my sunburnt nose.

When 5th grade ended, I was a swelling body consumed in curves, new smells, and puberty. Of all of my girlfriends, I was the first to officially become a woman. It happened when I was ten, and the realness of shedding blood for four days and discovering patches of skin that used to be bare now traced in black pencil strokes of hair...well, it was barbaric.

Kimmie predicted my evolution into adulthood before anyone else. She poked the bubbly protrusion on my chest and said, "Knew it. You're like one of them baby prostitutes. Know what I mean?"

I didn't, but I nodded and ignored the fact that my friend was poking my boob.

The summer of 2001 ended in a bleak cloud of darkness and rain, which heavily contrasted with the dry brightness previously maintained by June and July. I went down to Audrey's on one of the rainiest of days, the petrichor filling my entire body, and Tracy showed us how to shampoo our hair in the rain. The three of us ran outside in nothing but our bathing suits. We drizzled shampoo across each other's scalps and proceeded to lather, rinse, and repeat over and over again. TJ eventually joined us, but that was only because Todd ordered him outside to shower off so they didn't have to use any water.

"Saves money," Todd bellowed.

I made the joke that it would take more than just one rainstorm to wash away all of the dirt on Ray. Tracy decided to test my theory by lugging Ray from his camper and telling him to use the shampoo in his hair. He didn't even know what to do with it. He held the Suave bottle in both of his hands, like a child holding a Sippy cup, and he looked at the bottle and then back at us. I told him to turn it upside down over his head and squeeze like he was using a bottle of ketchup.

When he listened, a dollop of coconut shampoo oozed across his black hair and he squealed like a girl.

Fortunately for him, it only took one rainstorm for Ray to wash his hair clean. He took advantage of our girly burst of adventure and began washing his arms, legs, hands, and his beard. By the time the shampoo bottle was empty, Ray looked halfway decent, and he didn't smell like the inside of a kneepad. He was so eager that he asked us if we were going to wash ourselves in the rain again. Tracy told him, "If you buy the next bottle," and Ray agreed.

The thing about Ray was that he was nothing but an innocent boy, trapped inside a middle-aged man's body. I'd learned parts of his background since I met him, in 1999. Audrey liked telling me the story about how Ray fell in love with a girl in high school, so he bought her a car; the girl took the car, left school, and never came back. As much as I wanted to discredit her story, Ray sadly confirmed it any time Audrey asked him, "Didn't that happen, Ray? You told me it did!"

He owned a little Subaru and kept it decorated with animal key chains and laser lights that zapped across the floor mats. There were times that he got so angry with his car that we could hear him crying from the house. One time, Tracy motioned me to her bedroom window, and the two of us watched and listened as Ray kicked his car, tears flying down his dirty face. He was saying things like, "After all I've done for you, this is how you treat me?" He'd kick a tire and throw a rock, bawling like a toddler. It was the funniest, saddest thing I had ever seen.

Despite his tendencies, I liked Ray. He was innocent and nice to me. He was serene and giving to everyone. Any time Tracy needed something from the store, Ray offered to drive to Brownsville for her. If she was ever unable to take the kids to the bus stop, Ray volunteered to get up early that morning and take them all the way to Gunners Valley School.

We only washed our hair in the rain one time after that, and that was when TJ spilled an entire gallon of fresh sweet tea on the piece of carpet in the kitchen. After Tracy spanked him until he was nearly unconscious, she asked me and Audrey to get in our bathing suits and wash the carpet outside in the rain. We drizzled dish soap at our feet and pretended we were kneading wine with our toes.

Ray wasn't allowed anywhere near the kitchen carpet while we were cleaning it, so he stood off to the side and sang along with us. While Audrey and I stepped in rhythm, Ray scratched at his black hair and underneath his armpits.

In between scrubs, we could hear TJ screaming and crying from Audrey's bedroom.

That summer at the Lego house wasn't just about rain-washing and outdoor-shampooing. Almost every day, we took walks up and down Bear Run Road, collecting wild berries in our shirts and writing our initials in the gravel dust. Most nights, Audrey and I counted stars on the trampoline. She named hers Pretty Olivias, and I named mine Planet Nameks. We waded in the creeks, we took hikes in the Appalachian lands behind her house, and we even camped out in the backyard.

One day, we discovered a vast wall of beaver dams surrounding a waterhole a few miles deep into the woods behind her house. When we ran back home to tell Tracy about it, she told us to avoid the beaver dams altogether so we didn't scare them off. In her words, "They're makin' our nature, so you best leave it alone."

Our most foolish summer endeavor was when we stole some of Tracy's artificial tanning lotion. After we applied a copious amount to our pasty legs, our skin morphed into a sickly, burnt-orange color. Audrey walked around calling us the Carrot Sisters. She wasn't exactly wrong. The color wouldn't fade for another few weeks. We would still have orange legs when we started 6th grade.

Despite it all, I wasn't ever distracted enough to forget about Ryan.

He clung to my brain, a piece of memory too stubborn to ever walk away; I spent many hours trying to massage him out of my head. It didn't matter that Scott and Kimmie would forever play the matchmakers, seemingly the only two people still trying to keep Ryan and I linked with some invisible bond, a thread not meant to unravel; because no matter how hard they tried, the miraculous link would never take effect.

When I started 6th grade that year, on my first day of school, I stepped up into the bus and refused to look in Ryan's direction. When I stepped off at Gunners Valley School, for once I didn't look back, I didn't fake an itch on my shoulder, and I certainly didn't verbally tell him good-bye.

I knew that we were divided when, a few days into the school year, Ryan was walking down the hallway, and I was walking towards him. The only two people in the corridor, we avoided eye contact, kept our mouths wired shut, and passed one another without even a glimmer of recognition. That was the sign; it was time to move on.

I spent the remainder of 2001 ignoring Ryan. I pretended that I didn't know his name. It was physically painful to will my brain into forgetting the littlest of details, even my personal favorites, like the tiny scar on the side of his jaw and the oily, almost-blue hairline that bisected his solid black hair. I even dated two boys in my 6th grade class, but the relationships never lasted longer than a few months, and I always thought of Ryan the moment I was single.

What we had the summer before, writing our history on the back of Kimmie's bedroom door—it was almost as if it never happened. That was the part that hurt the most.

My first day back in 2002, I shared a table during 6th grade homeroom class with a girl named Lilith Anderson. She preferred to be called Lilly, with two ls. The reason she grabbed my attention was because she leaned over the table and, after grabbing both of my hands, she said to me, "You are heartbroken. I can read palms."

I managed to reply, "Sit with me next period."

She did.

That same day, the class was observed for the biannual Phys Ed checkup. Laney and I sat together on the gymnasium floor. Lilly was measured first. She came out of the office and said, "Four-eleven, one-hundred pounds." Laney went next, then me.

After we shared our results, the three of us learned that we were all the same height and weight. 4' 11", 100 pounds.

We celebrated by congregating on the gymnasium floor and sharing details of our first day back from Christmas break. Laney got a bunch of new football jerseys, Lilly got an electric piano, and I got *Mario Party 3* for the N64.

After that day, the three of us stayed close: phone calls every night, passing notes in the hallway before or after recess, flirting with the cutest boys in class. Lilly wasn't allowed to have friends stay over at her house because her parents were going through a bitter divorce. She told us that maybe by 7th grade, after they had split for good, Laney and I could come over. Until then, Laney and I hosted the sleepovers.

Starting that month, Lilly rode the same bus as us. She and her older brother, Bradley, were now a part of Bus #35. She explained to us over lunch that her grandfather passed away during final arrangements of her parents' divorce, and her grandfather's house near Bear Run Road now belonged to her father, Gary. Her mother was unemployed, so Lilly and her brother moved in with her father on Postlewaite Ridge.

Laney and I always tried to be the first ones on the bus after school, so we could snag two empty seats across from each other: one for her and Lilly, one for me and Audrey. Kimmie now preferred a seat by herself, but at least she helped us out when we were claiming seats every afternoon.

Right after my birthday, the three of us girls crammed ourselves into the same seat so we could talk about all of the boys we liked. That was how I found out that Lilly used to have a crush on Ryan, too.

Laney told her pretty bluntly, "Abigail's been in love with him since we were kids." She looked over at me with empty eyes. "Used to, at least. Do you still like him?"

I couldn't lie. "Sometimes." Ryan still found his way in my memory. He still managed to tug at my heart just a little bit even when I wasn't looking at him. The thought of him alone, how I remembered him over a year ago, was enough. I hadn't seen him for longer than two seconds in so long, I wasn't quite sure what he looked like anymore.

If I was brave, I would have turned around in the seat right then to find him, but I wasn't a bold girl.

She rolled her eyes. "You are so backwards sometimes, Abigail Delia." Laney always called me by my first and middle names.

Lilly pushed us closer. The smell of her lip gloss was so strong I imagined a bucket of blueberries in our laps. "He is adorable, in that nerdy-boy kind of way, but I think I wanna date Jace Cross."

She moved her lime-green eyes over her shoulder for a moment. I followed their direction and saw Bradley sitting with Ryan. Neither of them was looking at us, thankfully. "My dumb brother and him are like, best friends now. How could he be friends with my brother? He's so gross."

Most afternoons, Lilly asked to be kept up-to-date with everything I knew about Jace. In return, she salvaged what information she could about Ryan, thanks to his growing friendship with her older brother. I admitted that I didn't know much. Randomly, I confessed that Scott once tried to get Jace and me to date during one of the school dances, but I turned Jace down by saying, "You look like Harry Potter." It wasn't one of my proudest moments.

Regardless, Lilly kept her side of the deal, and even though almost everything she told me was stuff about Ryan I already knew, I never once told her to stop. She unraveled her memory, and I held my hands out and caught the threads as they danced in place. The hardest part about listening to Lilly was learning that she probably talked to Ryan every weekend.

A pang of jealousy ripped through my body hearing her talk about what he wore to bed when spending the night with Bradley (plaid pajama pants and a white t-shirt). The realization that Lilly has probably talked to Ryan more times in a few months than I have over the course of three years was easily the most damning.

I watched her small hands speak as she tried to explain, down to the finest of detail, what Ryan looked like when he woke up every morning. Instead of focusing on her voice, I focused on Lilly's features: poker-straight dark brown hair, bangs as long and thick as mine, a narrow, pointed chin perched underneath a set of full, symmetrical lips, and bright green eyes atop round, always-red cheeks. She was one of the prettiest girls in the 6th grade.

The fact that most classmates said she and I looked like twins was a little uplifting. The only discrepancies between us were our eye color (hers were green, mine were pale blue) and our smiles (my teeth were straight and coffee-stained, yet hers were pearly white and jagged).

Finally, she threw herself back in the bus seat and exhaled mightily. "God, that was a ton of stuff. I hope you don't want more than that, Abigail."

I didn't have it in me to tell her that I was too busy tracing the mountain-top edges of her crooked teeth to listen to her lecture on Ryan.

On the last day of 6th grade, Laney dared me to sit on the bus with Ryan.

We had already spent most of the day playing Truth or Dare with our classmates. Many first times happened and records were set during those last few hours as 6th graders.

For example, I dared Lilly to lick Laney's ear, and Zane dared Lilly to write on the inside of one of the girls' restroom bathroom stalls. He absconded to the girls' restroom when no teachers were looking so he could see it for himself.

Somehow, I managed to not only ascend the bus steps and walk down the aisle without an ounce of nervousness jetting through my pumping veins, I also passed my usual seat, where Audrey was flashing me a mischievous, inspiring grin, without any last-second tremors of regret or fear before I plopped down next to Ryan.

Behind us, I heard Bradley groan, "Oh, shit, she's doin' it."

My method of attack wasn't as graceful as I expected it to be. First, when I threw myself down on the seat, Ryan nearly side-swiped me with his arm, he was so suddenly startled. Second, I shouldn't have moved so fast to anchor myself down in the seat because one of my backpack straps smacked him on his little shoulder and he rubbed at it like it was a bee sting. Third, the leather cushion beneath us exhaled at my body weight, and its breath sounded like a stretched fart.

Immediately, I shrunk in my own skin, "Umm, that wasn't me, I swear."

"Hi, Abigail."

"Oh, yeah, hi."

As we watched the rest of the students pile onto Bus #35, my eyes moved across the tops of seats to find Laney and Lilly sitting together. Across from them, I hadn't expected to see Kimmie sitting with Audrey, but the two of them bobbed and tossed backpacks around, their blonde hair appearing and disappearing like a lighthouse beacon.

At once, all four of them turned around and locked their eyes on me. I froze in place.

Ryan nudged me with his shoulder. "So, uhh, why are you sitting here today?"

Gulping, I searched for a decent response in my lap. I didn't find anything. "I wanted to?"

"Don't you think it's weird, though?"

Now I looked at him.

It had been months, maybe even a year, since I took the time to look at Ryan for longer than two seconds. The shape of his face had changed since the last time I saw him, and I found it incredibly odd how the length of his cheeks and the curve of his jaw could morph and shift like that. Little pencil lines of facial hair traced the outline of his upper lip and parts of his chin. Even the size of his eyes, somehow, wasn't the same. Instead of seeing big bulbs of brown, I looked into beady, dark orbs hooded back against his face.

My eyes found his hands resting in his lap. For whatever reason, my vision dashing across the contours of his veins sent a wave of chills down my spine.

He didn't give me a moment to elaborate. Ryan's hands flew out in front of us, and I watched them dance as he spoke. "I mean, you're my best friend's little cousin, so it's kind-of like, taboo, y'know? Here you are, sittin' with me on the last day of school, so it's gonna grow and grow and grow all summer, and when I start high school, fuck only knows what they'll say."

What was he talking about? What would grow, who was they, and why was it taboo?

The bus lurched out of idle. The two of us momentarily lost our balance, and we each pressed our palms against the seat in front of us to remain stable.

We didn't say anything for a while. Ten minutes into the bus ride and all we had managed to say to one another was, "What are you gonna do today?" and "Yeah," and "That's cool."

I wasn't ready to accept the fact that Ryan was not the same little boy I first met three years earlier. It was almost impossible to talk to him. His attention returned to the window after every statement, even if he had asked me a question. At one point, I reached out and touched his leg, a gentle tap to motivate him to look at me for once when I responded, but he jumped back, and he blinked six or seven times while drilling me with his hard, warped eyes, and I held my tongue and apologized.

As the bus catapulted up on Red Cliff Hill, as our backs pressed hard against the seats at the 45-degree slope, Ryan shifted and faced me. My heart trembled at the sudden closeness of our faces. "Hey."

"What?"

"I just want you to know, I didn't have a birthday party last year. So I don't want you to think that I didn't invite or you anything like that."

Last year, he would have turned 13; in a few months, he'd be 14. For only two months of the year, we were one year apart.

My hands ran over my bare knees. Grass stains from that day's game of Freeze Tag painted my knee caps. I locked my grip. "I wasn't. I didn't. You gonna have one this year?"

"If I do, I want it to be just like 2000." His voice softened. It painfully crept through one ear and out the other. "I don't think I'll have another one, though. I wish I could just go back in time, y'know? Like, go back to when we were kids and everything was good."

"Why can't you?" I laughed while shaking my head. "I mean, why can't you have another birthday party, not go back in time, of course."

The bus turned near Red Cliff Church. My knee brushed his. Immediately, we gravitated away from each other like negatively charged magnets. My face burned. Momentarily, he stared out of the window until his cheeks were white again. I wasn't going to tell him that I could see his reflection in the window, and that his cheeks were definitely still blushing.

Ryan sighed through his nose. "I don't think my mom wants me to have another. That one wore her out pretty good." Faintly, his lips stretched into a smile.

"Oh, God. Is it because I dropped my McFlurry in her car?"

That got him to laugh, but I wasn't trying to be funny. "Yeah, Abigail, that's exactly it. My mom won't let me have any friends over anymore because a cute girl dropped ice cream in her backseat."

Cute?

The bus stopped at Bear Run Road. Over my sudden catatonia at hearing Ryan call me cute, Audrey's voice cried out, "Abigail, you comin' or what? C'mon, let's go!"

I shook my head out of its suspended blip in time. Did Ryan just admit that he thought I was cute?

Personally, I saw myself at quite possibly the worst-looking phase of my life: long, frizzy hair streaked orange with Sun-In, chubby cheeks, a small smile, and hips so wide that I bumped almost every bus seat down the aisle. From the front, I looked like a 25-five-year-old woman; but from the side, I looked like a 10-year-old boy. It was absurd.

Since starting my period the year before, my body underwent multiple, unexplainable shifts. While my chest still grew, my legs did not. I hadn't grown since Christmas, remaining at 4' 11" while Laney and Lilly both exceeded the 5-foot mark. Most days I saw myself in the mirror, and the image returned in a Fun House, where my hips and arms were lop-sided and my stomach was spilling over. It was frustrating trying on jeans anymore; either the waistbands were too loose or the legs were too long.

Despite my personal insecurities, Ryan still found me cute?

As I slid from the bus seat and slipped my backpack over my shoulders, Ryan reached out and barely grazed my hip with his finger. It was almost like he was trying to hook a finger around the belt loop of my jeans. "Hey. Have a good summer."

Just like that, he slumped back into the bus seat, pressing his temple against the window and tracing the outside vegetation with his swollen eyes.

I felt hands tap my backpack as I walked down the aisle. Each time, I saw a different face: Lilly, Laney, or Kimmie. All three of them were giving me the physical congratulatory gesture, that I was a brave girl for accepting Laney's dare. I didn't know I was holding my breath until I stepped down from the bus and got light-headed. Panicking, I gasped and splayed my hand across my chest. "Oh, God," I said aloud. I kept saying it. "Oh, God, oh, God, oh, God."

The bus kicked up tiny gravel, lurching down Red Cliff Hill. Its exhaust curled around my ankles, holding me there as Audrey motioned for me to get in Tracy's car. Immobile in my own thoughts, I panted and gasped. She hung out of the car window now. "Abigail? You okay?"

"I just sat with Ryan Mills on the bus."

She rolled her eyes. "Yeah, duh, I know, I saw it."

My eyes widened in horror. "He said I was cute."

The car sucked Audrey back in, and not a second later, the back door was tossed open, nearly swinging straight off the hinges. She ran at me, pebbles and gravel rolling underneath her pink sandals, and she grabbed both of my hands and tossed me left and right.

As our feet stretched up and down and off the dirt road, Tracy honked in succession with our celebratory dance. I caught a glimpse of her behind the windshield. Instead of being frustrated, she appeared eager. A bright grin split her red face in half.

Instead of driving us home that afternoon, Tracy drove us into Stream Ridge for vanilla cones and fountain pop. I recommended bringing Todd back a Reese's Cup flavor blast. As she handed me the Styrofoam container, Tracy flicked my knee cap with her hard, long fingernail. "Sis, you're growing up too dang fast, y'hear me? Stop it, or else I'll be fightin' boys off of ya with a shovel and my fists."

I swallowed a melted mass of vanilla ice cream. "I told you, I don't wanna grow up."

She steered the Ford Explorer back on Route 352. "Yeah, yeah, don't we all, Sis."

Seven

The weekend after the 4th of July, Lilly called and invited me to spend the night with her at her father's house. Lilly's family was currently split, and divided across different parts of Stream Ridge. After her grandfather passed away, her father inherited the farmhouse on Postlewaite Ridge, at the same time he was finalizing his divorce with her mother, who was currently living with her parents in the Stream Ridge Trailer Park until she could find a place of her own.

On most weekends, Lilly stayed with her mother at her grandparents'. Bradley, on the other hand, was not close with his mother at all, so he preferred to stay at the farmhouse with his father.

As my mother drove me across Red Cliff Hill to Lilly's father's house, she flicked a cigarette butt out of her window. "What do you and Lilly plan to do this weekend?" I glanced over at her worn face glowing in the summer sun. My mother's freckles were fading against her pale skin. She was working too much and not getting enough sleep. I almost felt bad asking her to spend her last hour before work taking me to my friend's house.

I shrugged my shoulders. "I don't know. We'll probably just hang out, watch some movies, whatever."

As we bobbed and dipped along Postlewaite Ridge, I pointed at a two-story house with flaking red shutters. "That house, right there." Lilly advised me that I wouldn't be able to miss her house once I looked for fire-red shutters and a big willow tree in the backyard. Both were accounted for as my mother slowed the vehicle's speed.

Lilly came from a poor yet hard-working farming family. Her father, Gary Anderson, actually worked for the same labor company that my father did. Even though he made a lot of money, most of it went to Lilly's mother, Linda. Alimony, she once told me.

Gary basically worked to support his ex-wife. Any money he made from the farm—livestock, meat, chicken eggs—helped put food on the table, clothes on his two kids, and paid the bills. Lilly didn't complain about it too much, but Bradley usually had something nasty to say about Linda on the bus. He called her things like Welfare Queen and Trampy McTramp. I once heard him tell Ryan that Linda recorded herself wearing nothing but lingerie and sent the video to one of her many online boyfriends. All of that Lilly denied, so I denied it, too. From what I heard from Lilly, I liked her mother.

My mother narrowed her eyes at the dilapidated wooden porch and the untrimmed weeds framing the sidewalk. "And this is Gary's place?"

"Now it is, yeah. It used to be her grandfather's, but now they live here." I opened the car door and jumped out. "When do you want me to call you?"

"Tomorrow night is fine." She scratched at her hairline. Her silver roots were showing. That was another sign that I knew my mother was exhausted; she was so vain about her silver hair that she rarely stepped out of the house with her roots showing. Two boxes of burgundy hair dye waited for her in her bathroom closet.

Right as I went to close the white Ford Explorer's door, Bradley emerged from the side of the house. My heart jumped into my mouth. Glistening in sweat and dirty, he was shirtless and giving me a narrowed, hard look. Even from far away, I noticed bulbs of mud caked in his dark eyebrows.

In typical West Virginia fashion, he swung a pitchfork around his waist and jammed it in a mound of loose soil near the house's side. When the pitchfork's rusted teeth vanished in the earth, he produced a can from his denim pocket, plopped a wad of chewing tobacco in between his bottom lip and gum, and claimed his spot by marking the dirt with his spit.

I made a noise. I didn't mean to. He glanced at me again, his expression sideways and confused. Sweat dripped down the center of his chest, and the tips of his brown hair were pointed and soaked. He didn't have a farmer's tan. His entire body glittered like copper. Bradley spit again. Tobacco saliva dripped down his chin. "'Sup, Abigail?" Naturally, he went for an old-fashioned bucket before walking around the back side of the house.

I reached forward to shove the car door closed, but my mother immediately held up her hand. "Abigail. Who is that boy?"

I held the door in place. "Bradley. Lilly's brother."

Her voice trailed off. "You never told me she had a brother..."

I got lippy. "You never asked."

"Abigail Delia." She reached for another cigarette.

My eyes rolled to the back of my skull. "Mom, he rubs snuff. That's so gross."

"He is still a boy." She judged him the same way she judged the dilapidated porch and the knee-high weeds around the driveway. Returning from behind the house, Bradley jerked his head up once, another welcoming gesture, as he made his way up the porch steps and through the front door. His boots looked two sizes too large, and they were both untied. The ends of the laces snapped like firecrackers with every step he took.

My mother watched him the entire way. "And how old is he?"

I rolled my eyes. "Mom, it doesn't matter. It's *Bradley*." Even from outside the farmhouse, I could hear the laces snap and crack as he shuffled his feet across the hardwood floors. It seriously bothered me that he never tied his shoelaces.

"Call me tonight." She quickly added, "And tomorrow night."

"Okay, okay. Bye, Mom."

I closed the car door and ran up the wooden steps. They creaked with each of my fast, heavy footsteps. The busted screen door screamed as I stepped inside. A lot of the netting was cut, so I pricked a few of my fingers as I pulled the door shut behind me.

Bradley's voice came from somewhere in the house. "Lilly's upstairs."

"Okay, thanks." I leaned down to take off my sneakers, only to notice that not a single pair of shoes was in front of the doorway. Realizing that Lilly's house was one of those homes where you didn't have to take off your shoes as soon as you stepped in, I kept them on as I trudged up the old stairs.

Even the stairs chirped as I made my way up. Clearly Lilly lived in the kind of house that would always tattle if she tried sneaking out.

The house was nice on the inside, definitely not what I had anticipated when my mother first pulled up in the driveway. It reminded me of an outdated country home, with knick-knacks and old, blue stitchery everywhere, and everything smelled like homemade biscuits and gravy. I didn't need to call for Lilly when I reached the top of the stairs. I knew which bedroom door was hers by the magazine cut-outs of cute boys all over the face of the door and her name in jumbled letters in the center. LILLY, but the I was a 1.

As I opened the door, she jumped up from her bed and rushed over to me. "Yay, you're here! You're here!" She smelled like expensive perfume. The gloss strewn down her legs told me that she just shaved them. Lilly must have been one of those girls that always needed to look and feel her best, despite not leaving her house or seeing anyone else aside from her father and brother. I yearned for that kind of self-appreciation, but I wasn't as motivated.

I didn't waste any time. Holding my arm up as high as it could go, I dropped my overnight bag so its *thud* rocked the old farmhouse. The floorboards cracked and cried underneath the weight. "Your stupid brother almost got me in trouble. He came out without a shirt. Without a shirt, Lilly. He was practically naked in front of my mom."

She looked away. "Well, it's hot out. He's been working outside all day." I noted that she was taking her brother's side by defending him.

Maybe I didn't quite understand her position, because I didn't have a brother who went to school during the school year and worked in barns and hayfields during the summer. Instead, I had a popular, spoiled older sister who would always run off to her grandparents if she asked our mother for something and didn't get it. She didn't understand hardship or work ethic unless she broke a nail getting into the car.

We both took a seat at the foot of her bed as if we had been doing it for our entire lives. One thing that Lilly had that I didn't have was nice clothes. She went shopping almost every weekend with her mother, so she would always be wearing something new on Mondays at school. While she readjusted her spaghetti-strap shirt and white shorts, I relaxed back on my arms wearing my basketball warm-up t-shirt and denim shorts my sister cut for me from an old pair of jeans.

She jumped up and reached for a CD case on one of her bookcase shelves. "Avril Lavigne okay? It's her new album."

I nodded. "Go for it."

For the next hour, Lilly and I talked about boys. We didn't leave any classmate, friend, or friend of a friend unscathed. She was particularly fond of Jace, and I was still holding on to the dismal, small chance that Ryan would eventually ask me to be his girlfriend.

As for Lilly, she'd committed a relationship faux pas by dating an under-classman. Girls weren't supposed to date underclassmen, but she did; they actually dated for a long time (two months). His name was Landon, and the reason they broke up was because Landon's older brother, Damien, flirted with her extensively in between classes and during recess, and she was overwhelmed by the Bowman brothers. She told Damien to leave her alone, and told Landon that he was a pansy for not sticking up for her.

It started getting dark. Lilly got up from the bed, for the first time in the last two hours, and opened her bedroom window. The house was exceptionally large and Gary didn't like running both air conditioners at the same time, so Lilly and Bradley had to rely on the huge windows in their bedrooms for cool air. The air smelled like dry hay and onion grass as it filled her bedroom. She pushed back her curtains. "So, get this, I was—"

Suddenly, her bedroom door swung open. Lilly didn't seem too startled when her brother appeared. She didn't even flinch when Bradley held up a hand, said something incoherent, and vanished into a bathroom. I hadn't realized there was a bathroom in Lilly's bedroom until that second. As soon as he closed the door, she stepped away from the window and slumped back down on her bed. "You'll get used to it. It's the only bathroom in the entire house."

I jumped back. The bed wriggled. "Really? But this house is so big."

"Yeah. Dad's working on building another one downstairs, but he's always busy." She nodded towards the closed bathroom door. "He's only using it right now because you're here. Normally they just go outside if they have to pee." She squeezed her lips together and cheesed hard. "Sometimes, they pee right off the porch!"

"But what if he's not peeing? What if he has to go, *you know what?*"

She shook her head. "I know him. He won't do that unless nobody is here."

I looked around her bedroom. Her walls were wooden paneled, like mine back at my house, but her room was a lot bigger, and it had such a high ceiling that I couldn't imagine how she cleaned her ceiling fan. Her carpet was soft and fluffy, but definitely in need of a vacuuming. Dirty clothes were scattered all throughout, and her television desk and set needed a good dusting. I snickered, "When was the last time you cleaned?"

She gasped. "What? I just cleaned!"

"No. I bet you stuffed everything under this bed or in your closet." I pointed at her small television. "I can literally see dust on that."

"So? I put away—" On cue, Lilly closed her mouth right as the bathroom door swung back open.

Bradley took one step away from the bathroom. He predominantly focused on his little sister. "Why do you keep shuttin' up when I come out? What are you talkin' about?" He fluttered his green eyes, the same ones that Lilly had, from their father. "You talkin' about boys?"

She readied a pillow. "Shut up and get out."

He looked right at me. "You're friends with Audrey Springs, right?"

What? Was Bradley talking to me, about Audrey? I moved my eyes to Lilly. She was just as confused as I was. I didn't see any kind of worrisome glimmer in her eyes, so it seemed okay to respond to her brother. Nodding, I lowered my eyebrows. "Uhh. Yeah, why?"

"Tell her I said hi." Bradley then walked towards the bedroom door and shut it behind him.

Oh my God.

Lilly jumped up and started pacing in circles. I, too, leaped to my feet and started prancing all around her bedroom. She stammered in excitement, "Oh my God, oh my God, oh my God. My brother has a crush on your friend!" She slapped both of her hands on her red cheeks. "My brother likes a girl? Oh my God, he likes a girl! He likes your friend! He likes Audrey Springs!"

Bradley definitely didn't seem like the kind of guy to like girls. He was the kind of farm boy who only thought about the farm and nothing else. Even the one time when he sat on the bus with Laney, despite him giving her flirtatious grins and nudging her with his shoulder, he never once went over the top, like blatantly doing something that meant he had a crush on Laney.

Audrey, on the other hand, he avoided like the plague. She tried talking to him a few times on the bus, mostly if he and Ryan were sitting together and I was trying miserably at making small talk with Ryan, but even then, he would look out the window and pretend to ignore us.

Still celebrating, even though I wasn't technically sure why we were celebrating, I shook my hips and threw my arms in the air. "Everyone likes Audrey." Lilly bumped me with her bony hip.

"Yes, but we're talking about *my brother*. He's disgusting." Her voice got cautiously quiet. "Sometimes, he wears the same shirt two days in a row." She pointed at me. "And, get this, listen, and he also talks to random girls on the Internet." Now she was pointing at her carpet. "At night, he'll be up until like, five in the morning, chatting with weird women." I figured out she was pointing downstairs, not at her carpet, which was where the family computer was. "And I bet he watches porn."

I frowned. "Eww, stop."

"It's true!"

"Okay, okay, your brother's a perv, I get it."

Lilly reached out and grabbed a chunk of my dark brown hair. "C'mere. Lemme fix your hair. It's out of control."

We spent most of the night giving each other makeovers. Masterful in the craft of hair, Lilly curled my long, dark hair in thick chunks of volume and shine. She finished every piece with a spritz of glittery hair spray. By the time we were finished, her entire bed was covered in a thin sheet of multicolored sparkling squares.

My love of drawing came in handy when I applied her makeup. I was able to carefully navigate her eyelids with an eyeliner pencil, and I dabbed the perfect amount of blush across her high cheekbones.

It took us almost thirty minutes to wash everything off our faces before we funneled into bed together. That night, we learned that we slept in near-identical fashion: one leg out, one leg in, pillow on the left side of our face, and a stuffed animal for personal comfort. Before we closed our eyes indefinitely, Lilly uttered under her breath, "You're me, I swear," and I firmly agreed before falling asleep.

The next morning, Lilly wanted to listen to Bradley's new P.O.D. CD. We waited impatiently in the sill of her open window, the sounds of the outdoors filtering through her thin curtains and the vegetation growing outside her window. She flicked a piece of fuzz outside after plucking it from one of her pillows. "We'll wait until they're workin' before I run over."

Lilly's green eyes were the exact colors of the bed of leaves next to us, their veiny olive skins nearly transparent as the sun pushed through their seasonal shade.

In a single gust, the aromas of cow manure and sweet hay filled our noses. It was an oddly invigorating smell. Both Lilly and I inhaled and exhaled at the same time, spilling the outdoor smells directly into our starving lungs.

When we heard Bradley and Gary firing up the lawn mower outside, Lilly told me she would be right back. Fast, she snuck in her brother's bedroom and burst back into the hallway exhaling like a mad woman. She waved at me as she explained, "I had to hold my breath. His room stinks. He stinks so bad." I closed the door behind her as she bolted straight for her CD player. It was the same one Audrey had, an old, outdated thing from the clearance rack of Walmart.

Lilly's eyes grew as music came from the boom box. Finally, it was working. "You know, if you like Ryan so much, I can try to convince Bradley to invite him over. I mean, he comes over sometimes, so it wouldn't be obvious that I'm doing it for you."

My stomach pretty much rolled straight of my body and sprawled out next to my feet, it was so overwhelmed with excitement. I held up a hand. "Don't do that. I don't wanna seem like I'm desperate or anything like that."

"Just let me know." She leaned over and turned the volume up louder.

We spent the rest of the day replaying her brother's P.O.D. CD, *Satellite*, until we knew all of the lyrics. Before we sang P.O.D. songs together, I knew how to harmonize with Lilly. She was already one of the best singers in Stream Ridge, and she was only in 6th grade. We had been singing in the Gunners Valley School choir together since 4th grade. She was a soprano, and I was an alto. Our instructor, Mr. Banks, favored us over the other students, because our balance was alarmingly perfect.

Our balance was so perfect that he gave us one of the duets for the annual spring concert. Lilly and I performed "Only You" by The Platters, and when we finished our duet at the spring concert, everyone in the audience gave us a standing ovation. They clapped for at least ten seconds.

It was the first time I ever sang in front of a crowd without the backing of the entire choir, so I was overcome with nervousness and nearly threw up all over my white dress shoes.

The audience didn't even affect Lilly. She just stepped up to the microphone, flipped back a piece of hair, expanded her lungs, and sang. We grinned at one another during our performance. Her confidence guided me through the lyrics. Her powerful, high-pitched voice practically reached out, grabbed my hand, and carried me in all of the right directions, across all of the right notes. It was because of her I learned progression, how saving my voice's power for dramatic effect, usually at the end of the bridge of chorus, could send chills into anyone listening.

It didn't matter that most, if not all, of those in the crowd were standing for her. Lilly was a talented singer, a 12 year old with a powerhouse voice fit for a middle-aged woman who lived on Broadway. I was pretty much in the duet only to harmonize with her, to complement her voice, and that was perfectly fine with me. At least after the concert, Mr. Banks congratulated both of us, not just her, on our performance.

By the time it was dark outside, Bradley came back in the house after finishing his farm work. When we heard the front door downstairs scream shut, Lilly quickly fetched the CD from the player, inserted it back in the case, and ran back to her brother's bedroom to put it back. While she was gone, I grabbed a bunch of old magazines from underneath her bed and opened them all around the floor, giving the impression that we spent the last few hours reading articles about French kissing boys and finding perfect boyfriends, not stealing her brother's CD and listening to it so much that it was lukewarm when we were done.

My mother picked me up on Sunday after we returned from church. As I jumped in the car, she sniffed only once and made the comment, "You smell like cow."

I smiled and affirmed in the proudest of tones, "Yup! I sure do!"

The summer ended in perhaps its smoothest exit. Audrey and I accepted the disappearance of the sun and the return of the cold dew in the morning, and we started 7th grade wearing matching BFF necklaces. Meanwhile, Lilly and I spent most weekends together watching Tae Bo workout videos and writing songs on her electric keyboard.

Kimmie and Ryan were unavailable most of that summer, on account of band camp for the Stream Ridge High School marching band. Not that it would have mattered, since Kimmie was now a big-shot 8th grader and Ryan probably didn't know who I was anymore.

By that September, everyone in my class had accounts for MSN Messenger. I created my email under the watchful eye of my sister. Diana guided me on the right path so I didn't come up with a lame account. She gave me advice on what emails needed. After I asked to have blue angel somewhere in my email, my sister created me an account: blue_angel_2008@hotmail.com, the 2008 the year I graduated high school, the number that everyone was supposed to use, an indication of that person's age, something like that.

My contact list wasn't as populated as my sister's, but it was full. My friends on MSN Messenger included Audrey, Lilly, Laney, Kimmie, and more. Some of my sister's friends even added me, even though I didn't know who they were so I never initiated a conversation.

One night, I snuck on MSN Messenger after watching *WWE Raw* with Patrick, something we did every Monday night until 11:00 PM. Nobody in my contact list was online, so I nearly logged off until I was greeted with a notification.

Someone with the email a_nightmares_fear@msn.com wanted to be my friend on MSN Messenger. Definitely curious, I accepted the notification and was almost immediately greeted with a message from that contact:

```
hey aggs
```

Aggs? That was a first. I didn't have any nicknames attributed to me, aside from Nyla's brilliant Six Pack Abbs, which I hadn't heard in years, thank God.

Quietly, I keyed in a response and hit the Enter key:

```
hey who is this??
```

My toes bent at reading the next message:

```
its Ryan
```

Oh. I bit down on my bottom lip while I typed back:

```
hey what's up??
```

Then my teeth unclenched from my bottom lip, and I readied another message:

```
how did u get my email?
```

Ryan was a painfully slow typer. The only reason I could type with such grace and speed was because I spent a lot of time on the computer writing in Microsoft Word. His response came in a few seconds later:

```
Kimmz gave it to me so wassup??
```

My smile practically glittered in the dim light of the dining room:

    not much...cant sleep so im online passin time

His next message came in blindingly fast:

    spend it with me

I read his message over and over again. Each time, my esophagus drained, and my mouth grew dry, and my heart trembled like a butterfly in a palm—everything was suddenly so real.

When I asked Ryan why he was up so late, his response chilled me:

    i don't really sleep...ill prob be up for another
few hours

My message was just as cryptic as his, but at least I purposely attached a romantic gesture:

    here...let me send u something...its a lullaby

I sent Ryan an audio recording of me humming Aeris' song from *Final Fantasy VII*, something I illegally downloaded using Napster shortly after watching Ryan and his friends play *Final Fantasy VII* back in 2000. The only reason I knew the song was because I listened to it on repeat during many of my writing sessions. Back then I was under the impression that I could reel him in as a boyfriend if I admitted that I knew her song by heart. Everyone knew that Ryan was in love with Aeris. The only fictional character he loved more than her was Sephiroth, the villain who slayed her.

Yet, there I was, a 12 year old humming into a tiny microphone perched above a computer monitor, the song from Napster playing faintly behind me.

Ryan didn't immediately send me anything back. No message, no recording. It took him a while to finally acknowledge the so-called lullaby I hummed for him. Eventually, MSN Messenger asked me if I wanted to accept an audio file from Sephiroth, Ryan's username. I adjusted the volume of the speakers before accepting, unsure if the message would play automatically. After estimating a low-enough volume, I downloaded the file and played it. I didn't want anything he sent me to wake up my mother or Patrick, ultimately grounding me for two weeks.

He wasn't humming. He wasn't singing. Instead, I listened to the recording expose the utter exhaustion in his voice, and his whispers came at me from the belly of the computer desk, "Aeris' song. Oh. Aggs, you're pretty cool, y'know that?"

I sent him a sly message:

```
yes I do...^-^
```

Another audio message came in, and I accepted it, too. His voice seemed heavier now. "Send me another one."

We stayed up until after 3 AM sending audio messages back and forth. By the time I managed to find my bed and close my eyes, my brain was like a shell holding every single recording he sent me, playing his voice over and over again, doing its best to ignore the indication of pain in his breath, wondering why a boy like himself was unable to find sleep, instead staying up at odd hours during the night.

As much as I wondered about the severity of Ryan's sleep schedule, I didn't dare ask him such a personal question.

I was nearly tempted to when I stepped onto the bus the next morning and saw his brown eyes cradled in pools of dreamless purple, the rings in twos and threes underneath his bottom eyelids. Instead, I waved to him; he tried a smile, but it faltered, and I sat down with Audrey.

That was the first time I ever wanted to forget something about Ryan.

I wanted to erase my memory of what total emptiness looked like on his pale face.

For Labor Day weekend, Kimmie invited me to her grandparents' house for a cookout. It was there that I watched a slew of fireworks explode in fiery glitter above my head, with Ryan no more than three inches away from me. He and I shared the padded seat of a single four-wheeler while Kimmie and Laney lay atop a blanket crocheted by her Mawmaw. Every time a firework exploded, he offered his own descriptive identities. "That one looked like fire water. That one, the tip of a cigarette. I liked that one. Oh, my favorite, did you see it? Definitely electricity."

During one of those short breaks in between launching fireworks, Ryan admitted to me that his favorite movie was *Event Horizon*. When I asked him what it was about, he stated with a rigid, electrified voice, "It's fucking sick. It's so fuckin', *fuck*, I can't even describe it. Like, it'll scare the shit out of you. It's one of the reasons I can't sleep. I keep seein' shit from that movie. It's so cool, but man, I just wanna close my eyes and not feel like someone is watching me."

As he told me this, I stared at him with a filling sense of urgency. Since when did his vocabulary consist of mostly the f-word? Since when did his brown eyes become swallowed in dark, purple rings? Since when did his hands shake so vigorously that he physically had to suppress them underneath his thighs, just to appear relatively normal?

It didn't make sense to me that a boy could change so much in a matter of seasons.

Ryan, now 14 years old, was a stranger, a new boy that I didn't know anymore: a troubled friend that I continued to stare at for the rest of that night, risking the sanity of my shift into adolescence to remember his new features. I wanted to learn about the physical struggles stretching across his face, so that I could spend the next few months learning how to make them all better.

Eight

By the time track season started my 7th grade year, I was chucking the discus over 60 feet and keeping hold of batons during 4x100 relays, though I definitely wasn't the fastest or slowest of the legs. It was the last year that Kimmie and I would be on the same track team, so she voluntarily sat with me every bus ride to and from track meets.

Almost every time, she reminded me, "Ryan still likes you."

Usually, I responded with something like, "Yeah, I know," because I was still worried about his transformation. Nobody seemed to notice it as much as I did. That, or I was the only one not accepting his change. Without a doubt, he was no longer the little boy that I first met in 1999. Something was wrong. Nobody should appear the epitome of enervation like that, especially a 14-year-old boy.

His change wasn't all bad. After spending that evening with Ryan watching fireworks at his grandparents' house, he began to acknowledge me more frequently on bus rides. It wasn't every day, but it was at least once a week that I heard him call out my name, just so I'd look up and see him give me a white-palm wave. He was as pale as I was.

By the time it was May of 2003, I was talking to Ryan on a daily basis. Every morning, Ryan waved at me on the bus. Every afternoon, Ryan would say aloud, "Bye, Aggs," when I grazed down the aisle. His nickname for me, Aggs, spread across my group of friends, and his. Eventually, I was on track to complete 7th grade as Aggs and Aggs alone. No more Abigail, no more Abigail Delia, and certainly no more Shorty or Kiddo.

The weekend after Ryan's birthday, he caught me online at 4 AM and sent me a rather unexpected message:

```
me and Bradley are goin riding 2morrow u guys
wanna come??
```

A lot of things went through my mind at that moment. Why was Ryan online at such an early hour? Did he just wake up, or had he not gone to bed yet? I was up, because I was suddenly obsessed with walking Bear Run Road before 5 AM so I could dance through morning fog and watch the sun come up from behind the Appalachian hills. I knew Ryan didn't have quite that excuse. He didn't seem that romantically involved with his own aura. At least, that was what I told myself, every time I refrained from getting out of bed in the morning.

I knew my mother would refuse my request to go four-wheeler riding with Ryan and Bradley. It was just at the Springs Reunion a few weeks before that she caught me and Audrey four-wheeler riding with her older cousins—and cans of lukewarm Bud Light perched between our knees. We lied and said the cans of beer were for the neighbor boys, when we'd actually just spent the ten minutes before that shot gunning some other cans at the Morris Cemetery. They were lingering in the ditch somewhere along Bear Run Road.

For whatever reason, I didn't get grounded. I believe my mother was so overwhelmed dealing with my rebellious, sexually-driven older sister that she figured my lapse in judgment was a one-time thing.

If Audrey and I snuck away with Ryan and Bradley, we just needed to get out of Bear Run Road without getting caught and we were fine.

There was also the fact that my mother just hated four-wheelers. It had nothing to do with the fact that Ryan was an older boy and Bradley an even older boy, asking me and Audrey to go away with them in the woods, without any adult supervision.

So I didn't sound as nervous and reluctant as I was, I typed a message that could dodge his interests and keep me honest:

```
My mom is asleep, but I can ask her in the morning.
Is that ok?
```

My heart jumped a little when I read his message:

```
well that just means im gonna have to steal u ;)
```

My insides immediately leaped from one type of matter to another. My organs were instantly liquefied and sloshing around inside of my stomach. The sweat surfacing on the pads of my palms caused the computer mouse to slip a bit out of my grasp. Even the webbing between my toes was quickly filling with perspiration. I was so nervous typing back that I carelessly misspelled tons of words:

```
We'll seea bout that. I hav eto go to bed. I'll
talk to you tommorrowe.
```

I watched the computer shut off. A black screen stared back at me.

"Okay," I said to my blurry reflection, mocking me. "What am I supposed to do now?"

The first thing I did the next morning was call Lilly.

I didn't leave any feeling untouched. Like a patron in a confessional booth, I let loose all of my emotions in a single phrase as I paced the kitchen, pink pajamas trailing behind me, coffee mug in hand, hair still unbrushed, new glasses probably crooked. "Okay, so last night, get this, I'm wishing Ryan a late happy birthday because I'm a horrible person and almost forgot, and I am awake at 4 to do my fog-walk thing, and so I'm talking to Ryan and he suddenly asks if I want to riding with him and your brother, four-wheeler riding, and then I tell him I don't know, and out of freakin' nowhere, he says he's gonna steal me, Lilly, what the heck, like, who even says—"

A series of muffled sounds echoed on the other end of the phone. Lilly groaned, "Ugh, sorry, I had the phone pulled away because my brother is stupid. Now, what were you saying?"

My lungs started weeping. "Noooo."

So I said it all again, with less run-on sentences and more breaths in between syllables. The sun peaked out from the kitchen window. The walls glimmered in bright yellows and whites.

Lilly hummed. "I still think Ryan has been in love with you forever."

I took a sip of coffee. My half-and-half started to marbleize with the coffee. "Everyone keeps saying that, but like, nothing has happened. I watched fireworks with him. That's like, the gist of our—whatever this is."

Lilly snorted. She and Audrey had the same kind of laugh now. "You're so hopeless. 'Oh, Ryan Mills, I love you so much. You are my sunshine, my angel, my *darling*.'"

I nearly choked on coffee. "*You* are hopeless."

She made a noise in the back of her throat. It was either a whimper or a catalyst of thought. "I have to tell you something."

"What?" Now that I wasn't unraveling all of my complicated teenage girl feelings, I didn't have to pace the kitchen, so I sat down at the table. Bills lined my mother's side of the table. At least now all of the bills were paid on time.

It wasn't like the summers before, when we lived paycheck to paycheck. My mother still worked at the Country Cupboard, and Patrick got promoted again a few months ago. He still worked for the coal mines, but he was working on the surface instead of underground.

Lilly closed her throat and made some sort of smothered squealing sound. Then, in the same exact manner I demonstrated before, she unleashed complete and total emotional chaos. "After trying again and again and again, I finally got to talk to Jace, and he came over to my mom's house the other day, and we sat around and talked about stupid stuff for hours and hours and then when he left he kissed my hand and told me to call him!" She paused just long enough to breathe in and breathe out. "We're getting ice cream at the Dairy Dump next weekend, when I go to my mom's again!"

That was the only reason Lilly liked visiting her mother at her new house in Oldestown, so she could go on walks and coincidentally walk by Jace's house on Gunners Valley Road. He lived less than a mile away from her.

"Is your mom gonna drop you guys off and leave? Or will she be there, too?"

Lilly's mother wasn't like my mother. Linda's body was chiseled with perfection and muscles in the shapes of sun-kissed peaches and little mounds of burnt dough. She was a retired professional body builder. She lifted weights twice a day. Her arms were bigger than my thighs, and she was toned in all of the right places. She must have been Native American or something, because her skin was a sheet of molasses stretched across her muscles, almost like the finest leather, and she had long, permed black hair.

Despite the animosity between Bradley and Linda, Lilly liked her. I liked her, too. I always made her do her Duck Face in public, which always rendered me breathless with laughter.

Lilly smacked her lips together. She must have been eating or drinking something. "I hope she just drops us off. She just got a new car, an old Camaro, so I'll probably ask her to drive around Stream Ridge so people can see me and Jace together in the Camaro."

"Your mom is so cool." As I said it, I quickly looked around the kitchen and living room, just in case my mother was somewhere nearby. I didn't want her thinking that I liked Linda more than her. My mother was nowhere to be found. She was still in her bedroom, smoking.

"You should come stay with me at Mom's this weekend."

I stopped playing with the fuzzy, pink feathers rimming my pajama shirt collar. "Really? Your mom will let me?"

"I'll ask her. She has a computer now, too, so we can even talk to everyone online." Then she said something that caught me off guard. "She also has a webcam. We can video chat with whoever we want."

I took in a deep breath like I was prepping myself to jump off a high diving board. "Umm, okay, okay, we can video chat with people. But what if they don't accept?"

"If you're talking about Ryan, he will. And if he doesn't, we'll video chat with someone else. You know that him and Jace are like, best friends, right?"

Ryan's friendships were nearly identical to mine. During the school year, Ryan was best friends with Jace. As soon as the school year ended and the summer started, he was best friends with Bradley. Just like I was best friends with Lilly during the school year, but I was best friends with Audrey during the summer.

The concept of double dating was so apparent now. Me and Ryan, Lilly and Jace.

I jumped up from the kitchen table chair. "We could go on a double date!"

"When?" Lilly seemed just as excited as me.

"Well, not this weekend, because you need to go on a date with Jace by yourself, but maybe after that? Like, we can have your mom take us to the movies in her Camaro?"

"Abigail. The Camaro only seats four people."

I struggled, pulling a knot out of my hair. "Yeah, well, she can stay home and I'll drive."

"Pfft. You'd drive us into a ditch."

"Really, though. Would you wanna double date?"

"Duh."

We started plotting immediately, but our plotting had to end after only five minutes because my mother needed the phone to call Patrick. Before I hung up, I made sure to tell her, "You better call me right after the date. Tell me everything. Or wait until I come over."

"Okay, bye!"

Lilly was my only friend who ever said bye when hanging up the phone. Kimmie and Audrey never understood the concept of a proper farewell.

That afternoon, Audrey came over with her boom box and bathing suit so we could swim in my pool and listen to Avril Lavigne's new album, *Let Go*. We lathered ourselves in multiple layers of tanning lotion. She braided my hair to one side, and I fixed hers in a messy bun at the base of her neck. In between songs, we rummaged through the pool house refrigerator for forgotten cans of pop. All we could find were opened bottles of Arbor Mist wine that my mother had discarded weeks earlier.

Risk takers, we each took a few sips straight from the bottle. Moments later, we were spitting and dry heaving in the nearest trash can.

The sounds of four-wheelers harmonizing with the song "Unwanted" caused me and Audrey to lean up from our relaxed sunbathing naps. We removed the logs of towels covering our eyes to find Bradley and Ryan casually waiting at the base of the pool deck ramp. Both of their t-shirts were a few shades darker with summer sweat, and flecks of cut grass lined the bases of their necks and along their jawlines. The look fit Bradley almost perfectly. Ryan, however, looked out of place. His shirt wasn't red. He was wearing rainbow-lens sunglasses and his hair was gelled to one side.

Apparently I was supposed to answer Ryan by that afternoon on whether or not I could go four-wheeler riding with him and Bradley. Frustrated with my lack of response, he decided to take it upon himself to fetch Bradley and drive to Bear Run Road to weed an answer out of me.

I pointed down at my house. "If my mother knows you're here, I am dead. I'll ask her, okay? Just don't get me grounded."

Ryan had a piece of grass in his eye, or he actually meant to wink at me. "I'll get you somethin'."

Was that his way of flirting?

They put their four-wheelers in neutral and rolled down my backyard without making a sound.

Two days later, Audrey and I were on her front porch swing, my head in her lap, a *Cosmo Girl* draped in between her hands in front of us, and again, the sounds of four-wheelers roared in our ears. Glancing up, yet again, we discovered Ryan and Bradley parked in her driveway, wearing similar looks and expressions from two days earlier.

Before we could even say a word, Todd stormed out of the Lego house threatening the boys with his shotgun. They sped off in one of the largest gravel clouds ever made on Bear Run Road.

As Audrey and I lay in her bed together that night, she asked me why I hadn't asked my mother if we could go four-wheeler riding.

Finally truthful, I admitted, "I am scared of being alone with them."

"Oh." She rolled over after that.

It wasn't the danger of the four-wheeler ride that turned me away from asking my mother for permission. The idea of being alone with a boy, with two boys, two boys that were older and more experienced than I was...it terrified me.

The third time we found Bradley and Ryan uninvited in Bear Run Road was the last weekend of July. Audrey and I were on one of our daily walks up and down Bear Run Road when we heard the agonizingly familiar buzz of four-wheeler engines getting closer and closer. We immediately tightened the t-shirt cradle of blackberries in our hands, an effort to protect our inventory from the oncoming dust cloud.

Ryan and Bradley drifted down the bend and played chicken with me and Audrey. At the last second, Bradley slammed on the brakes, but his back tires slid on the gravel and the front of the four-wheeler clipped both me and Audrey on our sides. Our hands unlocked from our t-shirt cradles and our days' worth of berry pickings rained down at our feet. Instead of asking if we were okay, all four of us dropped to our knees and tried to salvage as many of the blackberries as we could.

It wasn't until we shared what was leftover with the boys that they turned off their four-wheelers and apologized. Ryan particularly nodded in Audrey's direction. "I expected you of all people to run out of the way."

"You don't know me," she countered.

Then he looked at me. "You still haven't asked, have you?"

I looked to the ground for answers. "Well, look, I really don't think she'll let me. She hates four-wheelers. She thinks they're the devil."

Ryan made a strange noise in the back of his throat. "Well, can't you sneak out?"

"If I snuck out now, she'd know."

Bradley shot a bullet of tobacco saliva over his shoulder. "We'll make sure you girls are okay. It ain't about us gettin' you hurt."

"I know that," I snapped.

Audrey held up a hand. I pretty much traced the shape of a lightbulb flickering above her blonde head. "My mom and dad are going to some sort of banquet on Friday. They'll be gone all day."

She paused, as if she expected one of us to interrupt her. Noticing that we were waiting for more, she continued, "When they leave, I'll have them drop me off at Abigail's, and then Abigail can tell her mom that she's coming to my house, and you can pick us up and nobody would even know."

I kicked at a blackberry-stained rock. "You know, that'll probably work."

"Really?" Ryan nudged me with his shoulder. I wanted to nudge back, but I was actually already sore from the four-wheeler impact from earlier.

"Yes, really," I affirmed. "You'll get your four-wheeler ride."

Bradley smacked the back of Ryan's neck. The force, complemented by a fresh layer of sweat, sent a blindingly sharp snap all throughout Bear Run Road. Audrey and I hissed vicariously at the impact of Bradley's palm on Ryan's neck. He massaged the palm print gingerly.

"Dude, fuck, sorry. But this is cool. It's about damn time," Bradley said, flashing Audrey a calculated look. "If your dad decides to chase me with a shotgun again, I swear—"

"If you weren't so dumb, he wouldn't have to." Audrey now had something in her eye. The wink was contagious.

Nine

That Friday, Ryan asked me to send him a message on MSN Messenger as soon as we got back from walking from my house. Everything went as planned: Audrey told her parents she was coming to my house, they dropped her off on their way to the banquet, she waited for me outside, I asked my mother if I could go down to Audrey's, and she said yes.

Audrey and I had barely walked through the Lego house door before I rushed right for the computer, connected to the Internet, signed on to MSN Messenger, and sent him the message:

```
Come get us.
```

The message itself was exhilarating. My veins pumped pure adrenaline straight to my heart. It felt like my heels were levitating off of the plywood boards beneath us.

When I pressed Enter and the message was delivered, something fuzzy coursed through my entire body.

He responded almost immediately:

```
on our way ;)
```

He must have been sitting at the computer, impatiently waiting for me to message him.

That meant Audrey and I had about twenty minutes to get ready.

We dolled ourselves up, knowing perfectly well that we would probably get super dirty, muddy, and smelly by the time the four-wheeler ride was over.

Audrey wanted to wear one of her nicest shirts, but I called her an idiot and told her to change, because she would ruin her shirt; it would get stained, and her parents would know she went four-wheeler riding with boys.

We met in the middle when I suggested she wear one of her nicer shirts—a white blouse with a ribbon collar and sleeves that split at her elbow—because it was already stained with grease, and she called me a genius. She even put on a pair of old blue jeans without my suggestion, so I guessed she was learning.

Unfortunately, I wasn't the brightest when I met Audrey at the end of my driveway and we walked back down to her house, because I was wearing my newest gray sweatshirt for Morgantown High School that my mother got me for a discount at the Walmart in Morgantown. As much as I wanted to take it off, I was only wearing a slightly transparent camisole underneath. Audrey was bigger than me, so none of her clothes fit. At least my shorts weren't new, so I could ruin them and just lie to my mother and tell her that I fell in the woods.

Audrey offered to braid my hair, like she always did. Then I copied her and pulled her hair back into a messy bun at the base of her neck: the same way we styled each other's hair the week before, the first time Ryan and Bradley invited themselves over to Bear Run Road.

"So, you do like-like Bradley after all?" I asked while applying blue mascara. Blue mascara was popular back when we were in the 6th grade, but it was more like a personal favorite now than something to wear to fit in.

"He's okay. He smells like oil."

I handed her the mascara tube. "I like him. He's always very considerate when I stay with Lilly."

She made a face. "Is this blue?"

"Yeah, just put it on. It looks cool." I reached for one of Tracy's bottles of Victoria's Secret lotions, and I began lathering my arms and legs with a fragrance called Love Spell.

Audrey dropped the blue mascara on the bathroom sink. "Abigail, don't use all of that. That's Mom's good stuff."

"I'm not. Do you want some?" I held out my hands palms-up with lines of purple lotion in between my skin creases. "I have extra."

"Yeah." Audrey held her arms out like a zombie and I lathered her up.

Gravel crunched outside the open bathroom window. It was a funny thing that I heard the gravel moving around outside before even noticing the humming sounds of the four-wheelers kicking down to neutral.

Audrey gurgled the last of mouth wash and nearly missed the sink as she spit, then sprinted off to the front porch. I wiped away the excess mouth wash dripping from the corners of my mouth before doing the same, but I wasn't as graceful or in tune with Audrey's Lego house. My arms brushed against the unfinished door frame of the bathroom before I made it outside. I hissed in pain for less than a second.

The first thing Bradley said to me was, "Hey, you're bleeding."

I gave him a death glare. "Nice to see you, too, Bradley."

Audrey stepped in front of me. "Where are we goin', anyway?"

Bradley killed the ignition on his four-wheeler. Ryan followed suit. It was a lot quieter now. "You guys ever been to the abandoned house up near Steel Run?"

Audrey and I traded glances. "No. Where is that?"

Ryan's throat gurgled, and he spit mucus near Audrey's foot. She stepped back in horror. "It's near my house, a few ways from the bus stop."

I laughed. "I've never been on the bus longer than Kimmie's stop, so I have no idea what you're talking about."

Bradley nodded behind him. "Just get on and we'll show you."

With Audrey still in front of me, I shoved at her in the direction of Bradley's four-wheeler. Her voice softened as she got closer to Bradley. "Am I riding with you?"

Naturally, Bradley flashed her a *Duh* look, and rolled his eyes.

Ryan patted the black seat behind him. "It shouldn't be too hot." His rainbow lenses dipped down his nose. He pushed them back up his oily face.

I lowered my chin to hide the red glow emanating from my neck. "Okay, thanks." Hoisting my legs over the four-wheeler seat, I dropped myself down directly behind Ryan. He was still considerably frail for a 14 year old.

My lap pressed against his back. As soon as it happened, my heart bounced off every single rib in my rib cage.

He snickered over his shoulder. "You smell nice." Why did he have to snicker?

My heart was now literally gripping at every single rib bone and wringing it out with some kind of supernatural, bottomless force.

I croaked, "Thanks," and then buried myself in my own personal embarrassment.

Nobody wore helmets, which only frightened me a little bit. As we wheeled out of Audrey's driveway and started up Bear Run Road, I calculated the possibility of being in a wreck. The rate that Ryan and Bradley were driving was at a pretty safe speed, so it wouldn't technically be our fault if we were in an accident. With Bradley and Audrey in front of us, I paid close attention to Audrey's blonde hair whipping at the base of her neck. It was easier to focus on that—it was *safer* to focus on that—instead of studying the warmth of Ryan's skin underneath mine as I held on to him.

We were a few minutes into the ride when Ryan started wriggling. I assumed that he was fidgeting because of my hands, so I pulled away to give him more room to work with. That didn't last long. While still driving, he jerked his head around and snapped, "Don't let go of me." Without even breathing, I shimmied back up on the four-wheeler seat, my thighs squeezing his tiny butt, and I snaked my arms back around his paper-thin waist. He snapped again, "Don't do that again," and turned back to face the road.

"Okay, sorry," was all I could say.

When we passed my house, I ducked my face into the back of Ryan's sweaty neck. On the rare chance that my mother happened to be looking out the kitchen window, through the wall of vegetation and trees separating our house from Bear Run Road, I hid my face and hoped that she wouldn't notice. As I pulled my head back up for air, a hint of salt lingered in my nose. Ryan smelled like a hot day in July. It made sense.

Bradley revved his four-wheeler engine. Audrey squealed like a madwoman and started pounding away at his shoulders. Her voice ricocheted off the thick walls of trees strewn around us. She wasn't even considerate in her threats. "Bradley Anderson, you best stop it! I'll bust you, you redneck heathen!"

At the end of Bear Run Road, the two four-wheelers bucked over a pothole. I saw Audrey's body literally catapult into the air. She was in the air, not touching a thing, for at least one or two seconds. Her scream bounced as she smashed back down onto the seat. In between her wailing cries, Bradley's laughter broke free when she gasped for breath.

That was when Ryan's left arm let go of the driving handlebars, and he placed his arm atop mine and yelled, "Hang on!" When it was our turn to drive over the pothole—it was so large, it was physically impossible to avoid unless we wanted to go face-first into a pile of scree or roll down a hill—Ryan eased off the gas, and we somewhat glided over the pothole.

My chin smacked off Ryan's back, right at a vertebrae bone. His foot slammed on the brake and we skidded across the last patch of gravel on Bear Run Road. He looked back at me. "You okay?" Shockingly, he was using a motherly tone with me.

I rubbed my chin and smiled. "Yeah, I'm fine."

Bradley's four-wheeler screeched to a halt in front of us. It didn't faze Audrey a bit, as she continued beating on Bradley's shoulders, back, and anywhere else she could physically punch the life out of him. "Hey, lovebirds, what the fuck you doin'?" He pushed back at Audrey, laughing through his nose. "You hit like a girl."

Still facing me, I saw Ryan's cheeks flare up underneath the rainbow sunglasses, which meant he saw my face mimic his, like he was looking in a mirror. We couldn't stop staring at each other. I wasn't hiding my glance as it followed the contours of his face, his pale little face with that morning's toothpaste crusting at the corners of his mouth, and the poof of hair that seemed to permanently push up at his hairline.

There was no doubt about it that he was studying me just as I had him. His eyes were pointing right at my little button nose, at the river of freckles across my cheeks, and at the strands of wet bangs clinging to my oily forehead.

Bradley revved in neutral. "I can't stay in the middle of the fuckin' road like this all day! Let's go!"

I broke away first by looking down at the tops of my silken thighs and squeezing Ryan with my knees. "Go, before Audrey kills him."

"Okay, okay, hang on." Ryan eased his hands atop mine, and he magically dropped my arms around his waist before returning his grip to the handlebars, revving us out of Bear Run Road and onto Red Cliff Hill.

My eyes caught a glimpse of a grin stretching across his sunburnt face.

The ride from my bus stop to Kimmie's was at least fifteen minutes, so it took us a little over twenty or so to get where we were going. On the way, we zoomed past Lilly's house. In the short second or two that her bedroom window was in vision, I couldn't tell if she was home or not.

As much as I wanted her to see me, I also didn't want her to see me. I wanted her to see me on the same four-wheeler as Ryan, as some sort of proof that I defeated the odds and managed to sneak away from my house and go on a four-wheeler ride with him and her brother. I didn't want her to see me having fun with her brother, which seemed to be a best friend taboo if I was actually enjoying myself in the company of her so-called disgusting, gross, piggish, pervert of a brother.

Right as Ryan pointed up and said, as loud as he could above the popping four-wheeler engine, "It's somewhere," I knew that was a sign that we were almost to the allegedly haunted house of which he and Bradley spoke. When we drove to a fork in the road, instead of continuing on the recently paved path that would eventually lead us to Oldestown, we instead diverted left over a dilapidated bridge sprayed with lime-green moss and onto a road that clearly hadn't been maintained—or even considered—by the state of West Virginia in years.

It was an abandoned strip of gravel and jagged ground, with pieces of the earth literally jutting out of the soil in shards of pure stone.

The pothole on Bear Run Road had nothing on the potholes, cracks, caverns, and sinkholes on the road that Bradley guided us on. At one point, as he toned down his four-wheeler speed, he used just two wheels to traverse a complicated turn. I knew that Audrey was unaware that she and Bradley nearly tipped over into the ditch; if she had been, she would have burst into screams and started beating up on Bradley again.

Instead, she clutched him for dear life, her cheek pressed against his sweaty back, and I could see her eyes were squinted closed.

Ryan tapped my hand with his. His palm was caked in a film of sweat. "Lean this way." As he stood up, only his feet planted on the four-wheeler skirt, I let go of him and wrapped my fingers around the carrying cage behind me. Leaning with him, we were able to carefully go about the same complicated path on which Bradley nearly tipped.

I knew just by looking around me that no cars had driven on this path in years. There was no way such a thing was possible. If a four-wheeler could barely make it, a car wouldn't have made it even a few feet after the bridge. Any car would probably have been too heavy for that frail little bridge, so they wouldn't have even made it to that point.

Up ahead, I saw Bradley kill the ignition. He and Audrey shimmied off the four-wheeler seat together. As Ryan parked his four-wheeler next to Bradley's, he opened his hand and said, "After you, m'lady." I laughed in his face as he helped me from the four-wheeler. His fingers lingered atop my knuckles long enough that I was able to feel the lines and contours of his calloused fingertips on my skin. It was the first time I tried to speak to someone using just my skin alone. I wasn't sure if it worked.

Ryan was hard to read any more. He wasn't as clear as water, like he was when we were kids. I was unsure if he was kidding, like any other 14-year-old boy, or if he was trying to flirt with me. Even after our fingers pulled away, his hand gently brushed mine as we jumped down. It was the kind of thing that happened by choice, not something that happened accidentally. He willed his hand to brush mine. He wanted that to happen.

Audrey pointed down the hill. "Oh my goodness, that house is *creepy*."

Where we parked the four-wheelers used to be a driveway on top of the hill, leading to the house on which Audrey was fixated. I tore my eyes away from Ryan long enough to find the Victorian-style house perched neatly in between a few smaller hills.

The abandoned home was creepy for many reasons. Just on the outside, some boards were painted black, some scorched by what looked like fire residue, and there were broken beer bottles and empty beer cans littering the porch that surrounded the base of the house. I took a few steps forward. "How did you find this place?"

Bradley sniffed hard and proceeded to hack and spit snot near Audrey's feet. She jumped back and cursed. "We were off smokin' some dope and—"

"Don't tell them that." Ryan marched along with me. "Just tell them about the house, you dipshit."

"Fine." Bradley ushered Audrey to walk in front of him. The four of us walked sideways down the weed-infested hill. "So, we were off ridin' and shit, and we come across this path, and then we found this place. This place is fucking creepy." He launched another snot bullet near Audrey's feet. She turned and called him an asshole. "We haven't been inside yet. Saved that for you two. That way, you guys can hold on to us and be all like, 'Oh, save me, boys, save me from the evil spirits and ghosts and demons!'"

Now I knew where Lilly got her mocking voice from. She and her brother used the exact same tone when they teased someone.

I hesitated before stepping onto the broken-down wooden porch. I waited until someone else went first, Ryan, before I planted my tennis shoe on the broken boards. "Do you know anything about this house?"

"Nothin'." Bradley's untied work boots made heavy, hollow thumps every time he took a step. "We really did wait until we got you girls before goin' inside. Hey, there's a nail there." I stopped walking. Sure enough, glancing down, an upturned nail had nearly wedged itself into my heel. I kicked it aside.

Bradley continuously plucked at the collar of his gray t-shirt. I never liked wearing gray, because it was too easy to tell when I was sweating. Bradley was definitely sweating. Audrey's forehead was now oily with the heat. My cowlicks were frizzing at my temples. Ryan kept wiping his forehead with his arm. It was a superbly hot day for late July.

When we stepped into the house, we were standing in the kitchen. When I thought about an abandoned house, I thought about cobwebs, empty rooms, and eerie messages written on the walls. This house, though, was different. The fact that everything seemed to still be there—kitchen utensils in the drawers, what was left of a wooden kitchen table, dishes, cups, and mugs—made it even more eerie. We couldn't even see the floor, it was so covered in debris and papers. Newspapers were everywhere. I knelt down and sifted through some.

Underneath just a few pieces, I uncovered what looked like an old bra. I quickly put the pieces of newspaper back and furiously wiped my hands down the front of my sweatshirt.

There were a lot of holes in the floorboards. Audrey nearly got gobbled up three or four times because she never looked at where she was going. By the third time it happened, I didn't even stop my conversation with Ryan. We were talking about how it was super strange that the family, whoever they were, left everything behind—a sign that they needed to leave in a hurry—and the sound of someones's foot slipping into a hole echoed throughout the house. Bradley would grunt, and he would pluck Audrey from the house's mouth, and we would carry on.

It wasn't just the kitchen that contained remnants of a home. Everything in the living and dining rooms seemed frozen in time and exposed to the elements. A sofa and dining room table were still in the ordinary home locations, where every family had their dining room table and sofa. The papers-on-the-floor thing was common everywhere—in the living room, dining room, up the stairs... Newspapers were scattered all throughout the first floor of the home. None of the windows were intact; there were just broken shards and triangles jutting from the window frames.

As we approached the foot of the steps leading upstairs, I noticed something sparkling in the sunlight. I reached down and picked it up. It was a nametag, a keychain for a key ring. Rectangle-shaped and blue, the tag had a rainbow on it, and the name Jake was in gold on the bottom.

Ryan grabbed my hand that held the keychain. I sucked in my breath and held it there. "Who the fuck is Jake?"

I shrugged and pulled away before they could hear my lungs gasping for air. Exhaling, I blew hot air into the crease of my elbow, pretending to yawn. "Diana collects weird things like this. I'm going to give it to her when we get back."

Ryan placed one foot on a step. I gasped. Audrey, overhearing me, gasped, as well. Desperate, clingy, I reached for him, the pads of my fingers still shy enough that they didn't quite touch him. My hand levitated at his shoulder blade. "What are you doing? You're going up there?"

He turned to look at me over his shoulder. His dark eyebrows lowered. "Uhh, yeah?"

Audrey reached out, too. She was practically my reflection, fluidly moving with me, the only discrepancy between us being her white-blonde hair. "We shouldn't go up there. This place is too creepy. Let's just go home."

"Home? Fuck that." Bradley pushed me and Audrey aside, and with his big untied boots leading the way, they both carefully traversed the dilapidated staircase. The sounds the staircase made with each of their steps was enough for me and Audrey to step back, as if the boards would break into pieces and fly in our faces at lightning-fast speeds.

Only about two of the boards broke, unsurprisingly underneath Bradley's bulky, cement-caked boots, and the boys eventually made it to the top. Audrey and I followed moments later. We were able to use the fresh holes in the steps to determine the weakest places, dodging the lack of support in those spots and ascending elsewhere.

Audrey and I literally walked up the stairs in half the time it took Ryan and Bradley, and although I wanted to blurt out that we beat them and that we were better than them, as the four of us turned to walk down the small hallway upstairs, we all froze.

We literally stopped moving, stopped talking, stopped breathing, stunned by what greeted us there.

Audrey held on to my shoulders. She was standing behind me. Ryan wasn't in front of me, so my trembling hands climbed up Bradley's back instead, and he didn't push me away. The four of us huddled together, hands on shoulders, palms on shoulder blades, knees buckling, teeth grinding.

My eyes were unable to translate the object in front of us. I was looking at it, but for some reason, my brain digested it all wrong, and it became a wormhole of sorts, a curse, a totem that was trying to warn us.

Right in front of us stood a mirror. It stood because it was so large, an object that perched on lion-paw pedestals, the reflection glass held together with metal rivets of fired leaves and vines. Its mouth was so large that I was able to peer around Bradley's shoulders and Ryan's head and still see all four of us, our eight eyes growing in size the more we tried to understand just why and how a mirror of this sort got in a place like this.

We silently gawked at our disfigured, wobbly reflections in that black-framed mirror. Something shifted in all of us then, when we put the pieces together, that we were rummaging through an abandoned house, that we were peeking into a family's personal business that did not involve us, that we were trespassing on quite possibly a crime scene left forgotten.

There was no doubt about it. Someone—maybe a previous tenant or a bunch of curious kids like ourselves—had moved the mirror to the top of the steps, to a point where you didn't see it until you crossed over the last step. It was alarming that the surface was free of any blemishes. It had no flakes of dust or scratches or lingering fingerprints, almost like someone just recently wiped it clean.

I felt Bradley's shoulders shift underneath my grasp. Then I felt his body vibrate before I even heard his voice.

"The fuck is this thing? A mirror? Fuckin' Satan's mirror?" His voice was hard, almost as if he was trying to break the mirror by speaking. I never would have guessed in my lifetime that I'd hear fear in Bradley's voice, but that was why his voice was so weighted.

Audrey screamed through clenched teeth, "It was waiting for us! It's *right there!*" She rocked my shoulders. "Abigail, put that nametag back. It's cursed! It's cursed!" She stepped back a bit, her clutches releasing me. Predictably, not two seconds later, she was back.

"You think everything is cursed," I told her.

That didn't mean I thought there was no supernatural tie to the Jake keychain in my hand. First the Jake keychain, now Satan's mirror. What was going to be next? Would we find a dead body, or discover a hole to an alternate universe?

Slowly, the four of us thawed our ice-cold blood enough that we were able to finally peel away from one another. Audrey removed her hands from my shoulders, and I let go of Bradley. He readjusted himself by rolling his shoulders back and forth.

When Ryan didn't move an inch, we all looked at him. He was in the front when we all faced the spooky mirror. His back facing us, we couldn't see him; we couldn't see his face. All we could see was the back of his head: his fluffed black hair, the top bleached orange, the specks of dirt clinging to the sweat on the back of his neck, and the curious scab right behind his left knee. Bradley nodded to me, so I reached out and touched Ryan's shoulder, "Hey, are you—"

He jumped, turning 180-degrees midair, and flashed his hands in my face, "Ahh!"

Audrey jumped clean off the floorboards and hollered, "Oh Lord, *Jesus!*"

I shrieked and proceeded to punch each of his bony shoulders. His laugh vibrated every time my fist made contact. "You're such a jerk! We thought you were possessed!"

"I didn't think nothin'," Bradley countered.

As we each turned in different directions, we noticed that there were only a few rooms upstairs. We went to work fast.

Exploring each of the rooms together, we decided the first one looked like it was meant to be some sort of attic; it was dark because it had only one small window. The window itself was covered with a horde of cobwebs and dried-out spider nests. We decided to leave that room unsearched at full capacity, as soon as we noticed a few sets of dirty lingerie clinging to an old clothes rack.

Even worse, as we turned to leave that attic room, Ryan's foot kicked the side of a dirty mattress. That mattress was so dirty we weren't sure if it was covered in dust, mud, or old blood. We didn't stay long enough to study the elements. Audrey shoved us out of that room, and we closed the door behind us. It didn't even stay closed. The doorknob was missing, so Bradley football-shouldered the door until it nearly snapped the wooden frame.

The other two rooms were pretty boring, considering the first was the prime example of an abandoned crime scene. Nothing scary or haunting popped out at us as we rummaged through dresser drawers and closets. Audrey found an old pair of glasses, and she was about to put them on her face until she noticed a nest of baby spiders hanging from one of the lenses. She dropped the frames on the ground, stomped on them, and cursed in the Springs Native Tongue, "Gosh darn, them dang spiders, I nearly saw Jesus!"

Then she realized her error when the baby spiders, which just looked like ants as they scattered from the bent frames and broken pieces, started to make their way towards her feet, so she jumped around and screamed for Jesus some more before we exited that room and called it complete.

We were a group again, bundled together in the narrow hallway, as we approached the only remaining room unsearched. Ryan held out his arm. I stopped walking, Audrey and Bradley both apparently not paying attention as they walked into me. "That's the last one." In front of us, like a twin of Satan's mirror, a closed door was perfectly placed at the end of the hallway, as if it was waiting for us to open it and unleash some ancient West Virginian curse.

Turning, his warm eyes climbed my body. I couldn't tell if he was trying to find out if I was nervous, or if he was *looking* at me. The anticipation of opening the last door weighed more than my desperation for him to look at me again. Ryan quietly asked, "Did you want to go in?"

Looking to Audrey for an answer, she shook her head so fast that her face blended into a blur of blues and blondes.

I, on the other hand, tilted my head, "Ehh, I don't know. I think I'm good."

"Move." Bradley, as always, the southern gentleman that he was, pushed me aside as he went for the closed door. He was on a mission to drive out everyone's memory of his voice practically trembling when we first met Satan's mirror. I saw a heart-shaped pool of sweat staining the back of his gray t-shirt. I nearly laughed at myself, discovering the only romantic characteristic of Bradley was his sweat stain.

I heard Audrey's voice squeak behind me, "What if—"

Bradley hissed back, "Shh, shut up, you." As soon as his hand wrapped around the rusted doorknob, the three of us kicked it into high gear and sprinted up close behind him. Even though we were terrified for what was on the other side, there was no way we could miss a chance like that. *Anything* could be behind that door. A dead body, an old book of spells from some missing witch or wizard, or maybe even a place where rednecks had clandestinely been brewing moonshine.

I whispered my first question to Audrey. "What if we find a body?"

She drew a cross atop her heart.

I tested her again. "What if we find a *live* body?"

She double-crossed her heart.

Bradley didn't even countdown or anything. He just waited until we were right behind him, the most courteous thing he had ever done, and then he opened the door.

The room was bright. I didn't expect that. The walls were painted white, so the sun bounced off in bright rays all around. It was so much light that I had to lift an arm to shield my eyes with my elbow. In a corner sat a car-shaped bed, still in what looked like perfect condition. The sheets appeared free of any dust and debris.

Ryan pointed at the walls. "Look."

There were five or six childish paintings of characters like Lucy and Charlie from *Charlie Brown*. Clearly, a toddler had painted them, for they were just blue and black lines with dots for eyes. Even the small dresser across from the bed looked nice. It was white, with the letters A, B, and C on the front. I smiled at the teddy bear lamp perched on the top of the dresser. It held on to a set of multicolored balloons, the balloons the source of light when plugged in.

I stepped forward, curious and intrigued, "Hey, we—"

"Abigail, *stop*."

Someone grabbed my arm and yanked me back hard. It was hard enough that I lost my breath and stumbled back on my right leg, like stepping in a pot hole. My knee buckled out of place, and I wobbled to one side. When I turned, I expected to find Audrey clinging to me or something, her way of begging me not to step closer to the room because it would inflict its curse on me and we would all be doomed.

Instead, I came face to face with Bradley. He was clutching my arm so tight that I actually wanted to cry out in pain. His fingers constricted around my bicep with so much force that my skin around his fingertips paled in comparison to the rest of my arm.

He wasn't looking at me, though. His eyes were peering right above us, large and horrified.

Slowly, I raised my glance to the ceiling. What I found there was strange. Something that no matter how long I studied, no matter how long I stared, I would never be able to understand.

There were stuffed animals nailed to the ceiling above us.

Tons of stuffed animals and claw machine plushies dangled above our heads. At least twenty or thirty little teddy bears and Troll dolls and plushie cats were nailed by their imaginary hearts across the ceiling. I wanted to scoff at the near-perfect amount of space in between each victim. If I took a pencil and drew lines in between each nailed mark, I knew for a fact that a grid in precise measurements would surface.

That was the epitome of how difficult it was to swallow the reality hanging above our heads. There I was, standing underneath a vineyard of dead stuffed animals in a children's bedroom, thinking about drawing lines so I could create a grid for angles and shapes.

What was Audrey thinking about, as she studied the stuffed animals perched above us? Were Ryan and Bradley also thinking of something completely unrelated to the kindergarten nightmare enveloping us?

Nobody said a word. We stood there for a moment, long enough that Bradley attempted to reach up and touch one of the stuffed creatures, his fingernails failing to touch anything by at least five or six inches, and then he swallowed and took action. He pushed us back until we were out of that God-forsaken bedroom.

As he closed the door behind him, he ordered, in a stern voice, "Let's go," and we didn't fight him. Carefully, all together, like some happy little family, we held on to each other as we went back down the stairs and step by step back to the front porch and out of the house completely.

Something strange happened to me when I saw those stuffed animals, and it followed me outside the abandoned house as we stood on the precipice next to the four-wheelers. My body couldn't stop shaking.

Audrey held on to one of my arms the entire time we walked downstairs and back outside, and Ryan willed himself to hold on to the other when Audrey called out, "She's shakin' somethin' awful."

As we propped ourselves back on the four-wheelers, I was still trembling in my own skin. It wasn't so much fear that incapacitated me. The initial discovery of the abandoned house didn't even compare to the ceiling of stuffed animals. How was something so harmless so grippingly horrific?

My mind worked my memory far beyond its capacity, and I hummed in thought while Ryan kicked on the ignition and ordered me to hang on. He must have recognized the song I was humming, for he bravely placed a hand atop my knee and said, in a soothing whisper, "That's right, Aeris will make this all better."

That didn't help.

The stuffed animals didn't end up there by themselves, of course, which meant someone took the time to line up at least 40 plushies and nail each one of them to the ceiling. It seemed like something that would take hours to complete. Who had the time to create something like that? Who even thought that nailing kids' toys to the ceiling was a great idea?

It was impossible to wrap my brain around everything boxed away in that abandoned house: the Jake nametag, Satan's mirror at the top of the steps, the dirty lingerie and mattress upstairs, the child's room in immaculate and presently occupied condition (aside from the upside down graveyard of stuffed animals on the ceiling).

During our first break from riding, Ryan asked me, "Hey, you gonna be okay?"

And I lied and said, "Yeah," because I didn't know how to say anything else aside from "Yeah," at that moment. My inventory of speech was gravely empty.

The whole time we drove through pits of mud, grinding up the backcountry of West Virginia, even when I should have acted tough—when Bradley offered me a hit off a joint that he and Ryan shared—I still couldn't shake the image of that bedroom.

The only comfort I found was clinging to Ryan's little body, pushing against him as we dwindled down in speed to approach Bear Run Road, and he didn't push me away or call me a baby or tease me by going faster. That was a relief. His pace was slow after we searched that house. He was comforting, protective; when my body would explode in bursts of shakes, he'd coo to me and say, "It's okay," as gently as someone could when speaking over four-wheeler engines and Audrey's never-ending screams and cries to Jesus for help.

Bradley waved goodbye as he and Audrey continued down Bear Run Road so he could drop her off at Mam's. I ordered Ryan to stop a little ways after my house, near the abandoned cabin in between my and Audrey's houses, so my mother would think I was walking back from Audrey's house.

As I stepped down from the four-wheeler, he touched my arm. "You gonna be okay? You're fucked up right now." His eyes were bloodshot. I wasn't sure if it was from the air whipping at his face while he drove or the marijuana he and Bradley had smoked earlier.

I opened my mouth to tell him that I didn't like hearing the f-bomb in his voice, but instead, I shrugged my shoulders. "Yeah, sorry. I'm just, that was weird. I didn't like it."

"What do you think happened to that place?" Ryan turned off the four-wheeler. He was either doing it because he was going to stay for a bit, or he wanted to talk to me without having to yell over the engine. He had already been yelling at me and Bradley for the past two hours.

I moved my eyes over to the cabin behind me. "I don't know." I pointed. "That place is abandoned, too, but it's not as creepy as that house. That house was… God, I don't know." My hands rubbed together before I even realized I'd willed them to do so. My body was doing what it wanted to, without my brain letting me know what it was going to do next, and I wasn't sure how to accept that.

Everything I did, everything I saw, somehow translated to stuffed animals tortured and impaled on a kid's bedroom ceiling.

"Don't let yourself be afraid. Know how to do that?" He, too, stepped from the four-wheeler and approached me.

It wasn't until he was within arm's reach that I noticed how short he was. I hadn't grown since the end of 5th grade; I was still no taller than 4'11", so Ryan couldn't have been any taller than 5'7". With a long torso and short legs, he was at a decent height to match mine. My eyes levelled our heights by physical marks: his chin matched the top of my head.

My heart jerked. "Umm. How?"

He was so close to me now that I smelled the oil on his clothes and the marijuana on his breath. "You can train yourself. Be around things that scare you."

I swallowed hard. "I don't know what scares me."

Ryan reached out. He almost sighed. "I scare you."

My eyes looked up at him. Growing up, I always saw smashed morsels of food clinging between the corners of his mouth, something Kimmie always joked that he was saving for later. His cheeks were far less rosy now. They were nothing more than pale structures stretching as his skull took new shape, changing into his teenage transformation.

When was the last time he smiled, just because? Focusing more and more, my eyes uncovered the lines of facial hair complementing his upper lip. The moment I tried to look away, a glimmer. Since when did he get his ear pierced? Where did his dorky glasses go?

Then I saw dark pools underneath his eyes. My mother wore the same kind of blemishes. She was an insomniac.

Overwhelmed, I stepped back a bit. Gravel ground against the heels of my sneakers. I couldn't seem to accept that he was not the same little boy I met back in 1999.

He was right. He did scare me. He scared me because I didn't know him anymore.

Was that why I didn't want to go on the four-wheeler ride with him and Bradley? Because he was like a stranger to me now?

I placed my hand over my chest. It was suddenly hot and cold at the same time, and it was impossible to breathe. Even as he continued to stare down at me with a rudimentary yet darkly handsome smile, braces and all, I wanted him to do it. I wanted him to kiss me. Fierce, hungry, painful. I wanted him to push me down until my back cradled against the dirt road, and I wanted him to climb my body like a mountain, and I wanted him to claim me, mark me, whatever he could, and—

His lips brushed the tip of my ear, a movement he must have planned in order to accurately deliver just enough oomph to weaken my knees, and he whispered down to me, "I'm gonna message you on MSN later, and I'm gonna teach you how to not be afraid."

My knees did weaken. Ryan quickly reached underneath my elbows to hold me up as my body collapsed. He righted me back in place.

I whimpered, and when I heard it myself, I stepped back and quickly cupped my mouth. Then a gnat hovered over the tip of my nose, and I reached up to swat it away, only to knock my black glasses down my nose. As I pushed them back up in place, blinking away the spots and smudges lingering on my eyes, Ryan laughed with one of those breathe-out-the-nose laughs, and he reached up to rake back his black hair.

After he calmed a bit, he nudged me with his small hip and then slid back onto his four-wheeler. "I hope you had fun today, Aggs." He didn't say goodbye before he turned the key in his four-wheeler and gunned it out of sight.

I stood there, wrapped in my own thoughts, still in the embrace of my unnatural desire to just give myself up and over to him without a care in the world, and then I hated myself—more than I ever did before—because it took me this long: it took me so many years to realize how much I wanted Ryan. I didn't want him like a teenage girl wanted boys. No, my fury for him was something new, something primal, something that Kimmie and Laney and Lilly told me about many, many times. It was something that not even they had experienced, but they, too, desperately wished for a relationship fueled by blue fire and the feeling of rolling around in roiling embers.

When Bradley finally drove by, he was surprised to see me still standing in the road. He stopped and narrowed his eyes at me. They were watery, and tear tracks cut through the layer of dirt stretched across his cheeks. I could tell by his eyes, and by how quickly I first heard his four-wheeler and saw him, that he was driving way too fast. He patted the seat behind him. "You wanna ride up to your house?"

I thought I said no, but I couldn't even hear anything. I may not have said anything, actually. He ended up waving and driving off, so I at least told him that I was okay, but I didn't know if I even spoke. No matter what I did, no matter what I saw, I thought of Ryan. He was in the bed of leaves in the ditch. He was swinging from the braches above my head. He was walking next to me.

As I walked back home—more like tiptoed, because I was my own fragile entity afraid of splitting in half at even the smallest of careless steps—I imagined that he was standing next to me, walking with me, talking about growing up together. Ryan's voice went in one of my ears and filtered out the other. I actually talked back, aloud, oblivious to the fact that I was talking to an imaginary thing in the form of a teenage boy.

He asked me if I still liked Digimon, and I said to the trees, "Yeah. I'll always like Digimon." Then he asked me if I still liked Aeris, and I said to the gravel at my feet, "She's sad to think about, but I like her."

And then he asked me if I liked him.

Blushing, I kicked at a rock and mumbled, "Yeah, I do."

Then he was gone.

Ten

Lilly and Jace's first date was horrible.

Everything went according to plan, at first. Lilly convinced her mom to drive the Camaro around Stream Ridge, and when they picked up Jace on Gunners Valley Road, they rolled down the windows and blasted classic rock music. Linda allowed them to sit in the back seat alone, and she purposely moved up her rearview mirror so she wouldn't see anything, but Lilly admitted nothing more happened than Jace touching her thigh and telling her that she looked pretty.

They stopped at the local ice cream parlor, Dairy Dream, for hot fudge sundaes and banana splits. Linda stayed in the car to give Lilly and Jace privacy as they sat at a picnic table underneath a willow tree.

As Lilly told me this over the phone, I imagined the scene straight out of a romance novel. Lilly's straight hair blowing in the wind, Jace's hooded eyes glittering in their hazel magnificence, the willow tree practically singing as it swayed around their in-love bodies. The sun perched at the tippy-top of Dump Hill, so it cast an orange glow over Jace's vampire-pale skin and Lilly's tanning shoulders.

In my head, they were two seconds away from kissing—and then Lilly said, "But, Abigail, God, he threw up all over me. Twice."

My imagination shattered into a thousand tiny pieces. I cackled. "What? No way."

"Ugh. Yeah."

Lilly wasn't sure if Jace was lactose intolerant, or if he was just feeling ill, but apparently he was putting on a façade when he was eating his banana split. At first, she noticed that his skin had transformed into a pale-green color, and the pools underneath his eyes were shiny in beads of sweat.

Moments later, he upchucked his ice cream. The vomit splashed in his plastic container, and the impact was so strong that chunks of banana and warm, liquefied milk kicked up onto Lilly's blouse. She was a champ, however, a preteen in love, so she calmed the situation by getting him napkins and somehow swallowing her gags as she patted away the milk vomit. She washed her shirt using the water fountain behind the building.

But then Jace threw up again, in the Camaro on the way home, and then Lilly wasn't a champ anymore: she got grounded because of it, as if it was her fault he got sick.

"How long are you grounded for?"

She scoffed. "Until the end of summer. Really, it wasn't even my fault. It wasn't my puke. My mother can be a real bitch sometimes."

I felt the poison in Lilly's words as she spoke about her mother. I decided to switch the conversation's subject to something less troublesome for her. "So, get this. A few days ago, I went riding with Bradley and Ryan."

She gasped. "What? When?"

"Bradley didn't tell you? Well, we went to that aban—"

She gasped again. "Do you think Jace likes blonde hair? I dyed my hair today."

"Uhh..." I blinked. My mouth slightly hung open at the bottom of the phone, my chin pressed against the plastic curve of the receiver. Bringing my lips together, I frowned. My mood soured. I actually laughed at her. "I was talking about the abandoned house, the four-wheeler ride."

"Yeah," she began, her tone ending with another scoff, "but now we're talking about my hair. Do you think he'll like it?"

I almost said, "I wasn't finished," but it wouldn't have mattered.

It started shortly after Christmas break the year before when Lilly started to act differently. Laney and I both noticed that she was sometimes difficult to talk to, because all she wanted to talk about was herself. It wasn't just us who noticed it, either. Kimmie once made the comment that she never saw Lilly *not* playing with her hair or looking in her compact mirror. Everything about her appearance had to be pristine before she was social. It made sense now why she looked so pretty when I first spent the night at her house the year before; she had to look her best, had to be in her best clothes with freshly curled hair, just to see me, her best friend who could care less.

At first, Laney and I both denied her narcissistic behavior. We denied it because Lilly was one of our best friends, and even Laney and I both had our own negative quirks. Laney always canceled plans at the last second, and I had the horrible habit of delivering backhanded comments, like, "That shirt would look good if you didn't do your makeup so ugly like that."

Lilly's quirk was her conceited nature. Her blood ran ostentatious.

She was also territorial, more so than me, which made talking about Jace like walking on ice. If I ever agreed with her that Jace was cute, she would say, "Maybe you shouldn't talk to him anymore," or "I don't think you should talk about him like that."

After I caught on to her odd behavior, to be on the safe side, I usually refrained from saying anything more than, "Yeah," or "No," when talking about him.

That didn't mean she wasn't able to say similar things about Ryan. The last time we both talked about him and his dark and mysterious new hair colors, I admitted that Ryan looked like a darkly handsome guy, and Lilly agreed, which defaulted my response to something like, "You shouldn't talk about him like that." I literally threw her own words back at her. My intention was for her to realize how ridiculous she often sounded.

She countered without faltering, "Why not? It's not like I'm going to steal him from you."

Had I ever responded to her remark like that, Lilly would have ignored me for an entire week.

Apparently, the rules only applied to me. She was immune to her own regional laws.

All of our conversations had to be either about her, or have her in them. If I wanted to talk to her about Ryan or Bradley, and it didn't involve her for any reason, she would change the subject. If Laney wanted to talk about basketball, Lilly would start talking about cheerleading. She mastered the subject change so well that, more often than we liked to admit, Laney and I didn't even notice it until we were five minutes into a conversation about Lilly's latest favorite movie.

That was just how she was. Had Laney or I said something about it, it wouldn't have helped. To avoid arguments, we usually gave in. That was much easier than trying to sit Lilly down for an intervention. After all, she was part of the Anderson family, who were all masters at winning arguments, regardless of logic.

We didn't want our friendships to be ruined because we picked on her for her quirk. Lilly never once called us out on our quirks, even though we all knew about them. It was just one of those untouchable subjects between friends, and we respected that as best we could.

On the phone, she smacked her lips together. "My hair still smells like chemicals."

I sighed and forced humor in my voice, "All blondes are hot, so you'll be okay."

Lilly snickered. "Well, of course I'm hot."

She couldn't see me roll my eyes.

Slightly frustrated, I lied and said that my mother needed the phone to call Granny. Lilly made another lip noise. "Okay. I'll be on MSN after Mom goes to bed. LYLAS." *Love you like a sister.*

We spent the next few days calculating our double dates with Ryan and Jace. Since Lilly only trusted herself to sneak on the phone for no more than five minutes, we usually just rambled facts without saying anything in complete sentences. Lilly was able to spit out facts much faster than me; she was the fastest speaker I had ever met. Our choir teacher even joked that Lilly spoke her own language. He referred to it as Lillyanese.

Eventually, we managed to put our facts together and come up with a game plan. The four of us would attend the first Stream Ridge High School football game together. The goal was for me to ride the bus home from school with Lilly, Ryan with Jace, and Lilly's mother would pick everyone up on Gunners Valley Road. The only downside to attending a football game together was Lilly only being able to sit with us during third quarter. She was one of the best flutists in the marching band, and her only break was right after halftime.

Late one night, as I got up from the computer to refill my coffee mug, I came back to MSN Messenger to an unread message blinking orange on the bottom of the screen. Opening the conversation box, my stomach turned in fear at seeing Ryan's account. His message was quick, to the point:

    r u ready??

At least that meant he hadn't forgotten his promise days before, his promise that he would teach me how not to be afraid.

Or that he had forgotten, and that was just the beginning of one of his eerily flirtatious efforts to steal my attention.

Gulping, I keyed back:

```
Yes.
```

Ryan typed for a while, but his message wasn't as long as I expected it to be:

```
one day u should walk in the woods behind my house
and close ur eyes....and then i'll come find u....
```

He sent a second message detached from the first:

```
aggs i wanna find u
```

I gulped again.

Was that how boys his age flirted with girls my age? By tempting them to do foolishly unthinkable things to force them into positions of vulnerability?

As much as I wanted Ryan to somehow turn into my knight in shining armor and save me from some sort of horrible demon, I didn't want to play the damsel in distress card. I was brave. I could face spiders and snakes without even flinching.

Unsure of how to appropriately respond, I tested his near-threat:

```
Why should I trust you?
```

A message flew in at an instant:

```
u shouldnt trust me
```

How many times could I gulp in an hour?

Index fingers on F and J, I considered my next response. It mattered. Our conversation was dependent on my next message, I knew that.

As I closed my eyes, I saw myself in a patch of dense woods skirted with fog that smelled like dry ice and ivy. Surrounded by vegetation and eerie four-eyed birds flying across my shoulders, I stood with closed eyes, just like I was doing in real life. And then I saw a figure emerge from one of the tree trunks. Small, dark, gliding like a specter, its ends dissolving as it moved closer and closer...

By the time it reached me, the wraith took form. Human form—it was Ryan. His eyes were red and glowing, his mouth barred with sharp teeth, black hair long and pulled back against his neck.

The moment one of his hands touched my shoulder, my veins filled with cold stone. Then I opened my eyes, and they, too, were red. My mouth pulled apart in a strange, struggling way, almost as if my lips had been sewn together, the thread splitting as I unhinged my jaw, and then a near-fatal noise escaped my lungs, and the two of us screamed out in harmony.

The computer chair screeched, a warning sign that I was one second away from crashing to the floor. Jerking my eyes open, I reached out and pulled at the computer desk, yanking myself back into place. My heart was racing. Sweat beaded my forehead. My armpits were suddenly damp. The coffee turned into turbulent waves of black in the mug.

My hands were suddenly so cold that it was unnervingly difficult to type. I tried another method before giving him any time to answer my first:

```
What would happen? Why do you want me walking in
your woods behind your house?
```

Ryan's answer worked:

```
cuz I wanna terrify you
```

He was already terrifying me. I didn't tell him that, though.

I acquiesced to his game. My heart was just a few short emotions away from charging right out of my chest. With a single finger, I responded:

```
Okay. I will. What are you going to do to me?
```

As soon as I sent that message, I literally lowered my head, dropped it into my hands, and I knocked myself on the forehead over and over again, repeating the words, "Stupid, stupid, stupid." I was practically inviting him to give me the most cliché of responses.

I read his response in more ways than one. It chilled me to the bones. It rocked my woman core. It did so much to me that I immediately signed out of MSN Messenger, shut off the computer, and went straight to bed.

His confession:

```
aggs if only u knew the things i wanna do to u
```

I couldn't sleep that night. The nightmare of what exactly Ryan wanted, and would, do to me, it sloshed around inside of my skull for what seemed like an endless, dark period of time.

It was hard to function after that conversation with Ryan.

How was a girl to continue on with her dull, boring life when a boy, potentially crazy, yet handsome and innocent, said something like that? Every time I thought that, I had to tell myself that Ryan wasn't a boy anymore. He was a guy. He was a teenager. He was this brand new kind of person. He was a new *thing*.

In many ways, he was a stranger to me now. I didn't know anything about New Ryan.

It wasn't until early August that I was able to spend the night with Lilly at her mother's house in Oldestown. Linda loosened her grounding on Lilly with one rule: as long as we didn't leave the house, I could come over for the night.

That night, Lilly let me sleep in her best set of pajamas. They were silky blue, with cartoon cats everywhere. We lay her in bed for the rest of the night, crawling underneath blankets as early as 7:00 PM. We held each other's hands, played with each other's hair, and talked about boys, dreams, and our future. Her small television set stayed on ABC, and we were in tears watching a marathon of *Whose Line Is It, Anyway?*

At one point, Lilly pointed up and said, "I swear, if you and I were old, and if we were men, we'd be just like Colin and Ryan."

I turned to her. "Who'd be who?"

She looked at my face with such a closeness that I saw the blackheads sprinkled along the slope of her nose. "You'd be Colin. You both have big, baby-blue eyes."

I had to smile. "And you'd be Ryan. He's tall and skinny and always has that face."

It must have been a full moon that night, because white-blue light filled Lilly's bedroom long after we turned off the television. She reached out and pulled back the curtain closest to her bed, and a block of light spread across her bedroom floor.

The more we talked about the moon, the more I found myself referencing Ryan, who seemed to be a topic of interest to Lilly. She asked about Jace from 2000, when I went to Ryan's birthday party and spent almost the entire day with both boys. I told her about the belly flops, *Chicken Run*, and the car ride back home.

She pretty much melted on the bed sheets when I told her, on the way home, Jace pretended to see a pack of wolves following the car, their noctilucous bodies blinking behind the spines of pine trees, and that we'd all made up wolf identities. Lilly made up one, too, right there on the spot. She gave herself beige fur, and her wolf name was Luna. I didn't tell her that that was Kimmie's wolf name, as if it mattered anymore.

As our eyes grew heavier, she said through a yawn, "Y'know, both of them are cute. Jace and Ryan. We'd be the luckiest girls in the world if we dated either of them."

Our conversation ended with that; Lilly had eased into sleep, and I did the same not long after. I used her breathing as a metronome to slip into my dreams.

I never told her about my conversation with Ryan, about how he wanted me to walk in the woods behind his house. I didn't figure Lilly would understand.

The next day, Lilly gave me a makeover. Instead of dolling me up, she branded me with her curling iron when she burned the right side of my jaw. My skin sizzled and popped almost instantly. Terrified and stricken, she pulled away, yanking my hair that was still rolled up in the hot iron. The two of us fell onto our elbows and nearly caught her bedroom on fire. Her mother screamed up at us from the dining room downstairs, "Girls! You okay?"

We screamed the word, "Fire!" in a joking manner.

Linda bolted up the stairs, using her toned, chiseled legs to throttle herself straight for Lilly's bedroom, and she tossed down a small fire extinguisher. Realizing that the two of us girls were stricken with laughter, she proceeded to bop us on the heads, legs, arms, anywhere she could with the fire extinguisher, calling us names like, "Heathen!" and "Fools!" and my favorite, "Tutu trouble makers!"

I wore a Band-Aid on my face for at least a week after that. When the mark had healed, it left behind a scar that looked like a caterpillar cut in half. At least, that was what Lilly told me when I showed her the scar and her unintentional artistic mastery.

Shortly before school started, I found myself online at odd hours during the night. The only reason I was up until after 5 AM on MSN Messenger was because Ryan asked me. He greeted me every time I signed on. We shared our favorite songs with one another. We talked about our favorite books. If we were feeling especially brave, we told each other our favorite parts of one another.

Ryan told me that he could eat my eyes like candy, they were so sweet.

I told him that the angle of his eyes, the arch of his dark eyebrows, made me weak in the knees, and that sometimes, I traced the shapes of his hands, remembered that shape, took it home with me, and traced it in my journal.

To that, he responded:

```
damn aggs...u know me better than i know myself...
```

Shortly before 8th grade started, I took part in perhaps the most uncomfortable conversation in my life. As I made my usual cup of coffee and approached the computer desk, signing on and looking for Ryan's username, I opened up the conversation box and sent him the standard:

```
Hey ^-^
```

He didn't like it when I messaged him first, but if I wanted to start trouble, my way of forcing him to flirt with me, I usually beat him to it.

My skin ignited in goosebumps when I read his message back:

```
let me tell u something
```

A lot of things drove through my mind as I read his message over and over again. Each time, it was something different: he was going to express his undying love for me, he was going to finally tell me his biggest fear, or he was about to share with me the honest truth that he did want to kiss me after our four-wheeler ride together. My cranium filled with all sorts of scenarios, the walls of my skull virtually cracking to hold everything. It was like my skull was plunging deeper and deeper into an oceanic abyss, and in seconds, my head was going to explode or implode, coming apart one atom at a time.

Fingers sprinting across the keyboard, I acknowledged him:

```
Go for it. ^^
```

His next message confused me:

```
aggs...u wanna take some morphine with me some-
time?? i want u to try it
```

I reached for my coffee mug three times after reading that particular message, and all three times I was shocked, for some reason, to find that there wasn't any more coffee. Pulling my legs up to my chest, knees against my collar bones, I tested myself. Did I know what morphine was? It was a word I had only heard of a few times at that moment, a word that my Granny once talked about when one of her friends was receiving chemotherapy for lung cancer. Another time was when my mother got a hysterectomy, and was prescribed morphine for her pain.

Why was Ryan asking me if I wanted to take pain medicine with him?

I didn't want to seem so naïve, so I did my best to appear knowledgeable and wise in my answer:

```
Morphine? Like Tylenol?
```

Clearly, I had no idea what I was talking about.
His response both complimented and offended me:

```
aggs...ur so adorable so innocent...ur like a
little deer lost in the woods...its what i take to
feel better i steal it from my mom have u ever tried
it?????
```

I didn't have any experience with morphine, or anything like it. Still assuming that it was another way to say Tylenol, I typed back a response a few moments later:

No. I think I'll pass. ^-^ Just be careful with
that kind of stuff, ok?

He tried one more time:

plz? i will take care of u i promise...

It was the first time I didn't give in to Ryan:

No, thanks. Really. Don't do anything stupid.

Ryan countered my order with a command of his own:

then dont tell Scott or Jace or anyone about this
i don't want any1 knowin about this

More worried than curious, I asked him:

What do you mean?

For the remainder of the night, Ryan explained to me the schedule of his
nights, a routine that he had been following for the past few weeks. When both
of his parents went to sleep, he snuck from his bedroom and searched for his
mother's purse. It was usually on the cluttered dining room table, the one in
front of the fireplace. After snagging just a few morphine pills from her purse's
side pocket, he would run to the bathroom, wash them down with water straight
from the faucet, then sign on to MSN Messenger and talk to me. He talked to
other people, like Jace, but Ryan made sure to tell me that I was his favorite. I
wasn't sure how to respond to that.

After I signed off (since I was usually the first one to go to bed), Ryan would
sneak back into his bedroom and play *Event Horizon* on his DVD player. The
only night when he didn't fall asleep watching *Event Horizon* was when I told
him that I wrote a poem called "A Nightmare's Fear," in honor of his email
account. That night in particular, he read the poem over and over again until
he fell asleep.

I felt proud reading his message about that:

```
i didnt need morphine that night I actually slept
cuz of that poem so thnx
```

Then Ryan delved deeper into his relationship with morphine, explaining that it was a controlled medicine that he liked to take because it made him feel hyperactive. He confessed that he liked losing control of himself, of the things around him, and that he was particularly fond of the delay when his eyes saw something and his brain translated it a few moments later. He painstakingly described the intense wash of colors his eyes digested shortly after he took morphine, giving me the idea it was almost like looking through a lens of concentrated color saturation.

When he finished telling me his riveting tale, I practically applauded his efforts and said something like:

```
You're really good at sneaking around, huh?
```

All he said to that was:

```
yup...snuck around with u, remember? ;)
```

Before I could quench his thirst, before I could admit that sneaking around with him and Bradley and Audrey was the best thing to happen to me so far that summer, he asked me if I wanted to know one of his biggest secrets. I gave in. Okay, I begged him to tell me. His message flew in before I could even reach for my coffee mug a fourth time:

```
i always sleep with five knives underneath my
pillow cuz i gotta face my demons
```

My first thought was, *That's Audrey's trinity.*

My second thought literally eased from my now-trembling mouth. Actual words squeezed from the nervous push between my lips. "What in the world are you talking about, Ryan Matthew Mills?"

First, Ryan told me that he liked taking morphine. Second, Ryan told me that his childhood teddy bear was actually five blades the size of a ruler.

What was next?

My toes curled at the thought of something else coming at me, something more dangerous, like that he once killed someone or that he was a father to some baby states away. I ended up using my toes like fingers and plucking both socks from my feet to alleviate the muscle lock.

As I sat there, completely quiet except for my heart as it pounded away at the base of my sternum, a child begging to be ungrounded and let free, I mouthed his message over and over again. Every time I silently recited his admission, something more came from it. Ryan slept with knives because his father abused him at night; Ryan slept with knives because he was a cutter; Ryan slept with knives because he was mentally unwell.

The worst: Ryan slept with knives because he wanted to die.

Which of those, if any, were true? What if *all* of them were true?

Carefully, I thought about my next set of words. I glued them together, pulled them apart, rearranged them over and over again, until I came up with:

```
You should take a marker and write Abigail on one
of them. That way, I can help you fight off them
demons. ^^
```

I didn't want to embrace the fact that he was popping pills and sleeping with weapons, so instead I dodged the subject completely. I treated it like a kid would react to coming face to face with death, focusing on something else completely.

It was a new skill, the fact that I was able to manipulate the conversation enough that it was now about me: something I probably inherited from Lilly.

It worked. Ryan took the bait, and he followed me:

```
i already think of u when i fall asleep
```

Closing my eyes, I sighed out my worries.
I made sure to tell him:

```
I think of you, too ...
```

Then I signed off for the night.

That night was the first of many that Ryan and I talked on MSN Messenger until morning. We were suddenly so close that the only thing stopping us from becoming boyfriend and girlfriend was that we both were afraid to give our relationship something tangible like those labels. Ryan didn't want the label, and I didn't want my mother to know that I had a boyfriend.

If she knew I was dating a boy in high school, she would do everything in her power to stop it.

The first step in solidifying our relationship was asking him to stop stealing his mother's medicine. Still unsure what exactly morphine was, I determined that it was responsible for his sudden shifts in personality. Just by reading our MSN Messenger chat logs, I knew when Ryan had just taken some. His lapse in character occurred every other night, usually after 10 PM, and he would transform into someone much more debonair. His efforts at flirtation were dense, and he ended almost every single message with ;) .

During his morphine episodes, Ryan was brutally honest. That was how he admitted to me about the morphine and knives under his pillow in the first place: he was high. His honesty often hurt, especially when he confessed that he probably never would have invited me to his first birthday party had it not been for Kimmie and Scott begging him.

There were other moments where I held back tears while rereading his messages, like how he thought I looked my ugliest when I was in the 6th grade, and that he hated my favorite t-shirt with a tiger on the front because, far away, he thought it looked like the state of Ohio and he hated Ohio.

The one that hurt the most: he stopped liking me one summer because he started liking Lilly. It was something he made sure to tell me was just a fluke, how it happened because I wasn't spending the night with Kimmie anymore and Lilly was now one of his newest neighbors, living with her dad in her grandfather's old house.

When he asked me if that made me sad, I lied to him. I lied to him with clenched teeth and tears welling in eyes begging to suddenly go blind, so I didn't have to read any more.

Our conversations were usually a duplication of the one the previous night, as if our memories were wiped completely clean while we slept. Ryan liked talking about angels and demons, and blacksmithing with his father and Sephiroth. That was how I learned just when he started to like me. It wasn't when Kimmie called me after the dolphin incident and told me he thought I was cute. It was during his birthday party in 2000, when I was able to match his knowledge of *Final Fantasy VII*.

Ryan admitted that he fell a little bit in love with me when I sent him the recording of me humming Aeris' song.

Whether or not he was still a little bit in love with me, I didn't ask. I didn't want to know.

A few days before I started 8th grade, I decided to abandon my time at the computer and instead walk around the backyard. It was a spur of the moment sort of thing; I didn't even bother showering that morning, or fixing my hair. It was similar to my short-lived 5 AM walks a few months before. Throwing my long, dark hair up into a loose ponytail, I frowned at my blemished reflection in the mirror and at the oily spaces of scalp between pieces of hair. I didn't even bother wearing something that matched. After I put on an old Pokémon t-shirt and a pair of basketball shorts, I stepped outside with my Walkman and listened to Ai Maeda.

An hour into my walk, I saw someone appear from the side of the house.

My heart Plinkoed its way down my rib cage, hitting every single bone as it descended to its miserable state. I stopped mid-step, heel perched on the ground, toes pointed to the blue sky, as I witnessed Ryan walking closer and closer to me.

His eyes were abnormally large, much larger than usual. Upon closer inspection, I noticed his pupils appeared severely dilated. When he didn't even say hello or explain to me why he was suddenly at my house, uninvited, smelling just like a fresh four-wheeler ride, I knew that something was off. Ryan kept brushing back his black hair, now topped with a patch of bleached orange, touching his lips, stepping in place. Was this how he appeared when he talked to me on MSN Messenger?

The dark pools underneath his eyes were painful to look at.

I finally had to interrupt his physical movement tendencies. "What are you doing here?"

Everything about him stopped. His words were like nails as my ears embraced them. "Do you want to sit with me on the bus?"

What?

The thing about still being in middle school but being romantically attached to a high schooler was that, had Ryan even been old enough to attend prom, I was unauthorized to attend as his date due to my age. The closest he could technically get to me was asking me to sit with him on the bus. If I accepted, that automatically defined me as his new girlfriend. It was a process all students my age understood. It was a standard that even high schoolers accepted.

The webbing between my fingers and toes swelled with a clammy film. I was suddenly so distracted with his question that I wasn't able to focus on the fact that he was seeing me, the real me, in all of my dirty, oily glory, with unwashed hair, and my face glowing and makeup free. Ryan noticed that I wasn't saying anything, so he asked again. "Do you want to sit with me on the bus?"

"When?" Was I supposed to say yes or no first?

I watched his smile glitter in the early sunlight. His braces practically danced like stars in the night sky, even though it was daylight and pink outside. "The first Friday. Lilly's been begging me and Jace to go to the first football game and meet up with you guys."

My shoulders moved with my sigh. "I'll try. I mean, I may be grounded now, because, y'know, some guy decided to just show up at my house." His face transformed into sheer cynicism. To soothe the tension, I managed to throw in a laugh. "My mother hates older boys. But she hates four-wheelers even more."

He scoffed. "Well, tell your mother that I am good kid."

"She knows that. She knows who you are. But you're not a kid anymore. You're a teenager."

"Yeah, maybe, but that doesn't mean I wouldn't treat you well."

I laughed again. "What do you mean, maybe? You're fifteen! That's a teenager."

"Even if you can't go to the game, will you still sit with me?"

My smile burned into my skin. "Yes. Yes, of course."

So he wouldn't get caught, I begged him to leave before my mother noticed him. The last thing I needed was to get grounded before school started. As he said his goodbyes, Ryan gave me a look fat with venom and said, in the coolest of voices, "Your hair looks like shit, but you look adorable," and then he ran off. I heard his four-wheeler kicking up gravel on Bear Run Road before I even heard it start up in my driveway.

The first thing I did was run inside and study my mother, who appeared unbothered on the couch. She was barely paying any attention to the television show, let alone to the four-wheeler noises vanishing outside. After that, I made sure to wash my hair. The embarrassment alone at Ryan seeing me in such a raw state was enough that I tasted something bitter in the back of my throat, and I couldn't shake the feeling of being watched. With hair clean but still wet, I ran down to Audrey's house.

She was sunbathing on the trampoline when I showed up. Even though Audrey was as pale as I was, she was able to tan if she tried hard enough. I just burned. Without any explanation, I asked her what I should wear to school the first Friday. She was confused, naturally, so I had to step back a bit and update her on my life over the last few days. Rather than being jealous that I was going to a football game with Lilly instead of her, she folded her legs like a mother in training and used the tips of her fingers to draw things on the trampoline bed, as if they would actually materialize.

Audrey taught me lessons from experience, things that she had done before to get a boy's attention. Most of her advice was inherent, but I didn't dare stop her. She was on fire. Flooding with energy, she reminded me that I needed to wear something nice that day, so Ryan would always remember what I looked like. She said for me to also wear my hair a different style that day, different than the days before, so that, too, would be something for him to remember.

Finally, when I asked her what we were supposed to talk about, she hummed in thought for a moment before saying, "Abigail, I just don't know, but if he's anything like Bradley, talk about redneck stuff. Mud, dirt, and cows."

I smiled. "I like cows."

"Well, there you go." She leaned over and wiped her palm across the trampoline, using her skin as an eraser to wipe away her drawings and plans from earlier. I never once told her that I had no idea what she was writing or drawing. Audrey worked in her own way.

Eleven

By the time the first Friday of school rolled around, I had my overnight bag packed to take to school with me. That was the easy part; the hard part was dressing myself that morning.

I went through all of my new school clothes in a matter of seconds, and nothing was good enough to wear on the bus. After rummaging through my wardrobe three times, I decided to wear one of my favorite shirts. It was short-sleeved with blue, black, and white stripes, and the collar was super white and formal. To match, I wore my white skirt from last year's Christmas concert and blue sandals. With minimal makeup, I managed to braid my hair into long pig-tail braids, hanging down in front of my shoulders.

If anything, I tried to wear as much blue as possible. I wanted to match Ryan.

Like Audrey instructed, I made sure to wear my hair in a different style than any other day that week. As for my attire, maybe Ryan wouldn't notice that I was wearing the same sandals three days in a row.

I walked out through the garage door with my mother and Diana. I shimmied into the Ford Explorer, and my mother looked over at me as I patted at the sweat pooling underneath my armpits. I was so nervous the sweat was literally rolling off me. I would have bet that there was even sweat between my breasts. Terrified, I fanned out the boiling area there by leaning over and letting the air conditioner blow straight down my blouse.

My mother reached over and placed her hand on my knee. Even that was covered in sweat. She virtually pulled away when she felt my skin was salted wet. "Abigail, you are beautiful. And I think Ryan is a nice young boy." She quickly looked at my sister in the rearview mirror; Diana was applying a copious amount of glittering lip gloss. "And I don't want to hear anything out of you, young lady, understand?"

It was just minutes earlier that Diana had chastised me for sitting with the dork on the bus. In turn I called her a bitch, and my mother ordered us both to knock it off.

It was basically a catcall as I timidly marched down the bus aisle. The younger kids didn't even pay attention to me. That I'd anticipated. Kimmie, Laney, Lilly, and Audrey, however, knew exactly where I was going. I had made sure to tell them on MSN Messenger or the phone as soon as I found out. All four of them gave me nice, brilliant, congratulatory smiles as I made my way to Ryan's seat. Kimmie even leaned up, her hair spilling over into the seat in front of her; she held a fist in the air and said aloud, "You go, little bitch!"

The bus driver warned her to watch her language.

It was all much like the dare Laney handed down to me years earlier, except now I was doing it by invitation. He wanted me to sit with him on the bus.

Glancing up, I saw Ryan sitting in the seat behind Pokey Harris. He was looking right at me, and I could tell by the twitching in his face that he was trying his best not to smile ear to ear.

Ryan moved his backpack out of the way, and I sat down as heavy as an anchor being tossed into the sea. He spoke through laughing teeth. "See? I told you it wouldn't be so bad. I knew you could do it."

It wasn't bad at all. The entire ride to school, we talked about things we'd never talked about before. Ryan knew that I was an 8th grader now, and that I would be going on the 8th grade trip at the end of the school year, so he told me about his adventures in Charleston. That was where the class went for their graduation trip. The capitol of West Virginia was fun, in that it was the closest to a big city that most of us kids would ever get. Ryan's stories, as he told them with hands flying this way and that, were enough that I hunched over in laughter.

Apparently, his hotel mates for the trip had been none other than Scott, Jace, and Cameron. On the third night, it was tradition for everyone to order pizza to their rooms. Instead of eating their pizza on plates, the boys used pillows as dishware and didn't think anything of it when they set their garlic sauce and breadsticks on the air conditioning unit. By the end of the night, after roughhousing and chugging four liters of Coke, the boys monkeyed around and knocked the garlic sauce off the unit. It spilled in the engine, and as smoke rolled from its gurgling mouth, the breadsticks changed color from white to black. All according to Ryan's word, of course.

Pokey must have overheard us talking about the 8th grade trip. He turned around in his bus seat and also told us his tales of misbehavior. Instead of asking for privacy, we welcomed Pokey into the conversation, and by the time the bus stopped at Gunners Valley School to let the grade school and middle school classes off, I was terribly upset that I would have to stop talking to both of them.

As I grabbed my backpack and overnight bag for Lilly's house, Ryan reached out and hooked his fingers on one of my backpack straps. I looked down at him, now that I was standing and he was sitting. His eyes were much smaller now, not like they had been when he first asked me to ride the bus with him. His cheeks flared red as he readied himself to speak. "Thanks for sitting with me."

My cheeks mirrored his. "You're welcome." I looked over at Pokey and smiled at his bedhead, swirled at the back of his scalp. "Bye, Pokey."

He waved. "See ya, Aggs."

As I stepped away from the bus seat, I caught a glimpse of the window message I had written minutes earlier. During a moment of silence, I had leaned over Ryan's lap, blew hot air on the Plexiglas, and wrote, *Hello, Ryan* next to his shoulder.

It was still there when I walked away.

The moment that I stepped off the bus, Lilly, Audrey, and Laney bombarded me with cheers and squeals and everything else verbally girly. The only reason Kimmie wasn't with them was because she was in high school now. As they enclosed me with congratulatory hugs, I shimmied to the side just enough to glance over my shoulder as the bus pulled out of the parking lot.

There, in the far back, I made eye contact with Ryan. Apparently he, too, was adamant about seeing me one last time before school started. I made sure to stay in sight until the bus disappeared around the bend, just in case he wanted to watch me the entire time, just as I had watched him.

Lilly sat with me during recess. We occupied the only picnic table shielded with a canopy of leaves, a picnic table that used to be 8th graders only; since we were the new upperclassmen of Gunners Valley School, we were able to claim it as our own.

As Lilly unraveled my braids, only to braid them in pig tails again, she bragged about how much she and Jace were in love.

I had to roll my eyes. "I know, I know. True love."

She and Jace officially became girlfriend and boyfriend sometime that August. They went to the movies every weekend, and he magically appeared in her bedroom window almost every night, the kind of gesture that only happened in young adult books. Jace had to climb one of the willow trees and fight off cobwebs every time he did it. They had their first kiss on their one-week anniversary. Lilly, naturally, said that Jace was the best kisser ever.

I didn't agree with her, nor did I disagree; I knew better than to do either.

Instead, I chewed on my piece of peppermint gum and listened to the leaves shake above us.

After school, Lilly gave me another one of her makeovers before she slipped into her marching band t-shirt and a pair of white shorts. Linda called us downstairs, so we funneled into her red Camaro and hightailed it down Gunners Valley Road.

When we showed up at Jace's house to pick him and Ryan up, I noticed that there wasn't enough room for everyone in the Camaro. Even worse, as the boys approached the car, Linda ordered them both to sit in the backseat. It didn't even faze Lilly. She hopped out of the car to let Jace squeeze in first, and she just naturally slid atop his lap. They had obviously been practicing lap sitting for a while.

I, on the other hand, stepped on Ryan's toes as I got out of the car so he could sit down. Then, when I tried to climb back in, my head got caught on Linda's seatbelt. She growled, then I smacked Ryan in the face and practically fell chest first on his scrawny legs.

Eventually, while Lilly and Jace were snuggling neck to neck, giving each other Eskimo kisses, I tried so hard to appear weightless as I sat atop Ryan's lap. He didn't seem to mind. From Jace's house to the high school, little by little, my body slid down from the side of the backseat and onto Ryan's thighs completely. Under my breath, I told him that he could move me if I weighed too much. His response was physical. He grabbed my hips and pulled me down on top of him. He never said a word.

Even after Lilly was dropped off at the high school for the football game parade, Linda told me to stay in the backseat with Ryan and Jace until we parked for the football game.

The football game itself was boring. Stream Ridge High School wasn't a prominent powerhouse in athletics, but for the size of their football team, they were dedicated until the last second. Lilly wasn't able to sit with us during the game, because she had to sit with the band in the set of bleachers in front of us. I sat next to Ryan, while Linda and Jace sat behind us.

Linda was recording the halftime show on her video camera, as Lilly had warned me she would earlier. She dropped the device right above my shoulder, her dark, permed hair swaying across my white WVU hoodie, and she said, in a hushed whisper, "Abigail, scoot closer to Ryan."

I turned and met face to face with the buzzing, moving camera lens. Embarrassed, I pushed Linda's mechanical eye away. "No way."

"Do it." She pointed the camera in Ryan's face, who was just as unhappy about it as I was. "Both of you, get together. You'll want this for the rest of your life."

Jace rolled his eyes. "Linda, really."

"Quick! Better do it fast!" Linda was pushing the video camera around, left and right, back and forth, like she was recording a professional basketball game.

Awkwardly, like we were on some sort of blind date and didn't even know one another, Ryan and I scooted closer together. My right knee touched his left knee, and then we sort of turned around to face Linda. She propped the camera on her lap and said, with a weird voice, "Ahh, yes, young love."

My face burned. There was nowhere for me to hide my reddening face. Then my eyes met Ryan's; he was sporting a look similar to mine. That was the start of it, of the staring contest. At least, I thought it was staring contest. Without removing his eyes from mine, Ryan continued to swim into me, through my eyes, asking my brain what it was thinking. So I showed him my thoughts with my own eyes, like they were some sort of doors welcoming him, and we did that for no less than two minutes.

I knew this because Linda jerked the camera away and snapped, "Geesh, get a room, you two."

Jace shook Ryan out of my glance. "Look, look at her. Look at Lilly." She was performing in the halftime show, playing her flute while prancing around in white shorts so short that the cusps of her butt cheeks peeked out when she leaned over the banister during timeouts.

We all looked at Lilly. There was no denying her gracefulness, her beauty, her poise.

I hated her a little bit right then, because I couldn't compare.

For the rest of the football game, Ryan and I sat like strangers next to one another. The only conversation between us existed in physical expression. While

Jace and Linda talked about Lilly and how pretty she was, how perfect she was, how much Jace loved her, Ryan and I spoke with our hands. At one point, he touched my knee. I responded by running my finger over the knee bone underneath his dark jeans.

Then he held my wrist, and I let him, and he held it for the rest of the fourth quarter.

He wrote words above my vein. Not understanding a single one of them, I usually flashed him a smile. Ryan's smile flashed more than mine. He still had braces.

On the way home, we reverted to our original positions on the backseat: Lilly on top of Jace, me on top of Ryan. The radio was busted. Linda punched the dashboard at every Stop sign, and even though she was undeniably the strongest woman I knew, she couldn't violently bring the radio to life. To dissolve the silence in the Camaro, Jace asked Lilly to sing a song. At first, she modestly refused. Her excuse, "No, I can't do that, I don't want to," seemed to work for only a moment.

As we passed under a streetlight, Jace's hazel eyes found me cradled in his best friend's arms. "Abigail? Will you sing with Lilly?" Lilly must have made a noise, for he shifted a bit in the seat, his leg brushing mine, and he cooed, "C'mon, please, darling?"

I leaned against Ryan's chest. It was so warm. "We can sing—"

Before I could get another word out, Lilly snapped, "No, I'll sing, I'll sing." She started singing one of her solos for the upcoming Christmas concert.

Meanwhile, I deflated against Ryan, a balloon losing air, my skin shrinking and losing its luster.

In the dark, I looked over and saw Jace close his eyes. As Lilly continued to hum in between lyrics, he pressed his forehead against her shoulder. The two looked like some sort of statue like that, certain features highlighted if we passed a streetlight or a patch of moonlight.

Staring at something so profound, so beautiful, it was hard to feel rejected by my own best friend.

I knew why she suddenly changed her mind about singing. Lilly was my best friend, but she was also self-centered, absorbed in everything about herself. I knew the only reason she changed her mind about singing was because she didn't want to share any attention with me. She had been like that since we became best friends, but it wasn't hurtful until then, right then, and I wasn't sure why.

About halfway through the song, Ryan reached over for me. In reaction I jumped a bit, which made him laugh.

He whispered, "*Shh*," and as if I weighed as much as a feather, he scooped me up and pulled me on top of him. My hair whipped against his doughy cheek. I knew this because I heard the cascading brush slap his face, the bristles as dry as hay. Ryan's hands molded into the curvature of my hips, and he gently wedged my body against his. Not a pocket of air existed between us.

At that moment, thrilled to the point that my blood was about to boil clean from underneath my skin, utterly intoxicated at the smells alone coming from his boyish features, I held my breath, the only thing I knew to do to settle the chaotic reverberations rippling from my heart, and I willed myself not to move.

Ryan laughed in my ear. The texture of his heated breath sent chills down my spine. "Don't be scared, Abigail."

I tried to speak, but only a whimper escaped me. A syllable may have crept through just enough to begin composition in the backseat of the Camaro, but it didn't materialize in a matter that Ryan understood. His fingertips traced the contours of my hip bones. How was such a silly, insignificant motion so paralyzing?

Lilly's gorgeous voice filled the car with pure, unfiltered sound. Jace absorbed her hymn while continuing to smother his face against her soft, warm skin. The two of them didn't have a clue that next to them, only a few inches away, Ryan hooked his arms around my waist, solidifying his grip on me so that it would be impossible for me to escape, with his fingers laced in the ratty, damp mess of hair resting at the back of my neck.

It was the closest I had ever physically been with a boy. It was right and wrong, and good and bad, and raw. Everything was suddenly so *raw*.

Closing my eyes, I prayed that his fingers didn't get trapped during their curious adventure. Probably turned off by the amount of liquefied sweat lingering there, Ryan's hand retreated and instead pushed around until it cupped at one of my ears. My stomach hiccupped. Then he pushed down at me, and I gave in. My head glided down to his chest, and I curled up into a little ball, my nose against his neck, my legs now magically somehow cradled atop his brittle thighs; we were now the textbook definition of cuddling.

We were composite sketches for an amateur artist, kids learning how to be with one another, open to make any changes necessary.

Was I supposed to fall asleep? Was that how it worked? Lilly and Jace were always cuddling, but that usually led to making out, and I definitely didn't want to make out with Ryan in Linda's backseat, in front of my best friend and her boyfriend.

Something moved next to my leg. I thought it was Lilly's knee, which meant she was changing her position with Jace. Then I realized she wasn't singing anymore. Wet, slobbery sounds filled my ears. A giggle smothered in skin, the washed sounds of clothes shifted, a female gasp, a male groan. They were making out.

Suddenly, I felt something slip underneath my hoodie, underneath my cami, flesh on flesh.

My throat closed. My heart tried desperately to climb out of my body, straight from my mouth. It felt like my spine was Jell-O, and my body wriggled against Ryan's chest, my legs bent and unfolded and twisted in his lap, and he continued to breathe in my ear, filling my head with his breath, and I just let him.

Finally, in my ear, hot breath exploded into word-form, and came with it a voice. "Shh," Ryan warned. His hand, now plunging deep in the crevices of my womanly features, traced the skin around my belly button before climbing higher and higher. My teeth were only seconds away from riving into thousands of tiny bone particles. I was grinding my fear straight out of my body.

While his mouth blindly searched for the lobe of my ear, his hand was trying to uncover never-before touched land on my body, a place that I wanted to save until I was older. The moment I felt lips at my ear, I felt one of his fingers trace the bottom curve of my left breast. From his lips, I felt something escape him: a groan, a laugh, something smothered and prohibited.

As soon as his entire hand encompassed the curvature of my breast, I cried out. At least, I tried to cry out. Something, a mix between a scream and a laugh, flew from my mouth before I even considered giving it some sort of filter. The lower part of my body grew firm with starch, and my sneakers collapsed atop his knees. The two of us painfully collided and unhinged in a reckless attempt of discovery and heat.

Immediately, Ryan pulled away and shoved me against the backseat frame of the Camaro. My cheek kissed the dry portion of Linda's curly hair spilling from the empty space of her headrest. She stirred only slightly.

It wasn't my cry that got Lilly's attention. In between her and Jace's hot kissing session, my elbow slammed against the window, the thud similar to a hammer on a board, and she sharply retreated from Jace's passionate hold. He used the moment of escape to take a half-decent breath of fresh air.

Lilly pushed away from Jace. She readjusted her shirt in the process. "What happened?"

Linda lazily chirped from the front seat. "PG-13, kids."

Ryan's hand still perched on my stomach. It hadn't completely withdrawn from unclaimed territory. His fingers drew circles in my skin.

My voice trembled. "Uhh...uhh, nothing." He kept drawing on my skin, and I kept trying to crawl away. Instead of understanding that I didn't want to do something like that, Ryan insisted. It was something I didn't expect. It was worrisome enough that I was determined to look into his eyes when the dashboard lights came on. I needed to see just how large his pupils were.

I hated how the more I tried to push him away, the harder he laughed in my ear.

"Boys," Linda called out. The Camaro stopped at the bottom of Jace's driveway. As soon as she reached up and turned on the dashboard light, Ryan's hand withered away like a nocturnal animal running from the sunlight. Now was my moment to read him, to read the expression that he had on his face while he went burrowing near my woman parts.

In the dim light, I saw it right there. I even whispered my disappointment. "No, no. No." I pretended I didn't see it, but I saw it. His pupils were large, glossed, ravenous for more.

Ryan was high. He broke his promise.

His brown eyes glimmered. He looked like he was about to cry. As best I could, I tried to appear unfazed by the obvious addiction swallowing his face. Instead, I must have shifted all of my facial features into the epitome of disillusionment, for Ryan gently pushed at my legs and uttered, "I need to get out," and I moved aside without even fighting for him.

Lilly actually stepped outside so Jace and Ryan could get out of the backseat. Before he walked away, Jace smashed his mouth against hers, and she leaned up into his kiss, her white tennis shoes barely touching the gravel. Her arms hooked around the back of his neck, and in their kiss, she was smiling, and he was smiling, and...

It was so *much* that I started crying. Right there, in the backseat of my best friend's mother's beat-up Camaro, I was crying because of how glorious my best friend looked with her boyfriend. It was glorious. It was gloriously awful. While the two of them put on the sweetest display of public affection, Ryan was looking down at the ground, making sure that no matter what he did, he wouldn't meet my eyes. He didn't even peer at me in the backseat. I lied to myself and said that he didn't want to see me because he knew I was crying, and he didn't want to know what that looked like.

The truth was, he couldn't stand to look at me anymore because I read the morphine in his eyes, and he saw just how betrayed I was.

Lilly got in the passenger seat instead of the back seat. She closed the door and said to her mother, "Jace is so perfect. He's so perfect, Mom."

Linda put the Camaro in reverse. "Uh-huh, uh-huh." The car wheeled out of Jace's gravel driveway.

Something smashed against the top of the trunk. I turned around and saw Jace and Ryan, in the whites and reds of the car lights spilling across their bodies, standing there. At least, one of them was standing. The other, Ryan, was literally laying across the back of the Camaro.

Humorously, he started yelling, "No! No! Don't leave me! Don't leave me!" His hands smashed against the back window. The feigned fear on his face softened. We made eye contact with one another, his cheeks lit up with reds and whites, the clear night sky providing a glimmering, misty backdrop behind him. The moment I saw a glimmer of hope in his eyes, the blue of the moon staring back at me, I leaned up and pressed my hand against his. Ryan's eyes trembled. His braces surfaced as his lips pulled away to smile.

I watched him say it. "I'm sorry."

I didn't say anything back.

Lilly immediately cooed. "Aww, that's so freakin' cute, Abigail!"

Linda wasn't about to play that game, however. She cocked the Camaro in gear and stepped on the pedal. The physical sciences tossed Ryan into the air and he came back down on the ground, side first.

Thankfully, only a few moments later, Ryan jumped up on his short little legs and ran around the Camaro at least three times. Jace, unwillingly to participate at first, joined in the last lap. They ended their run by yodeling and squealing and chanting in succession.

As we drove off, their bodies grew smaller and darker. I looked back; I kept looking back, until they were no more.

That night, the boys were supposed to sneak into Lilly's bedroom for a game of Truth or Dare. That never happened.

Instead, she and Jace got into a serious argument on the phone right after we dropped them off. I didn't know what they were fighting about, but it was enough for Lilly to be in tears when she hung up the phone. I asked her if everything was okay, and her response was terrifying. "I want to break up with him."

What? Wasn't it just minutes earlier that Jace was perfect and everything about him was perfect?

We didn't even sleep in her bedroom that night. She was so angry that she asked Linda to prepare the sofa mattress for us. We lay together in the living room with big, open windows beaming moonlight down on us. There wasn't anything bright outside, but it was cool being able to lean up just a bit and see a bunch of trees, the roads, and Oldestown. Lilly had the cordless phone next to her the entire night. She thought that Jace would call back and apologize, but it never happened. He never called back that night.

Instead of worrying about Lilly's relationship, I worried about my own—if that was even what to call it.

How was I supposed to trust Ryan as my boyfriend if he was still stealing his mother's morphine, the one thing I'd asked him—pleaded with him—to never do again?

As much as I wanted to talk to Lilly about it, I didn't want her knowing about it. That was Ryan's business, not mine, so Lilly didn't deserve to know something like that. Judging by the size of his pupils earlier, either Ryan just popped some during the football game, or he was well over his typical amount. That worried me so much that I nearly troubled myself sick.

Rolling over in the blankets, Lilly sighed in my ear. "Abigail. Do you think Jace and I will be together for a long time?"

I hoped so. I told her just that.

She rolled over onto her back. We both peered up at the ceiling, at the many cobwebs there that Linda didn't sweep away. "I don't think I love him anymore."

She sounded hideous, so I tried to find her hand underneath the blankets. "Why not?"

Lilly pulled away when my fingers found hers. Broken, she choked, "I can't tell you," and then she closed her eyes.

Twelve

In a matter of days, everything changed.

It seemed as if I blinked just once. That was all it took, and before that moment of black, everything was okay, everything was fine, everything was just as I had planned; however, the moment that my eyes fixed their blurry lenses and reassembled all of the colors and cool autumn days, nothing was the same.

Lilly and Jace broke up shortly after that night at the football game. She didn't disclose much about the breakup to me.

A few days after she was officially single, she ran up to me in the school hallway, grabbed both of my hands, and said, "Ryan and I are dating now. So, you should, like, date Jace. We can trade boys!"

She said this like it was *normal*–like it was *okay*.

Her cheers kept me anchored to the ground as she tried to swing me around. Rooted in the middle school corridor of Gunners Valley School, I watched in heartbroken awe as her dark hair fluttered around her shoulders, and the rose color biting her cheeks spread like blood across her tanned, smooth face. Relentless, she yanked at me one last time. I finally shoved her aside and snapped, "*Stop.*"

Lilly, naturally, gave me an up-and-down with her summer-field eyes, and she dipped her head to one side. "Really, you could be happy for me."

Of all the things to say to me, she chose something like that?

I didn't want to argue with her. I didn't want to cause a scene in the hallway. Swallowing the anger swelling in my throat, I wheezed through a fresh smile cut across my pale face. "That's really cool."

"Yeah, I know." She looped her arm with mine. "Let's go talk about him."

I obliged with a rock wedged in my stomach.

Despite appearing betrayed by my best friend, losing Ryan like that wasn't unexpected. Those few days after the football game, I avoided him out of confusion and discomfort concerning his morphine addiction. I refused to look at him on the bus. I ignored his messages on MSN Messenger, which were plenty and filled with nocturnal desperation.

He even showed up at my house on a four-wheeler with a batch of freshly picked wildflowers. Afraid to even make eye contact with him, I had pleaded with my mother to answer the door and turn him away. I was so heartbroken that my mother didn't even ground me because a young boy showed up at the house, which was her usual maternal mantra. Instead, she did just as I had asked. She accepted the flowers, tossed them in the trash, and made me another pot of coffee.

She only asked me once, "Is everything okay, Abigail?"

And I shot a look of, "I don't want to talk," into her veins, and she walked away.

I shouldn't have been so hard on Ryan. I didn't know what it was like to have an addiction, especially to such a powerful controlled substance. I had no idea the kinds of withdrawals he felt in between doses.

I was only 13 years old. My broken, betrayed heart weighed much more in my mind than Ryan's addiction, and because I thought that, I lost him. Instead of giving him a second chance, I tossed him off to the side, a ragged, abused, unwanted thing, and he lay like that until someone else came by to help him. Lilly.

Even though I wasn't shocked about Lilly and Ryan now dating, our shared group of friends was blindsided. Not a single person in our group of friends expected something like that to happen. It became apparent that Lilly and Ryan exchanged MSN Messenger accounts sometime before we initiated our first double date, something that didn't seem too suspicious at first, especially if she was trying to arrange our double date. After that night of us all sharing the back seat of a Camaro, however, they exchanged phone numbers and their most ambitious dreams.

They did that while she was still dating Jace.

Lilly still considered herself Jace's girlfriend while she spent most evenings blocking him on MSN Messenger and indulging herself by knitting together several romantic ties to his best friend.

After Lilly and Jace broke up, and immediately following Ryan's official status as her new boyfriend, his closest friends shunned him out of the group for his perfidy. By September of 2003, nobody talked to Ryan. Scott, Jace, Cameron, and the others punished Ryan for breaking Bro Code.

That's what Scott called it, at least. To which, he told me, "And Lilly broke Girl Code. You shouldn't be her friend anymore."

Instead of pushing Lilly away, she and I grew closer.

It didn't take long for me to move on from Ryan. Desperate, I clung to the idea of a relationship with one of my Internet friends, a young boy from Kentucky. We had emailed one another for over two years, and it wasn't until I practically sobbed at his virtual feet that we considered a relationship. The relationship eventually transformed into a hideous, draining creature that sucked the joyous life and hope out of me. Convinced that I probably wouldn't ever meet my Internet boyfriend, but too foolish to let him go and save myself from the trouble, I remained obsessed with the idea to the point that I lost myself in the make-believe world he and I created together.

By that October, I wasn't sleeping, afraid that if I logged off for even a minute, I would miss him. That was just the beginning. My grades suffered. I was having destabilizing panic attacks during every single one of my basketball games. All because I was in love with someone from the Internet, whom I would have done anything for just to see for a moment.

Staying in love with him pulled all of my emotions straight from my body, stretched them, poked them, even set some aside that were never touched again. Then my feelings were reconstructed, but everything was in the wrong place; I didn't know how to control the sudden urgency of my anger, of my confusion at the world's vendetta against me.

Small things bothered me. I couldn't look at dirty laundry without erupting in tears. It was impossible for me to see an old couple in Walmart without assuming their life was riddled with illness and debt, ultimately filling my veins with a painful empathy that lasted for days.

While I showed up to school every morning wearing mismatched shoes, unbrushed hair, and lack of sleep on my face, Lilly bragged about the perfection that was Ryan. If she was feeling especially spiteful, she usually looked over at me and said something like, "Oh, get a grip," as if my troubles of having an Internet boyfriend were a direct effect of her now dating him.

My inability to handle stress and understand that my best friend wasn't acting like a best friend didn't dissolve into my brain. My problems solidified and blocked the ports. Almost every day, I either lashed out at a friend or my mother for no apparent reason, or I just sat like an empty shell during class and refused to say a word for at least nine or ten hours.

Shortly before Christmas break, my Internet boyfriend dumped me with a poorly written email. He justified his decision by saying he wanted to see other people and not limit himself to just me. He had typed something like, "And I don't want to keep you from someone there, who may like you back." I was so angry that I kicked aside a few computer chairs, cursing, and was sent to the principal's office for detention.

A lot of things happened before Christmas break. My mother, who was unsure how to properly handle my prolonged episodes of total breakdown, admitted me to Chestnut Ridge, a mental institution in Morgantown. There, I was assigned to a therapist for biweekly sessions. After they exposed me to in-depth examinations, they prescribed me a medicine called fluoxetine. I was ultimately diagnosed with depression and bipolar disorder.

While that was happening, Lilly was continuing to try and pawn off Jace on me, still living her dream of swapping boyfriends without facing the uncomfortable realization that boyfriend swapping wasn't what best friends were supposed to do. She was continually ending casual conversations with phrases like, "Too bad you and Jace can't be as happy as me and Ryan," or, "Ryan is such a good boyfriend, you should have dated him when you had the chance," or the worst, "I love him."

She never once offered her shoulder for me to cry on after I was dumped.

It was no wonder I was essentially decomposing from the inside.

It wasn't until after Christmas break that things changed, things that nobody saw coming, things that nobody understood.

Lilly returned to Gunners Valley School in 2004 wearing gothic clothing from Hot Topic. She drew heavy lines of eyeliner across her eyes. Linda even let her dye her hair black with red streaks, and she cut it off right below her ears. She looked like an evil pixie on the front of a Walmart folder.

A belly ring fresh atop her belly button, spikes lining the edge of her ear cartilage, and a detachable silver ring hung from her left nostril—she was a new breed of herself, and it horrifically contrasted with the talkative, bright, colorful teenage girl who just last year had enjoyed wearing pink and glitter in her hair.

At the same time Lilly transitioned into that phase, Ryan was doing the same. He bleached his hair, painted his fingernails black, wore dog collars and studded wristbands, and even had new piercings. Lilly got her belly button pierced around the same time that Ryan got his lip pierced.

The two of them became the token goth couple in Stream Ridge, which garnered a lot of negative attention. Parents were concerned with the pentagrams on Lilly's backpacks. Classmates worried for Ryan, because of the Xs he'd drawn in Sharpie up and down his arms.

There was something wrong with Lilly and Ryan.

Their goth phase spread like wildfire in Gunners Valley School, and by the end of January, everyone in 7th and 8th grade wanted to wear black clothing with skulls and crossbones. Laney and I went to the mall together, and we each bought black t-shirts with red skulls on the front and little white bows on the sleeves. We wore them to school the next Monday. The moment that Lilly saw them, she scoffed and said, "You guys are copying me."

Laney lowered her eyebrows. "How the heck is this copying you?"

Lilly turned her nose in the air. "You just are. You don't understand." She loved saying that.

I didn't say anything.

It was in Lilly's nature to think that it was all her and nobody else, causing the goth look to take off like the latest fashion trend. The reality was that she just happened to be the first student at Gunners Valley School to shop at Hot Topic, literally three days after the store first opened in Meadowbrook Mall in 2003. It wasn't because it had been there the entire time and she was the first person to introduce black shirts and bloody skulls to the human eye in our town.

My and Laney's wardrobes expanded a bit. We both came from financially insecure families, so we didn't ask for expensive Tripp pants or leather corsets from Hot Topic. Instead, we were satisfied with the generic t-shirts from Walmart and the occasional choker from Claire's. I snagged an old pair of my sister's boots from her closest, which were black, leather, and came up to my knee, and Laney colored an old pair of white sneakers with a Sharpie. Laney called our phase, "Cheap punk."

We didn't immerse ourselves in the Gothic aura as much as Lilly had. We ventured off track only a little bit. It was enough to piss Lilly off, however. A few days before Valentine's Day, Lilly wrote a poem called "Influential." She passed it to me during Ms. Kendall's English class. Whining in her fake ghostly voice, she wheezed, "This is what you do to me."

My eyes skimmed her obloquy. I could barely finish reading the murderous, toxic words without vomiting on my desk.

> **I hate you sometimes / and wish you would go away / you make things worse / always**
>
> **You think you're dark / only influenced by me / making my life hard / hard to breathe**
>
> **Taking more than you know / yet I'll never tell / you please stop / maybe notice / my life / now a living hell**
>
> **In me fire has already spread through / crumbling my angel wings / only making me the stronger / beholding the few people / into my hell I'm bringing**
>
> **Go back to your heaven / you were perfectly fine / never come back / to this influential life**

At the top of the paper, she wrote,

> **Dedicated to more than one person...approximate #: 2, only females.**

She was talking about me and Laney.

No doubt the "people" she referenced to bringing into Hell with her were none other than Ryan and the so-called Wiccan friend she made on the Internet, a girl she only knew as Proxy.

Instead of showing the poem to Laney, I vaguely told her that we needed to avoid Lilly.

Eventually, we stepped away. If Lilly was my best friend, like she told everyone, then she wouldn't have written such a horrible thing. It was easier for Laney to stop talking to her; after all, Laney was best friends with Kimmie, not Lilly—so it wasn't like she was going to be friendless. The distance crushed Laney, however, and she couldn't understand why I kept telling her that Lilly was a nothing more than a mean girl.

I was used to Lilly's continuous verbal and psychological abuse, so it was nothing new to me. It was just something that I let happen far too often, and far too frequently. As my mother once told me, "Stop being a doormat."

There were other poems and notes (mostly notes) that Lilly would pass me in class. Most of them were negative, telling me, "You don't understand," or "I can't believe you," or "Just leave me alone and never talk to me again." Lilly's self-isolation phases usually only lasted about a week, because every Monday morning after a weekend, she would send me a note that said, "Hey, I'm sorry. Will you still be my best friend?" Like an idiot, I would always go back to her.

Her phases also coincided when she was arguing with Ryan. I was suddenly her long-lost best friend when he wasn't talking to her.

Some time in March, when Lilly was spending the night with me, she noticed that I was taking medicine with my coffee. Instead of asking me what I was taking, she snatched the medicine bottle from my hand and read the prescription aloud. "Fluoxetine." She looked at me with raccoon eyes. "What is this?"

I swallowed the pill. "I see a therapist. I didn't want to tell anyone."

She actually rolled her eyes at me and said, "You're not depressed. You don't know what it's like to be depressed." As if she was the sole person on the planet to have a bad day.

That was the standard of our friendship, anymore. I was myself, it wasn't enough for Lilly, and she constantly had to put me down because she was always *more*: more depressed, more melancholic, more dark, more whatever made her feel superior to me.

Even worse, I couldn't treat her like Scott and Jace had treated Ryan. I couldn't just leave her like that.

The school year was only a few weeks away from ending. On May 10th, Bradley brought a deck of cards to school, but since Audrey and I were still in junior high, we weren't able to play poker until the bus ride back home.

A lot of the upperclassmen were absent from the bus. Since it was so close to the end of the school year, seniors were allowed to take their final exams and then stay home for the rest of the year, until graduation. That meant my sister and her clan were still at home, napping away hangovers from graduation parties and avoiding filling out college applications.

Without a crowd, Audrey and I were able to snag a seat in the back of the bus. She was sitting with me at first, but then Bradley invited her to sit with him in the back seat. He was a senior, too, but he still went to school because he didn't want to stay at home and do more farm work. It was impossible for her to deny a cute boy anything, so she accepted and plopped down close next to him. She was still oblivious to the fact that he was in love with her.

I was sitting by myself, hanging over the back of my seat, with five cards splayed out like a Japanese geisha fan in my hands. I flashed Audrey cold, playful eyes. "I know I got you beat."

"Nu-uh!" She exchanged two cards from the deck. Her freshly painted pink fingernails turned the red backs of the cards into a collage of Valentine's Day colors. Bradley offered his left hand as a deck holder; otherwise, the cards would fall over the place with all of the West Virginian turns and hills in our bus route. Silver Canyon was especially topsy-turvy, but we had already ridden past it.

I watched her purposely brush one of her fingers across Bradley's fingertips. I could practically see a jolt of electricity in their subtle exchange.

Bradley looked over at Ryan, who was still holding his original five cards. "What're you gonna do? Trade or fold?" He nudged at Audrey. "Get back, you're hoverin'." Like an animal being disciplined, she peeled away from Bradley with sad, puppy dog eyes.

There was a sigh. "Fold." Ryan dropped his five cards in Bradley's lap. "I'm folding forever." The three of us traded expressions of confusion, worry, and anger, but none of us acted. Bradley at least rolled his eyes.

Ryan started to wriggle his way out of vision, but I could still see him. After all, he was sitting in the seat directly across from me. It wasn't normal for him to sit in the seat he was in; typically, he sat in the far back in the half-seat, the one for the Fire Emergency Door. That day, however, he broke tradition by opting out of that seat and instead taking the one across from me. In Bradley's words, "He probably wants to sleep."

Everyone knew about his sleeping problems. That was why teachers rarely disciplined him for falling asleep in class.

As he stuffed his backpack up against the bus window, Ryan dropped the bottom half of his legs into the aisle and lay back. I saw the smudges of black eyeliner all around his eyelids. Even his hair looked tired, now just a matted mess of orange on the bottom and black roots draped across his forehead in sharp, edgy chunks. His dark roots had sprouted no more than a few days after he tried to bleach it.

When Scott said his hair was strawberry blonde, Ryan called him a fucking faggot and told him to mind his own stupid fucking business. There was enough bite in Ryan's warning that Scott backed off. After that happened, Scott told me, "See why we don't talk to him anymore?"

Exchanges like that were typical now, pretty much expected.

In just eight months, Ryan went from wearing nice blue jeans and a basic black t-shirt to wearing Tripp pants from Hot Topic, white t-shirts covered in bleeding skulls or vulgar language, and eyeliner. Even his fingernails were painted black. His arms were overloaded with wristbands, bracelets, and plastic bands. There were just enough accessories to cover the cuts and scabs and scars strewn across the thin, pale belly of his left arm. I noticed the cuts almost immediately, but I never said a word. Nobody else did, either.

I looked at him every morning when I stepped up on the bus, and I saw him every afternoon when we were traveling home, but I still couldn't accept it. I couldn't accept that the Blue Ryan was gone. It had been months since he wore anything that wasn't black or bloodstained.

"What?" Audrey leaned up in her seat. The back of her white-blonde hair clung to the seat behind her. She always carried several volts of static electricity. "What do you mean, *forever*? You should still play!" She fanned her cards out in the aisle. The gusts of air barely moved Ryan's hair. He practically narrowed his dark eyes in annoyance. "C'mon, I'll show you, I have a horrible hand! You can win, I swear!" Now she was pushing her hands up and down, as if the motion was enough to work him to play back in.

Ryan snort-laughed, but then he closed his eyes. "Audrey, no."

Just like that, he propped one of his arms over his face, and he was gone.

Bradley snatched the cards right out of Audrey's pink nails. "I'm done. If this fucker here isn't playin', I don't wanna play." He was already packing cards away into their tight cardboard box, with jesters, kings, queens all over the front and back. Bradley and Ryan's friendship had dwindled shortly after Ryan got with Lilly. Everyone expected that. What everyone didn't expect was for Lilly to tell Ryan to stop talking to Bradley.

The only reason we all were playing poker was because Lilly rode a different bus home that day. She was going to her mom's house in Oldestown.

Audrey reached out and grabbed Bradley by the shoulder. She was the weakest of the weak. While she pushed him and pulled him this way and that he continued to roll his eyes, still packing away the card deck. She snapped at him, her lips pressed together, "But we just started!" Then she looked at me, with an expression of calculated desperation. "Abigail! Tell him we should keep playing!"

What was I supposed to say to him? Glancing over, I saw one of his legs slowly slipping from the seat's edge. In a few moments, the back of his leg would lose traction, and his booted foot would slam down. Ryan wasn't going to magically change his mind just because I asked him. Audrey was foolish to think that things still worked that way.

Shortly after Lilly and Ryan started dating, she told me that I wasn't allowed to talk to him anymore: the same thing she told Bradley. The worst part about her "request" was that Ryan followed it. He listened to her. It had been at least six months since I'd last said a word to him and he'd actually responded.

I handed Bradley my cards. "Audrey, we'll play another time." I, too, turned around and burrowed out of sight, falling far down into my own covered arms and solid black backpack.

It happened like that every day now.

The bus continued to bump along Route 2. Quite unexpectedly, I felt the space next to me sink almost at the instant I settled. Glancing over, I never would have expected to see Kimmie suddenly sitting next to me. We were still friends, but we never rekindled the friendship we formed the summer of 2000. She was only a freshman in high school, but she was already one of the most popular girls. Everyone knew her. Everyone was friends with her. She was in a long-term relationship with the same boy since 7th grade, Brent King, and the two of them were always, *always* holding hands.

She and I hadn't spoken in months. For her to suddenly appear at my side in my used-to-be-empty bus seat made me wonder if something was wrong. Before I could even ask her anything, she turned to me and then nodded over her shoulder. "See him? See him all fucked up like that?"

I leaned over. She was pointing at Ryan. "I wouldn't say effed up, but yeah."

Kimmie frowned. Her frown was razor sharp. "If you two would have kept dating, I bet he wouldn't be like that. He wouldn't be so fucking distant."

I had to look away from her broken face for a moment. Did that mean I wasn't the only person Lilly asked Ryan to shut out? I didn't know Kimmie as well as I used to, but I knew if something like that happened, she would never be able to forgive him. Walking on thin ice, I approached the situation as calmly as possible. "Do you not hang out anymore?"

She scoffed. I saw the necklace strewn around her neck bounce. She was wearing her boyfriend's class ring. "Hang out? He doesn't even talk to me anymore. He can hear me right now, and guess what? He's not even trying to defend himself, because he has no balls. Lilly fucking took them away, the bitch cunt."

Here I thought *my* situation with Ryan was troublesome.

I watched her grind her knuckles against her tanned knees. Kimmie was a few seconds shy of breaking skin and bleeding, I was sure of it. Eventually, she swallowed her anger, almost literally, and reached up to pull herself from the bus seat. As she turned back to look at me, I saw tears glittering in her eyes. "Abigail, that's not my cousin anymore. Lilly's fucking killing him."

Then she stepped into the aisle and went back to her seat.

As Audrey and I stepped off the bus for Bear Run Road, Kimmie called out my name. I looked over my shoulder and saw her nod in Ryan's direction. Laney sat next to her, a look on her face that matched Kimmie's, and she mouthed, "That's not him." My body felt riddled with ice. It almost caused me to freeze in place in the aisle. Had it not been for Audrey shoving at me to make me go, I would have stayed there for the rest of the day, the night, the year.

I was able to catch a glimpse of Ryan's eyes, peering up at me from underneath his bleached hair. Nothing could hide the terrifying gloss over his eyes. I hated it when his pupils were soaked in glitter. That part of him, unfortunately, still hadn't changed.

Lilly never talked about the morphine. She probably didn't know.

Audrey and I climbed into Tracy's Ford Explorer. TJ took his usual seat in the front, while Audrey and I climbed in the back next to the booster. She sighed through her nose. "Abigail, we had a good summer last year. What happened?"

I knew what happened. I knew what cut our potential summer in half. Her name was Lilly.

Yet I didn't have the heart, or the guts, to admit it. Instead, I shrugged it off, saying "I don't know," and left it at that.

Audrey asked me to call her when I got home, but instead, I was held up on the phone with Lilly. She was having one of her emotional breakdowns, and I was her only friend that she could use as a test dummy. Nobody else ever endured her self-righteous pity parties. That made me quite possibly the most foolish person ever.

There was something wrong with me, because nobody else would have stuck around for such emotional abuse. One day, she could be the cheeriest person in the world, telling me how much she appreciated my friendship and how I saved her from herself; the next, she would call me a copycat and tell me that she sometimes wished I was dead, because she hated just looking at me.

Her bouts were all too predictable, however. The only reason she ever asked me to come back to her as her best friend was for one of three reasons: Ryan was ignoring everyone (including her, because not even his personal demons spared his girlfriend), Lilly had already pushed away everyone else in class so she was temporarily friendless (she would ask me to come back as her only remaining option), or she wanted to brag about Ryan's perfectness in their relationship (pretty much the same things she talked about the summer before, except the name had been changed).

She inhaled without exhaling. Patiently I waited for her to purge, the sponge of my body unfazed by her approaching confession. "So, I need to tell you something."

"What?" I wasn't excited. I didn't seem interested. It was hard to be, anymore. It wasn't just because it was Lilly. The medicine turned me into a creepy, hollow corpse: a shell of a girl, without emotions or anything reactive.

I heard her close her bedroom door. She was at her mother's house for the week. "I'm sneaking to Ryan's after school tomorrow. His mom and dad won't be home." She paused. "We're going all the way, Abigail."

"*Whoa.*" I leaned straight up from my bed and said it again. "*Whoa.*"

I knew that Lilly and Ryan were doing things together, things that I had never done before—he first made out with her at the movie theater, and then, while they were watching *Gothika*, Ryan forced Lilly on top of his lap and he put his hand down her pants—but the two of them being in a house, alone? I knew they were perfectly capable of going all of the way. They were going to have sex, and I didn't doubt it for a second.

Maybe that was what Ryan wanted that one night after the football game.

I was breathing heavily now. "Are you sure? Are you ready for something like that?"

Lilly just turned 14. Best friend or not, I didn't think a 14 year old should be having sex. The only two students I knew of at Gunners Valley School who were having sex were Natalie Graham (who was 13 and pregnant because of it), and

Peggy Simmons (who had sex when she was 12, with her 13-year-old boyfriend, and told the entire school about it).

She hummed. "Yeah. I've been ready. We want this."

I hated when she did that, when she spoke on someone else's behalf. For all I knew, Lilly could have been begging and begging Ryan for sex for months now, and the only reason he was finally giving in was because he was tired of listening to her.

It also worked the other way; maybe Ryan wanted it, but Lilly was still reluctant. Lilly did that all the time, though. More often than not, she was just talking out of her butt, without the input or interest of the other party.

One time she used the word *we* in front of my mother, talking about nose piercing; I got grounded for nothing, and Lilly didn't even apologize. All she could say was something like, "What? I thought you and I could go together."

She had changed so much since she and Ryan started dating. It wasn't a good thing, either.

Diana knocked on my bedroom door. "Hey, I need the phone."

"Okay." The medicine altered me so much that I no longer fought with my sister over little things, which was a blessing in disguise for my mother. I started to open my door, "Hey, I gotta go. Call me tomorrow. I just—I can't believe you're going to do this." I bit my tongue before I continued ranting, ranting that I couldn't believe she had changed so much in just a few short months, that I couldn't believe a human being could be so manipulative and insecure, that I couldn't believe she would do something so *stupid.*

"We love each other," she affirmed. "We would do anything for each other."

Rolling my eyes, I hung up.

Thirteen

I got the phone call shortly after 6 PM.

Sitting at the computer with Microsoft Word open, a cup of cold coffee marbleizing next to the keyboard, I heard my mother call for me in between rings. When I picked up the cordless, I read the caller ID. ANDERSON, GARY.

What if it was Lilly's father, asking if I knew where his daughter was? With only a few seconds to spare, I prepared an impromptu speech about how his daughter was at Laney's house, and that I could call her for him, if he wanted me to. I knew better than to tell him the truth, especially if Linda was involved. I didn't want to come between those two.

I shoved my door into its cracking frame. "Hello?"

Nothing.

Maybe someone from Gary's house accidentally called me. That happened sometimes, especially with Bradley's masterful ability to always lose the phone in the couch. I asked again, a little louder, "Hello?"

Static. Something moved on the other end. Then I recognized a huff, a cloistered breath, followed by a series of uncontrollable sniffles.

Immediately, I wondered if a heartbroken Lilly was on the other end of the phone, still too timid to admit that she was wrong, that sleeping with Ryan was a horrible idea, that she regretted everything, or that it didn't even happen. Perhaps it was worse. What if they broke up because she turned him down, or he turned her down, and I was listening to her cry on the other end?

All of these thoughts rotated on a wheel inside of my brain, touching down long enough for me to creatively fill in some pieces: maybe Ryan didn't have a condom and Lilly didn't want to proceed. The whole time I turned Lilly's life into a soap opera of a young adult novel inside of my head, my eyes grazed up and down my black and white striped socks.

Giving her one last opportunity to say something, I released a ragged breath. "Okay, if I don't hear something in the next five—"

"Abigail." Lilly screamed my name through clenched teeth. That immediately got my attention. Then she coughed, choked on saliva, and her voice trembled on the hardest vocalization she would ever have to speak. "Ryan shot himself."

I laughed. I shouldn't have laughed. Why did I laugh?

Lilly said it again. Her voice heavy with tears, she screamed, and it sounded like she was underwater. "Abigail! He is *gone*. Ryan shot himself."

She wasn't saying what she should have been saying.

She never said, "Ryan is dead."

Something fish hooked my body somewhere near my neck. I felt the sudden pull at my throat and had to get down on my hands and knees to ease the sharp pain. Somehow I managed to still hold the phone in between my hand and ear, though it slipped somewhat and nearly toppled to the floor with me. Staggering, confused, I felt around the floor for my glasses, though they were still propped up on the bridge of my nose.

Now that I was sitting, I stared mindlessly at my toes as I waved my feet back and forth, left and right, in and out of focus from the orange sunlight bleeding into my bedroom.

"What?" I finally managed to ask. "What?" I said it again, over and over again, "What? What?"

Lilly wheezed like a siren dissipating down a thin alleyway. "Ryan is, is... he's gone."

I swallowed the impending regurgitation rising from the pit of my stomach. "What if? How when it?"

My mind was splitting in two. I couldn't even form a sentence properly. Something grotesque, something that made me eerily uncomfortable—the memory of Ryan running through the center of my brain—was wedged inside my head, the walls of my skull creaking as they shifted in place. As best I could, I leaned down and pressed my temple to my shoulder, but that didn't stop the horror. That didn't help anything at all.

Footsteps approached my bedroom door. At least, that was what I thought, so I quickly crawled to press my back against the door, preventing my mother from discovering me at quite possibly the weakest moment of my life. Instead, the footsteps stopped in the kitchen. I heard the small kitchen window above the sink ease open, followed by the ignition of a lighter and the intimate inhale of cigarette smoke.

Right then I imagined myself at the other end of my mother's Marlboro Light cigarette, receiving her nicotine exhalation, using it to fill my body with a toxic haze, just enough poison to coat myself in an impenetrable shield. Closing my eyes, I listened carefully to the noises happening on the other side of my bedroom door: the air conditioner, the smoking crackle of a cigarette, my mother's beautiful breath. I wanted to take in the moment, to take in whatever I could, long enough to distract me from the obvious.

Lilly's voice shattered my world of serenity, and it crumbled to my sides like broken shards of a mirror. "Abigail, I need you right now. I just, I can't, I am so scared. They're taking me to Mom's. I can see the red and blue lights from my bedroom window. Oh God, I can see it."

My eyes flew open. Brave, maybe a little naïve, I said to her, "I am coming over." Then I carefully set the phone down next to me.

I waited a few minutes before telling my mother what happened. As my body settled into a sort of recovering hibernation, I traced my memory of the last few years. I purposely outlined any smallest bit featuring Ryan and set it aside in a cozy little place next to all of my fondest moments of life, so that I could carefully study every detail, down to the little dye of color in his t-shirt and the texture of his tennis shoes as they splashed in puddles from a June rain.

At that thought, I drew up comparisons of the first time Ryan and I met, to the last time I ever saw him.

That first time, as I clutched my naked little body, with a battered dolphin plushie recovering its dignity only a few feet away, Ryan skipped through the basement, a carefree little boy with round glasses and that morning's breakfast crusted around his lips. I remembered how he didn't pay any attention to me: how he continued to ask me to use the computer, as if I was the only one who could grant him that access.

The last time was just three hours before, when we made eye contact as I struggled up the bus aisle to my seat with Audrey. I sat in the seat directly across from him (only the second time he ever sat across from me), so I could see his knees bounce three times a second, his hands run over his thighs, the back of the seat in front of him, and through his orange and black hair, until they finally hung cupped at his sides. Nothing could hide the lingering gloss in his eyes. That I would never forget.

He had blossomed into such a difficult, complex, dark book that I couldn't read him anymore.

The last time I looked at him was as I stepped from my seat to get off the bus. He wasn't looking at me. He wasn't looking at anything; he continued to stare out the window, perhaps seeing his own reflection, and maybe he was horrified by how much he had changed. There was a chance that he hated looking at himself through a layer of glass. Then Ryan closed his eyes.

I had already turned away before I could see him reopen them. Now I never would.

When I approached my mother in the kitchen, she looked at me with narrowed eyes. "Abigail?" Everything I heard translated to static in my mind, and I reached up to massage the electricity out of my ears. "What's wrong?" I stopped picking at my ears when she reached out and grabbed my hands.

Then I told her.

My mother cried before I did. The first thing she did after I said to her, "Ryan shot himself," was call one of her friends who volunteered as an EMT. After being put on hold for at least four minutes, someone confirmed the news. There were public safety personnel at the Mills residence on Postlewaite Ridge, and they were currently removing the body of a 15-year-old boy from the premises.

She dropped the phone down on the kitchen counter so hard it echoed through the house like a snapping mouse trap.

The instant she looked at me with foggy, red eyes, I morphed into a younger version of her, and I stepped into her arms and cried into her chest. The same orange glow that burst in my bedroom earlier grazed our bodies with generous, delicate hands, and the skin on my arms warmed as I clutched my mother harder and harder.

I bawled at the rate of a toddler first wrecking a tricycle. I reverted back to a child, begging for my mommy to hug me and make everything better. She split in half when she couldn't make the pain go away. She knew this, and she hated it; I knew it because she ran her fingers through my hair and uttered a bitter, harsh fact. "I am so sorry, Abigail. I am, I want to make your pain go away, but I can't, I can't," and hearing her say that sent me into a supernatural state. I froze in place. I didn't bat an eye or breathe, and I allowed the tears to traverse my cheeks and spill onto my mother's chest. Her skin glittered. Her skin cried.

Pulling at my mother's shirt, I cried out. "I need to see her! I need to see Lilly."

Diana suddenly stormed from her bedroom. She stepped into the kitchen, her freshly painted toenails shimmering purple in the orange light, and folded her arms across her chest. "What is going *on*?! Why are you guys crying? You sound like Aunt Judy's cats fighting over Wonder Bread."

I pretended she wasn't there. I begged my mother, again and again, "Let me see her. She needs me. Mommy, she needs me so much right now."

Diana pushed aside a kitchen chair. "Who? Who is Abigail talking about?"

Fighting tears, my mother finally said, "Diana, Ryan Mills is dead. He killed himself."

The cogs quickly jerked back on course in my sister's brain. She looked at me, repeated my pleas in her head, and immediately threw her arms down. "No. No, no, no. My little sister is not going to that witch's house! You are not letting her go! Don't you dare!"

I didn't need to see the tears in her hazel eyes to know that she was crying. Her typically soothing voice was hoarse, hollow, burned out; the tone my older sister was using was horrific. It was one of the few times that I listened to her, and I sympathized.

It also wasn't any secret that Diana did not like Lilly. She once told me that she didn't like my best friend because Lilly sucked the life out of me so she could continue growing. She said this after Lilly spent the night one weekend. When she left, she was all glimmer and blinding shine, but I shut myself in my bedroom and sat on my bed while listening to Linkin Park's *Reanimation* CD on repeat. My sister didn't know that Lilly and I had spent the entire night talking about Ryan and Jace. More so, Lilly talked about Ryan and Jace, and I just listened, because she didn't ever let me say anything. That was why I appeared so drained.

My mother's fingers ran through my hair. They smelled like cigarettes. She was pulling more and more as she yelled at Diana. "I can't let her friend suffer alone like that. Diana, one of your classmates has died."

"Mom. *She's* the reason he's dead, I bet you. I bet you!" A kitchen chair flew across the floor. "Abigail is *not* going over there!"

I tugged at my mother's shirt. "Mommy."

"Go pack your bag. I'll be there in a moment."

As I crawled back into my bedroom, I left my door open so I could listen to my mother argue with my sister.

I couldn't understand why Diana was so adamant about me not going to Lilly's. The fact that she showed a sliver of concern at all was much unlike her. As I pressed my face in the small opening of my door, I could smell my sister's Victoria's Secret perfume colliding with the salt of her tears. Her anger burned. It caught fire in her long, highlighted hair. "Mom, you are not about to let my little sister go to that house! She will *die!*"

My mother slammed something down on the kitchen table. "How am I supposed to help her right now? I don't know what to do!"

Now everyone was crying together but apart: my mother in the kitchen, my sister now in her locked bedroom, and me hanging in my open doorway. The moment settled shortly after my mother treated herself to three more cigarettes. Meanwhile, I clawed through my bedroom carpet looking for a miracle shred of Ryan's black hair, knowing perfectly well he had never set foot in my bedroom before.

My mother monitored me as I packed my overnight bag for Lilly's. She asked me how long I planned to stay with Lilly, and I responded by saying, "However long I needed to." At that, she recommended that I pack more than four pairs of underwear, and two more t-shirts.

The car ride to Linda's was quiet, sunny, and dense. My mind willed Ryan in every single capture of scenery as it passed. He was walking in the front yard of the Young residence; he was running along the highway, across from the Silver Canyon nursery; he was lying in the sun, in the fields right before Sweet Run Road. If I ever saw him too close to the Ford Explorer, I pulled back a bit, gave him more room to live freely, and then I went back to watching him immersing himself in the West Virginian hills along Route 2.

The only time my mother interrupted my peace was when she asked me to watch over Lilly.

I glanced over my shoulder. "Mom?"

I saw her knuckles whiten underneath her pale skin. The grip she had on the steering wheel entered catastrophic pressure range. "Abigail, she can't—she'll want to—you'll want to—"

Then she clenched her jaw and proceeded to tell me how Ryan was so young, too young, how he was such a promising young man, how he was a sweet boy even when he showed up on an ATV to sweep me off my feet, how she could never understand how someone his age could feel so lost, troubled, and hopeless that he would take his own life.

I couldn't have agreed with her more.

The more she remembered Ryan aloud, the more she shared her memory of him with me, the emptier I felt. By the time she drove up to Linda's house in Oldestown, I was nothing more than a skeletal figure wrapped in pale skin. I had no composition. I had no filling. I was nothing.

She got out of the car and gave me one last hug. As we pulled away, as I stepped away to climb up the brick wall around Linda's house, my mother grabbed me at both of my shoulders. She injected me with an important, final glance. "Abigail, I love you. Please, don't go." I knew what she meant. She wasn't asking me not to go to Lilly's.

I slipped away just in time before she heard me whimper. I threw my overnight bag over the brick wall, and she got back in the Ford Explorer and sped away.

Linda greeted me at the screen door. Her eyes were red, and I saw tear tracks separating her taut, leathery skin from its sleek, department store foundation. She reached out and touched my shoulder, just one shoulder. "Thank you," was all she said, and I stepped around her to find Lilly.

Listening for any signs, like crying or sniffing, I discovered noise coming from the living room. As I moved around the computer in the dining room, I found Lilly sitting on the couch, wrapped up in a blanket, with a phone to her ear.

I knew I'd never be able to forget what she looked like right then, the first time I saw her knowing that she was now alone. She was wearing one of her extra-small Emily the Strange t-shirts. Red and black striped socks poked out from the bottoms of her loose-fitting black pants. Her wrists were weighed down with endless amounts of bracelets, sweatbands, and an arm warmer on her left arm. She was right-handed. I saw a dragon stone glitter on her right hand. Skulls dangled from her ears.

She looked up at me when I appeared. My heart jumped a bit. Her face was twisted in reds and blacks, mascara smeared underneath one eye and dark gloss smudged just under her nose. I imagined she wiped her nose and got part of her lipstick.

It was the look in her eyes, however, that stunned me. There was nothing there. I wasn't looking back at anything. Just a torn face covered in raw pain, abysmal loss, complete and utter regret. Lilly was gone now, and it worried me that she might never come back.

She mouthed the name, "Laney," and I nodded.

She started to unwind underneath the blanket. Her body moved at half the speed it normally would. It was like watching a person wake up and crawl out of bed first thing in the morning. "Hey, Abigail's here now. I'll talk to you later. Yeah, I know. Yeah, yeah, thanks, Lane. Bye." She pressed a button and dropped the phone behind her on the couch. "How long can you stay?"

"As long as you need me to." My eyes searched the phone behind her. "Is Laney with Kimmie?"

Lilly sniffed. "Yeah."

"Good." As much as I wanted to split in two, one part of me taking care of Lilly and the other taking care of Kimmie, I couldn't do that. Not that I intended to choose sides, but I was meant to watch over Lilly and help her with Ryan's passing, and Laney was meant to watch over Kimmie and help her with Ryan's passing. We understood our roles as best friends to them: me to Lilly, and Laney to Kimmie.

As I stood in place and thought about it, I wondered if I should call Kimmie. Knowing her, she was handling her cousin's death with violence, like a beast ravaged with rabies, anger consuming every cell of her body and mutating it into something nefarious and untamed. I made a mental note to contact her as soon as possible, right after I helped Lilly.

Cautious, I stepped closer to her. "How are you feeling?"

She gave me a look.

I understood that look.

She cut me in half with her cold voice. "Did you hear about Jace?"

My lungs jerked sideways. I was almost too afraid to ask. "What? Oh, God, no, what?"

Lilly breathed out through her nose. "As soon as he found out, he stole his sister's car and drove it to Ryan's." Then she shrugged. "At least, that's what everyone's saying. A lot of things are going around Stream Ridge right now."

"Did it really happen? Did he make it?"

She shrugged. "They don't know where he's at right now. His mom called the house right before Laney, wondering if he came here." Her pause haunted me. "Abigail, he's missing."

Why couldn't I split my body in three pieces? One for Kimmie, one for Lilly, and one for Jace?

I would have to worry about Jace later. Selfish, I turned towards the dining room. "Let's go upstairs."

Then something happened that I never, ever would have guessed. Lilly reached out for my hand. When I grabbed it, she didn't let go. She held on to me as we walked from the living room, through the dining room past the computer, and up the rickety stairs to her bedroom. It wasn't until we stepped into her room and closed the door that she let go of my cold fingers and sat on the floor.

Lilly didn't sit on her bed, or in her poufy little couch-thing nestled in the corner.

Instead, she sat in the exact center of the floor.

It took her a moment to gather all of her strength and sit down, easing her body to the floor one muscle at a time, until her frail legs folded underneath her and she cupped her knees with her hands. A noise escaped the back of her throat when she was done. I was unable to determine if it was a good thing or a bad thing.

Standing there next to her, in the middle of her bedroom, I felt all four of her bedroom walls wash over me with a fiery, relentless grasp. My skin tugged and quivered. Everywhere I looked, I saw him. I saw him in the photos taped to every inch of her bedroom. I saw him in the movie ticket montage pasted above the head of her bed. I saw him in the artifacts piling up on her vanity: in the wristbands, the necklaces, the lazily folded hoodie with a red dragon on the front.

Every time I tried to look away from his chocolate baby eyes in every photograph, he was there, too. Ryan was everywhere, holding on to Lilly as they posed on a bridge in New Martinsville after seeing a movie; pressing his lips against her cheek as the two of them walked the streets of Fairmont hand in hand; lying in a bed of leaves with Lilly, smiles stretched across both of their weary, troubled faces.

It wasn't just the photos, however. Ryan existed in other things, in the movie tickets, in his leftover belongings, in Lilly's tears as she tried her hardest not to cry in front of me. I wished myself illiterate when my eyes came across a blanket of handwritten notes sprawled across a piece of wall near her vanity. Lilly called him darling, Ryan called her baby, and it sickened me that a couple so young could appear so mature, so in tune with one another, as if they were genetically created to complement one another for the rest of their lives.

Curiosity consumed me, and I took a few more steps closer to the notes. My fingertip brushed a pencil signature. As I pulled away, I sighed at the lead stain filling the spaces between the walls of my fingerprint.

Now I had Ryan's signature embedded in my skin. I quickly turned to see if Lilly was watching me. She wasn't. She had been staring at her toes since we entered her bedroom.

I moved over to the heart-shaped cutout of movie tickets above her bed. My eyes narrowed at one ticket in particular, for the movie *Elf*. It held a different importance to me than it did for Lilly.

She kept the ticket because that was the first movie she saw with Ryan. I kept the ticket because that was the last time Ryan was allowed to speak with me.

In mid-November, my mother worried that I was succumbing to my depression. I stopped getting on the computer. I didn't read. Frankly, if anyone called the house for me, I declined to talk to them. To brighten my mood, to lift me from my own self-isolation, my mother offered to take me and a group of friends to the movies, as long as they paid for their movie ticket. She even offered to buy them dinner at McDonald's after the movie. I knew that she couldn't afford to do that, and my friends knew it, too, but I accepted her offer.

Of course, I invited Lilly to come along, and I also extended the invite to Laney and Audrey. All three were eager to pile in my mother's Ford Explorer so we could listen to old CDs and sing along with the Spice Girls, a sort of tradition when my mother took me and my friends anywhere.

The day that we were to leave, Lilly begged me to ask my mother if Ryan could come. They had only been dating for a few weeks at this point, so she was still wearing bright clothes, and Ryan still invited Scott over to his house on weekends.

When I asked my mother, she was reluctant to bring Ryan. It had nothing to do with him personally. I knew this because she said to me, "Abigail, I think Lilly is taking advantage of you," and I tried to deny it by saying that she just wanted to bring her boyfriend along, and that it was okay since all of us were friends with Ryan. Unconvinced, my mother continued to warn me, "I am doing this for you. I am not doing this so Lilly can see her boyfriend."

It took me several tries, but I finally managed to shove back harder than my mother, and I said to her, "Mom. Ryan is my friend. He was my friend before Lilly." That she couldn't argue with, so she told me that he was allowed to come and that we would meet him at the bottom of Postlewaite Ridge on the way to New Martinsville.

The reason I remembered that day wasn't so much for the movie *Elf*. After the movie, we went to McDonald's, and my mother lost at the burp game. Ryan told her that she had to make sex noises because she lost. Everyone was shocked that he didn't apply the parental filter on my mother. Everyone knew that we weren't supposed to say the word *sex* in front of parents, yet Ryan said it in front of mine, and he said it more than once.

However, my mother didn't seem too troubled. Instead of making sex noises, she volunteered to do animal noises. For the next minute or so, she sang the songs of monkeys, birds, elephants, and coyotes.

We even stopped at Walmart on the way back home, which was a nice gesture from my mother. Audrey dared Ryan to steal my white coat and put it on top of a coat rack, a place that I couldn't reach, and I proceeded to chase him around the store as he tossed my coat back and forth like a surrendering white flag.

Eventually, an employee approached us and asked us to stop misbehaving, or we would have to leave the store. Defeated, but still smiling, Ryan handed me back my coat, and Laney admitted that it would have been cool to get kicked out of Walmart.

The only one who was not amused was Lilly. On the way home, she sat far away from Ryan. She didn't accept his hand when he tried to hold hers. When we dropped him off at Postlewaite Ridge, she told me that Ryan wasn't allowed to talk to me anymore in front of everyone. She said it so particularly that it was sickening. "Abigail, don't talk to Ryan anymore, okay?"

My mother gave me an *I told you so* look, and Laney and Audrey exchanged puzzled expressions in the back of the SUV.

Finally, I asked her, "Why not?"

Coolly, she said, "Because he chased you around."

According to her, chasing a friend around the local Walmart warranted the No Talk rule being activated between a girlfriend and boyfriend. I tested her threat a few days after the incident, when I tried to talk to Ryan on the bus about what he planned to do Christmas vacation. He didn't say a word. On MSN Messenger, away from wandering eyes on the bus, I sent him a message. He signed off.

I wasn't sure what hurt more: the fact that my best friend hoarded her boyfriend like some treasure, as if she completely forgot that he and I were friends before the two of them got together, or the fact that Ryan listened to her, and that he and I hadn't spoken since November of last year.

Lilly brought a disposable camera with her that day. She snapped a photo of me holding her stray cat. I was wearing her yellow and black Fox Racing shirt. She also took photos of Laney and Audrey, making faces in the back of my mother's car. She even took a photo of my mother driving. I could still hear her voice as she called out, "Mamma Grace, smile!" The photo that was produced from that moment showed my mother hiding half of her face with one hand, but it wasn't enough to hide the grin on her face.

At one point, Lilly asked me to take a photo of her and Ryan in the middle seat. They were holding hands, brightly smiling, cheeks grazed red with the oncoming winter air. The two of them looked the part of newly married couple.

Remembering that photo, I looked around her bedroom for it. I couldn't find it. There wasn't a single photo on her wall that depicted that day back in November. The only photos she had taped up on her walls were of her and Ryan drenched in black clothing, and forcing as much desperation into their eyes as possible before every camera flash.

I saw an empty shoe box on the floor at the foot of her bed. "What's that for?"

"Mom said I needed to start packing up his things." Her voice was cold and lifeless.

I reached down. "She's right. We need to pack him away."

My heart shot bubbles of ice into my veins. I shouldn't have said it like that. It came out of my mouth sounding so insensitive.

Lilly flashed me wide eyes; I looked at her and literally watched little, wavy lines of water rim her black eyelids. She froze, her chin turning into mushed pebbles of skin, and her thin, barely-there eyebrows pushed up over her eyes. The look was horrifying. She whispered, "I can't believe you just said it like that." Her shoulders pushed back. "He's not something to just pack away, Abigail. God."

I placed the shoe box on her bed. "Look, I'm sorry, okay? But we can't just sit in your room with him all around us." My eyes found one of the photos of him and Lilly leaning against a tree, arms around each other, bodies cloaked all in black and red. Ryan's eyes followed me as I walked closer to the movie ticket heart, all the pairs of his eyes photographed on every surface of every wall. "Do you want me to do it for you?"

She thought about it for a moment. "Yes, but leave me some." She sniffed, "Just, leave me a little," and she paused. I looked at what Lilly was looking at, which was the bundled up black hoodie near her nightstand.

Lilly crawled on her hands and knees, closer and closer to the hoodie, but I reacted fast enough to pull it from the vanity and drop it on her bed. She didn't say anything. She just looked at the hoodie, looked at me, and looked back at the hoodie, then she crumbled to her bedroom floor and began crying. I didn't want to acknowledge her. I wanted Lilly to feel as if she was in her own personal space, where nobody could bother her, where nobody could judge her, as she completely fell apart.

I knew what was expected of me when I agreed to see Lilly. I knew that it wasn't going to be easy. I knew that it would require much more than I had to offer to keep her at peace, or as close to peace as possible, as she dealt with her boyfriend's suicide. My mother made similar comments as she drove me there. She mentioned that I would have to grow up a lot faster than I wanted to, whether I planned to or not, in order to take care of Lilly. I didn't argue with her. She was right.

Moving the hoodie was a bad idea, especially since it happened right before I started plucking Ryan from her bedroom walls. The entire time I did it, while I removed the photographs, movie tickets, scraps of notes, and the little knick-knacks of his dog collars, wrist bands, and skull pins on her nightstand, Ryan's scent drifted in and out of my nose, in and out of my memory—like he was coming and going, staying long enough for me to see him, and then leaving the instant I thought he was there, that he was back.

His scent was unique, something that no other boy in my class wore. Ryan always wore a cologne Lilly bought him from Hot Topic for Christmas, so when I inhaled it, I didn't see anyone else. I only saw him.

Lilly begged me to not pack away everything. She begged me to leave something out, just one thing, but I refused. I didn't want to leave her anything. She tried sneaking a movie ticket into her shirt, but I stole it in time and dropped it into the shoe box. I noticed something glitter in her praying hands, and I had to unravel one of his silver necklaces from her knuckles as she begged for him to come back.

Things like that kept happening, over and over again, and every time I had to steal a piece of Ryan away from Lilly, I hated myself for hurting my best friend like that. I swallowed salt every time I watched her eyes turn to liquid and her body slither to the floor, hands searching for a piece of him, perhaps a black hair of his braided with her carpet: the same thing I had done back in my bedroom hours earlier.

How was I supposed to take care of my best friend when I myself was dissolving in my own body of salt water? Did my mother, did Lilly's mother, actually expect me to play the role of some superhero and keep her from taking her own life? I bit down on my own tongue, smothering my own selfish thoughts for the sake of my best friend's well-being, and I continued to pluck Ryan from the walls and pack him away in her Volatile shoe box.

After about twenty minutes, when her bedroom walls were completely clean of anything Ryan, I dropped the shoe box lid on top and scooped it up against my chest. "I'll be back."

"No, no, don't, Abigail." She started crying again, feverishly, as I turned and walked out of her bedroom. I didn't see her, but I heard Lilly crawling across her carpet to catch me. My heart thanked my willpower for not looking back, for not knowing what Lilly looked like as she crawled for me, her last attempt to keep her boyfriend's memory alive.

My brain, however, showed me some disturbing images: Lilly crawling through a floor made of nothing but Ryan's photographs; the ends of her fingers dyed red as she plucked away at his skin, a sea of bodies writhing underneath her, the bodies all ages of Ryan, from as young as five years old.

I made it about two steps down when I realized that I was clutching probably the last pieces of Ryan Matthew Mills in my arms. His last photos, his last notes, his last words—*Jesus Christ.*

Instead of taking the shoe box straight to Linda as she'd ordered me to do, I instead sat on the stairs, took the lid off, and dropped my head into the miniature coffin in my arms. I was holding on to a coffin, with the last bit of the real Ryan inside.

Realizing this, my arms pulled the shoe box closer, so close that my nose swam around in the notes and photographs, and I wept into the shoe box. I cried into Ryan's grave, the pain of losing him severing every nerve in my body except the feeling of him cupping my cheeks as I continued to lose myself.

My cries were quiet, quiet enough that Lilly couldn't hear me. She didn't deserve to see me like that, not when she was suffering far beyond what I could ever imagine. I needed to be strong for her. It was prudent for me to remain a solid structure around her, so she could trust me to hold her when she cried, and to listen when she needed to talk.

With the shoebox open and filling with my tears, I sniffed long and hard in between cries, in between hitched breaths, drawing out the last of his scent, pulling Lilly's leftovers into my brain, so I could keep them there for myself. He must have worn the same deodorant then that he wore back when we went on our four-wheeler ride last summer, because those were the types of memories flooding back into my head as I inhaled, a different piece of time coming with each breath: four-wheelers, the abandoned house, him wanting me to walk into his woods so he could scare me, the texture of his hot whisper as it glided over my ear.

No.

Disappointed in myself, I snapped the shoebox closed and stood. This wasn't about me.

This was about Lilly now. She needed me. There was no time to worry about myself.

Linda was sitting down at the kitchen table when I handed her the shoebox. I didn't actually hand her the shoebox. Rather, she jumped back a bit when I dropped it flat on the table. It made a sharp *snap* that echoed throughout the entire empty house. Her mouth opened, but I didn't give her time to speak.

Instead, I said, "Here he is," and marched right back upstairs.

Fourteen

I made sure enough time had transpired before I asked Lilly the ultimate question.

"What happened?"

Lilly asked me to sit down on her bed with her. I obliged. I wanted her to be as comfortable as possible as she took me through the last moments of Ryan's life, something that more people than just her deserved to know, something she couldn't keep all to herself. Others craved those answers. His friends starved for the truth.

She admitted that everything, at first, went according to plan. Her mother dropped her off at Ryan's, knowing that she would have to lie to Gary if he decided to ask where his daughter was. Lilly and Ryan waited until Linda's Camaro was out of sight before they started taking off their clothes. By the time Gary learned from Bradley that Lilly was not at Linda's and was in fact at Ryan's losing her virginity, he lost it. While Gary was rushing to his beat-up Chevy, Lilly was taking her shirt off and Ryan was pulling her on top of his lap.

As she spoke, she choked a bit. "My dad found me on top of Ryan. I wasn't wearing a shirt. Ryan wasn't wearing any pants."

I asked her the obvious. "Did you guys—?"

She shook her head. "No. We didn't."

As she continued to unravel the story, Lilly admitted that her father transformed into a beast when he found them together. He practically grew claws, his teeth protruding like a hungry animal's, the skin on his face wrinkling in incarnadine anger. She couldn't remember if she ran from the bedroom herself, or if her father dragged her out by her hair. When she tried to uncover those details in her memory, I saw the pain register in her face. Something twitched; she flinched, and leaned back a bit to tease the tension.

I knew Lilly was near the hardest part of the story when she leaned closer to me. She made sure her knee was touching my leg before continuing, as if it was a comforting enough gesture to massage her through the rest of the story.

While she ran from Ryan's bedroom, Gary threatened Ryan, knowing his weakest points, his most vulnerable shreds of adolescence. He threatened that he would never get to see Lilly again, that the two of them would never be together, that Ryan was never allowed back at his house, or allowed to speak to his daughter again. That went on long enough that Linda took Lilly outside and forced her into the vehicle.

Lilly didn't know when it happened—when Ryan shot himself—but it happened before she got to her father's house. It must have happened the moment Gary's foot left the Mills residence.

She finished her story with a strong, long inhale through her nose. The whole time she spoke, she cried without sound. Her hands danced up and down and around, and her eyes moved back and forth, and tears just dripped straight from her green eyes, yet her voice was unaffected. It was the strangest thing.

"My dad blames himself for what happened. He was too hard on him. My dad overreacted, and I tried to tell him that Ryan was different, but he wouldn't listen." She cleared her throat. "My dad hasn't stopped drinking since. Mom said she may have to take him to the hospital. I don't even want to see him right now."

I didn't know what kind of questions I should ask her. What was off limits? Anything?

I rubbed my hands together. "Did he leave behind a note?"

She shrugged. "I don't know. I don't know anything, Abigail. They won't tell me anything." She scoffed, "People are already saying that it was a suicide pact between me and Ryan. That's what Laney told me."

I had to ask. "*Was* it a suicide pact, Lilly?"

Something flinched in her green eyes.

It wouldn't have been the first time rumors swirled Stream Ridge of a suicide pact involving Lilly or Ryan. There were other instances, other moments of clarity fogged in her name. Just a few months prior, Lilly and I had devised a plan together to take our own lives. She and I wrote back and forth on notebook paper about the ways we could commit suicide. She said Ryan could steal his father's truck, and the three of us could go meet my Internet boyfriend in Kentucky. We would spend a few days together, the four of us, and then we would have sex so we didn't die virgins, and then we would have the boys kill us before they killed themselves.

The idea itself was unorganized and far too surreal to even commit. We went into so much detail about this plan that we used up over twenty pages of notebook paper, front and back, writing back and forth. Halfway through organizing everything, I referred to my mental state as the Monster, and Lilly piggybacked and said that her Monster was the same as mine, and that we needed to feed it in order to survive. We even went beyond that, saying that we were possessed and had powers, like reading minds, swapping bodies, and predicting the future.

It got to the point that one of us crossed the line, though I cannot remember who or what happened, but we stopped writing and stopped calling our mental state the Monster.

Linda liked snooping through Lilly's things, so one day, she uncovered our series of notes underneath her bed. She was only able to find the second half of the story, the one involving the Monster and not planning our suicides, though that was enough for her to worry.

My mother brought up the Monster in my appointment following Linda's discovery, and my psychiatrist upped my medication.

After a few moments, Lilly finally looked at me. "No. It was not a suicide pact."

I prepared myself to be my bravest. "Lilly, what happened tonight is a lot like what we wrote about back when we were gonna go to Kentucky. Back then, we did have a pact, and it involved sex and—"

She snapped, "I said *no*." I relented.

It didn't matter if she was my best friend or not. I still didn't know if I could believe her.

Lilly asked me to follow her to the bathroom. For the next ten minutes, I just stood by and watched her take a razor over the underbelly of her arm three different times. Each time a new red line appeared atop her pale skin, the blood cracking at the razor's teeth, she hissed, "This is for him, this is for me, and this is for the letter I never read." She collapsed against the toilet and dropped her face between her knees.

As small traces of blood dripped down her fingers, I wondered if there was a note. Just its existence alone would determine some form of premeditation. Maybe Lilly just needed there to be a note so she didn't feel so guilty.

It was dark by the time we emerged from the bathroom. Lilly and I made each other stand in front of the small mirror before exiting; trading glances, juxtaposing each other, we looked exactly like I had expected.

Lilly's swollen eyes were rimmed with purple welts. It was strange, the discoloration that tainted her, how she looked half-dead. Maybe it was her black and red hair that made her normally tan skin seem blue.

I, on the other hand, looked more like a homeless person than someone stricken with grief. My hair was unbrushed and knotted, with some of Lilly's blood caked in the ends. My eyes were clean and clear; they were wide open, not swollen, yet completely empty.

She nudged me with her shoulder. "Ever notice how much we look alike?"

I didn't give in. I didn't want to know whether she was talking about physical features or our clothes. Knowing her, Lilly could have been talking about anything. Instead of acknowledging her question with a response, I ignored it and walked out of the bathroom. She followed.

I asked her if she wanted to talk about anything else before we readied for bed. For the first time the entire night, Lilly stopped crying. After she wiped away the tears on her face, no more slipped into the familiar tracks. Then she looked right at me, as honest as she could be, as transparent as water, and she said, "Abigail, if you really are my best friend, you will make sure that I do not go with him."

She crawled in bed first. I followed her like a lost shadow. I rolled over so my arms held her close.

I didn't sleep. The image of Lilly hanging from a noose in her closet kept me awake. She eventually found dreams a little before midnight, and even though my arm was twisted underneath her and it was painfully uncomfortable, I didn't readjust. I didn't want to wake her up. I watched the numbers on her digital clock go from 1:00 to 2:00, to 3:00, to 4:00, to 5:00.

At 6:00, I closed my eyes, just for a moment, just long enough to taste sleep.

At 6:05, the sound of water running in the bathroom yanked me from my nap.

The first thought that crossed my mind was Lilly bleeding out in the shower, her body completely drained, an incision the length of her favorite arm warmer and the width of her favorite novel, *Rebecca*, drawn across her left arm. I struggled from the bed worried that I had failed her, failed her mother and mine, because I had let her die.

Not obeying hygienic protocol, I threw the bathroom door open just in time to find Lilly pulling her pajama shirt over her head. She wasn't wearing any pants or underwear. I didn't say a word as I stood in the doorway. My eyes looked her up and down to see if she'd cut herself sometime that night without telling me. She didn't say anything, either. At least, she didn't say anything as I looked over her naked body, examining every inch of pale skin for a mark that wasn't there before.

There was so much trust between us right then that she didn't even feel the need to shield her feminine features, nor did my eyes ever travel to those areas.

Finally, she pulled the shower curtain back and told me, "I'll leave it open so you can watch me." I told her that I didn't have to watch her, that I just wanted her to remove any razors so she couldn't cut. She shook her head, her black and red hair whipping against her bony little shoulders. "I need you to watch me."

Oh. Now I understood. I sat on the toilet seat and listened to her sing while she showered. She hummed the song "I Miss You" by Blink-182. After the fourth rotation through the song I joined in, offering my voice as the alto to her soprano, something we did with one another without even having to say a word. When she didn't tell me to stop, I knew then that parts of my best friend were coming back.

When she was done showering, she asked me if I needed her to watch me shower. I shook my head, but thanked her for her efforts. Lilly tried to leave the bathroom completely, but I told her that she needed to stay in the bathroom, where I could hear her, while I showered. As I stripped completely naked, I asked her, "Will you sing while I shower?"

Lilly nodded. "Of course."

As long as she sang, as long as she continued to hear her own powerful, beautiful voice, she was unable to hear me cry in the shower. I crumpled into the fetal position as she sang, and every time she got to the hardest of lyrics—"Don't waste your time on me you're already the voice inside my head"—I bit the side of my hand, clenched hard, jaw buckled, and I screamed without making any sound.

How was I supposed to be strong for Lilly when I couldn't even hear a Blink-182 song without thinking of Ryan, without every cell in my body unraveling from its nucleus?

After I showered and got dressed, Lilly apologized for me missing my track meet. The only reason she was apologizing was because it was the biggest track meet of the season, when all schools of all sizes came to Fairmont to participate. Even though Gunners Valley School was the smallest participant, our 4x100 team was undefeated. Her apology was on my behalf, since I was part of the 4x100 team. I told her that being with her was far more important than a regional track meet.

To pass the time, I recommended that we watch old VHS tapes that her mother had recorded, something we'd done many times before. Lilly readied us a bed of sheets and pillows while I rummaged through her bookshelf for some of our favorite VHS tapes. None of them were labeled. I memorized the content by studying the VHS tape itself. I knew our favorite one—the one of Lilly sled-riding with Bradley—was the tape with the chipped protective flap over the film, so I put that one in the VCR.

We laughed together watching her brother wipe out. We held each other and commented at how adorable Lilly, then 12 years old, looked in her one-piece pink snowsuit with frilly cuffs at both her wrists.

The end of the tape was approaching. We knew this because Linda, who was recording, told her kids to hurry up and get all of their gear, because they were going back inside. I threw my legs over the bed to get up and take the VHS tape out, but the film cut to something else.

Instead of seeing the usual static at the end of the winter segment, a new segment appeared.

I nearly vomited at what I saw on Lilly's television screen.

There, right in front of our eyes, were me and Ryan, sitting together in the bleachers at the football game from 2003. My stomach knotted as I listened to Linda urging us to scoot closer, to stop acting so shy, to be the lovebirds that we were. I almost didn't turn around to see what Lilly looked like as she watched her boyfriend and I move closer together, knees touching, cheeks catching fire, but I did. I saw me and Ryan in Lilly's green eyes. Her mouth hung open, and her eyes were dry, trembling, in utter denial.

Linda released a satisfactory breath. "Geesh, get a room, you two."

Instead of turning the VCR off, I just shut the television off. I did it so hurriedly that I accidentally shoved the television a bit off-course. One corner hung over the side of her dresser, exposing a fair amount of accumulated dust around the edges.

Lilly forgot to breathe. When she remembered, she gasped almost as if she was torpedoing straight out of water. I couldn't look at her. I felt as if the recording was a signal of my betrayal: that I somehow let her down over a year ago before I knew what was to happen, before she took him away from me, before *she* betrayed *me*. She blinked a few times, then slowly, she got up from her bed. "I forgot that happened."

Bile rose in the back of my throat. Lilly was a horrible liar. She didn't forget, she could never forget, how she manipulated Ryan out from underneath me, while simultaneously keeping Jace wrapped around her finger. She worked her magic on Ryan while she was still dating Jace, and she did the thing she'd vowed no friend should do: she went behind my back, after the boy I liked, and she didn't even feel like she did anything wrong.

She never even apologized. Not to me, not to Jace. She still hadn't.

Had it been the other way around—me sneaking online to use MSN Messenger at late hours and talking to Jace until dawn—she would have disowned me as a friend. She would have preached to me about the importance of friendship and how I broke a sacred vow; she would have played the victim tenfold.

Now wasn't the time, however, for me to call her out on her hypocritical ways. I needed to fix what just happened, even though it wasn't even my intention to see myself and Ryan together on her television. With eyes still glued on the carpet, I mumbled back, "I'm, umm, sorry you had to see that."

"Sorry that I saw him, or sorry that I saw him with you?" Her snide tone dripped like venom from her protruding fangs. Lilly could be an unforgiving, evil, venomous girl.

I straightened my posture on command. "That's not fair, Lilly. Don't even."

She rolled her eyes. They were still dry. "Let's go downstairs."

I gave in. I didn't want to argue with her, especially not while she was clearly still grieving.

As we made our way downstairs, she double-checked her arm to make sure it was fully concealed with her arm warmer. Lilly was foolish if she believed that our mothers wouldn't check our arms a few days after we separated.

The morning was quiet. I made Lilly a cup of sweet coffee, just the way she liked it, and I prepared mine black. We didn't talk. I offered her some quiet time, some personal space to roll around in her own head, to coat herself in the last memories of Ryan. She cried every now and then, something I expected. Each time I heard her sniff, I handed her a tissue from the box nearest me. Linda was pacing back and forth from the outdoor laundry room to the dining room.

When Linda had finished folding clothes, she dropped the basket on the kitchen floor and excused herself. My toes felt the warmth of the freshly dried clothes, and I slipped from the chair at the kitchen table and crawled inside the laundry basket. I did it because I was cold, not because I wanted to make Lilly laugh, which is what happened. She shook her head in humorous disappointment. "Abigail, God, you're nuts."

"It's so warm," I told her.

Lilly reverted to looking out the kitchen window. While she watched over the Appalachian hills, I looked around the kitchen for something to look at. My eyes found a calendar. It was May 12th, Wednesday—only a few more days until the weekend. Some random thoughts came and went, like what day the parents expected us affected kids to go back to school. Then I did more math in my head; then I thought about Ryan's viewing; then I thought about Ryan's funeral; then I thought about my birthday. All of those happened that week.

Linda returned to the kitchen. She looked at me twice, contemplated asking me why I was sitting in her basket of clean clothes, and then pushed the thought away. I managed to work up the nerve to ask her, "Do you know when the funeral is?"

"Friday."

Lilly finished sipping on her coffee and looked down at me. "Some birthday present, huh?" I wasn't sure if she was trying to be funny.

It took a moment for Linda to put the pieces together. She fixed her sports bra top and somewhat gasped. "Oh, Abigail, is that your birthday? Oh, no, that's awful."

"Yeah," was all I could say. My body withered into the warm clothes beneath me. I didn't say anything after that, and Linda didn't ask me to move out of her basket of clean clothes. I spent the rest of the morning contemplating how many birthdays I would go through before I forgot about Ryan. Would there be a year when I could celebrate growing a year older without seeing a casket falling into the ground?

Glancing outside, I was momentarily distracted by a spring shower blowing rain sideways against the window. The orange glow from the day before was still there, still reaching for me, but I didn't want to be found.

Later that day, Linda and Lilly's grandmother took us to Meadowbrook Mall. It seemed like a good idea, even though my mother didn't give me any money—not that I needed it for anything. Linda offered to buy me one t-shirt.

The car ride to Clarksburg was especially painful; Lilly's grandmother kept trying to make us laugh, but all she did was make us hate her. At one point, we were listening to Blink-182's self-titled album, and the song "I Miss You" came on, and Lilly asked for it to be put in repeat. Her grandmother kept starting the song over, right after the first few lyrics. We heard the phrase, "Hello, there" at least 20 times.

Eventually, Lilly yelled out, "Just stop it!" Her grandmother only laughed back at us and kept doing it.

There was even a moment when Lilly was looking out the back of the Camaro, so I couldn't see her face. I felt a raindrop splash against my cheek, though it was completely sunny outside. Trying to make her feel better, I tapped on her back, ready to yell out, "It's raining, y'all!" When she turned around to face me, I realized that it wasn't raining. The raindrop I felt earlier was actually one of her tears being catapulted into the backseat by the wind force of the open window. In the end, I never said anything, and she turned back around to cry out the window.

We went to Hot Topic, and Lilly bought a new pair of Tripp pants and an expensive studded, hooded sweatshirt. I didn't feel comfortable letting Linda buy me a t-shirt, so I decided to pick out another pair of striped socks for only $10. She told me not to be cheap, so she went and got me another pair. Lilly's grandmother held up a revealing piece of corset lingerie and asked if I wanted to get that instead. I was nearly tempted to surprise her by saying yes, but instead I said, "No, thanks, I don't have any boobs," which made Linda laugh but not Lilly.

I left the store with two pairs of striped socks, one pair blue and black, the other yellow and black.

That afternoon, Lilly and I went for a walk up and down Gunners Valley Road. We told one another that we weren't allowed to walk farther than Jace's house, and that we weren't allowed to cross the bridge that connects Gunners Valley Road to Route 352, so we walked back and forth a lot. Lilly liked kicking rocks as she walked. She pointed at one as it skipped at least four different times before sinking into the ditch. I nudged her with my shoulder, my way of saying she kicked it pretty good.

"We were going to grow up together, y'know."

Her comment caught me completely off guard. My foot stopped midair before it, too, could kick a rock aside. "What do you mean?"

At least Lilly wasn't crying anymore. Her eyes were swollen, puffy on the bottoms, and her cheeks were peeling and red, but they were dry. She tucked a piece of black and red hair behind her ear. "Me and Ryan. I didn't doubt that we were going to stay together all throughout high school, graduate, get an apartment together."

I watched our feet match one another in steps. Her left with my right, her black and red Volatile sneaker with my Punk Rose flats. We were both wearing Hot Topic shoes. I was reluctant to give in to her confession, my way of not letting her dwell on something that could never happen now. "We haven't even graduated middle school yet."

"Doesn't matter." She arched her head up towards the sky. "I don't think we're supposed to feel like this until we're older—like, a lot older, in college maybe—but I *do* feel it. I just, I just feel it and I know it is real. I felt it before he died, and I'll feel it for the rest of my life."

Right then, I believed her. I believed Lilly. I didn't care if I was too young to understand what was going on, my 13-year-old self believed in Lilly when she admitted these things to me. She was right to say that there was no doubt of the affection and perfection between her and Ryan. That was the only reason why I didn't ask her to use the past tense for "it is real."

Instead, she and I continued walking up and down the gravel road, kicking at stones, drawing names and shapes in the rock sand.

Every few minutes, she would remind me, "You're my best friend."

And I would confirm, "Yeah, I know."

My mother showed up a few minutes after we came back from our walk. She actually came up to the house to give Lilly a warm, cigarette-smelling embrace. Lilly managed to look away from her *Seventeen* magazine long enough to spill tears against my mother's shoulders and cry out Ryan's name three times. When they pulled away, I tasted something bitter in the back of my throat.

My mother went to Lilly for advice on many occasions. The few times that Lilly was allowed to spend the night with me, my mother would pick her up on her way home from work, and the two of them would talk about me the entire car ride. My mother asked Lilly how I was doing in school, if I was handling my medication well, what my favorite band was because my mother wanted to buy me a new CD. At times when I was disconnected from my own mother, I asked Lilly to help me build that connection back up, and in no time, my mother and I were back on the same level.

The two of them shared an unnatural, intimately close bond. Lilly didn't embrace me like I watched her embrace my mother.

My mother climbed down the stone wall first. Back at the house, I hugged Lilly and made sure to remind her to call me if anything happened. She hugged me a second time when I tried to leave. "Abigail, thank you."

I just smiled.

The moment I got into the vehicle, I turned to my mother and said through clenched teeth, "You shouldn't have let me come here."

"Abigail?"

I fastened my seatbelt and stared out the window. "Don't ever let me do something like that again. Please."

My mother put the Ford Explorer in drive.

Most students returned to school on the 13th, the day of Ryan's viewing. I was only slightly surprised to find Lilly on the bus that morning, but it was probably better for her to return to school instead of withering away alone in her bedroom. She smiled at me as I took my seat. I refrained from looking at the empty half-seat in the back of the bus, knowing that it was going to be vacant for the rest of the year: perhaps the rest of the decade.

My Uncle Dan, the counselor for the high school, offered counseling to any middle school student affected by Ryan's passing. I declined. Lilly and Laney did, too. We spent most of the school day with one another. Me on one of Lilly's arms, Laney on the other.

Every single teacher offered us a moment to grieve in silence. Though the gestures were made out of kind thoughts, they became tiresome after the fourth time. We skipped lunch completely and went straight outside for recess. While I listened to the new Blink-182 CD on my Walkman, Laney and Lilly created fortune teller flowers from notebook paper. According to them, I was going to

become an architect and marry 8th grade heartthrob Micah Sine. I laughed at
my options.

The rumor mill morphed into a conglomeration of sorts by the end of the
day. At Gunners Valley School, students continued to share the myth that Lilly
and Ryan planned a suicide pact. The only part of the story that they got right
was that her father intervened and sent the plan on an entirely different course.

On the bus ride home, Kimmie grabbed my arm and yanked me into her
seat. She asked me if I knew about the other rumor, the one that students at
Stream Ridge High School were spinning. For a moment, I believed the high
school rumor to have more depth and maturity than the middle school rumor—
perhaps Lilly wore some lingerie, or Ryan rolled a few joints before the two of
them attempted to have sex—but then Kimmie whispered in my ear, "It was
supposed to be you, Jace, Ryan, and Lilly. All of you were supposed to commit
suicide together."

I actually shoved her out of her seat. Kimmie crawled back up next to me.
"So you didn't know?"

My eyes were practically engulfed in fire at that point.

"Figures. That's what they're saying at the high school. Everyone's calling
Lilly a selfish succubus because she was supposed to tell you about it, but she's
a cunt and kept it to herself because she wanted all of the attention." Kimmie
wedged the tip of her tongue between her teeth, a sign that she was upset. It
was only after everyone returned to school that we learned Kimmie saw Ryan
after he passed away. She had snuck to his house once the red and blue lights
stormed the backroads, and she ran inside his house and saw what was left of
his body spilling of blood in his parents' bedroom.

Kimmie saw what nobody else did. In her mother's words, "He doesn't have
a face," but Kimmie returned that evening and told Nyla that Ryan, in fact, did
have a face, and then she crawled onto the couch and cried.

I clenched my fists in my lap. "What about Jace? Why wasn't he there?"

Kimmie sighed. "They're saying he stole his sister's car before Ryan died.
Almost like..." she stopped, and awkwardly tapped my knee. "I don't feel sorry
for Lilly. She can rot in hell. But I have this fuckin' hurt in my chest for Jace, and
I don't even know him." Then she asked me to go sit with Audrey, and I did.

Scott called me when I got home from school. He screamed that he couldn't
stop crying, and that he couldn't stop watching old VHS tapes of his class
during Christmas concerts and Easter shows, watching so he could see Ryan

with his little black mullet bouncing around, laughing, singing, shoving pretty girls and turning away smothered in red. I asked him if he needed me to come over. He declined. He wanted to be free in case Jace needed him, and when I heard that, I made sure to tell him, "You are a great friend, Scott."

He tried laughing. I heard snot shoot out from his nose. "If I was a good fucking friend, he'd still be here."

When I asked about Jace, Scott didn't say much more than what I already knew. Jace did steal his sister's car the day it happened. Even worse, he wrecked the stolen car because he managed to hit an old lady on Gunners Valley Road. Abandoning the car, he took off running. Nobody was sure what happened, but wherever Jace was going in his sister's car, he did not make it.

Slowly, Scott purged details from that night and the day later. He found out about Ryan's suicide when his mother called him downstairs, and he saw her crying, holding the phone in her hand. Then he got on the phone and listened to Mrs. Mackey, an EMT volunteer, talk about finding Ryan without a face, saying, rather bluntly, "He shot his entire face off."

Scott snapped back, "Fuck you, you fuckin' bitch!" Then he threw the phone and ran outside.

Soon, news spread that Jace was missing, so Scott and my Aunt Paula searched all over Stream Ridge for him. They managed to find a dark figure walking in between trees near the Field of Dreams. Scott and Jace spent that first night together sneaking into a nearby Catholic church, stealing candles, and lighting them in honor of Ryan. The whole time, they held one another; they collapsed to the dusty red runner in the church aisle, and they cried. Scott told me through the salt in his voice, "Abigail, we cried so fucking much."

The next day, Ryan's closest friends went to Jace's house for a sleepover. The boys played video games the entire day. Any time they played a multiplayer game, they designated a computer player as Ryan by using his personal favorites. Scott admitted that it wasn't as sad as it sounded, saying it was uplifting, almost cleansing, to play against the computer as Ryan's favorite character.

That night around the bonfire, the boys watched as Jace held his palm over the fire for at least thirty seconds. He never pulled away, regardless of the blistering welt swelling on the belly of his hand. He'd been wearing a bandage ever since.

When he stopped purging, he struggled to catch his breath. "Abigail, I just... There's so much."

"I know," was all I could say.

He never asked me how Lilly was. That was how I learned all of Ryan's friends blamed her for what happened.

A part of me agreed with them.

I never asked Scott about the second rumor, the one in which the four of us were supposed to commit suicide together. It was just that: a rumor, nothing more. At least, that was what I told myself.

Back at home, I stayed in my bedroom and listened to the Blink-182 album on repeat. By the fourth cycle, I knew all of the words to every single song. It was impossible not to liken a lyric to Ryan. Every single song was reminiscent of an unexpected loss, of love severed too soon, of a fond memory.

That night was the first time I fell asleep with headphones on. When I woke up the next morning, one foam piece was off and sandwiched between my pillow and my cheek. I vowed to never sleep with headphones on again after that, at the expense of breaking my headphones. I knew that we couldn't afford another pair.

The day of Ryan's viewing I stepped from my bedroom wearing wrinkled black dress pants and a white button-up shirt. My mother asked me to dress nice, but I didn't have a lot of dress clothes. My dress pants were the same ones from the 6th grade, so they were faded and worn. As for the white button-up shirt, I couldn't even remember where it came from. It was probably a hand-me-down from my sister, but I even second-guessed that.

My mother did a double take when she saw me step into the kitchen. "Abigail?" She paused. I didn't know why she paused. "Have you showered yet?"

I shrugged. The last time I remembered showering was at Lilly's, when I sunk into the fetal position and bit down on my fist to smother my own cries: so, two days before. The last time I brushed my hair was just a few hours before, when I brushed in succession with the song "Violence," which Laney and I liked to refer to as "The Bumble Bee Song," because the intro sounded like a bumble bee playing the guitar.

My mother looked nice, however. She was wearing a solid brown top with a heavy floral print, brown dress pants, and shiny brown shoes. Brown was my mother's favorite color.

Diana even looked nice, but my sister always looked nice. She always glittered in pink. She, too, wore black dress pants, but her top was bright pink with loose glitter, and sleeves that spread like flower petals at her elbows. Her heels were super high, and she fixed her hair up in thick, ringlet curls. Looking at her, it appeared that she was dressing up for a date, not a viewing for her classmate.

Normally, my sister would say something snarky to me, like how I was a skank for not showering, but there was something wrong with her. Her eyes were dilated, and she didn't look right at anyone. Her eyes were pretty much anchored to the floor the entire time. She only nodded when my mother asked if she was ready to leave, when typically she would snap back. She didn't even start a fight with me when I accidentally stepped on her foot trying to slip into my dress shoes.

We filed into the Explorer, and on the way to Cedar Rock, my mother kept looking at me in her rearview mirror. Every few minutes, she'd ask, "Are you okay?"

And I'd give her a look that translated to, "What the *fuck* do you think?"

And she'd look back at the road.

My mother approached the funeral home. She cursed under her breath, then she said, "Go ahead and get out here. I'll find a place to park." The funeral home was so busy with traffic that my mother dropped me and my sister off at the door. She had to drive a ways down the street just to find a parking spot.

Even the parking lot right across the road was packed full of cars, even SUVs and trucks sideways and tipping on grassy hills that definitely weren't legitimate parking spots. Someone's white SUV was about three inches away from slipping onto the muddy creek embankment nearby.

The line to view Ryan extended beyond the front double doors. My sister branched off from me while I stepped in line behind Cameron: the same Cameron from Ryan's birthday party, many years earlier. We said hi to one another, and that was it. Another classmate, Arnold Koontz, stepped in line behind me. He wasn't able to hold it together long enough to step inside. He peeled away from the line and collapsed to his knees on the front lawn, where he proceeded to pound at the grass while cursing underneath his breath. Nobody minded him. Nobody told him to stop.

Norma greeted everyone when they managed to step into the funeral home. She was wearing a brightly-colored shirt and skirt set printed with blue oceans, yellow trees, and orange suns. Her eyes were wide, dark, like black translucent vases filled with sparkling water. I didn't turn her away when she reached up and grabbed both of my hands. She offered me thanks for coming, and I found every morsel of strength and massaged it into one last effort to hold it together so she wouldn't see me come undone at the wake of her late son.

I wished I hadn't seen the apparent twitch in her left eye, the stretched Cheshire smile across her face. How many medications did she need in order to function semi-properly at her only child's viewing? It didn't matter. She was still human. She was still a mother. I didn't want her to be here. I wanted her to be at home, away from curious, judgmental eyes, so she could grieve at her own pace, on her own time, out of sight, just her and only her.

As she let go of my hands, she whispered, "Thank you, little Abigail." When she greeted the student behind me, I covered my face with both hands and cried without shame. My glasses pushed up and over my fingers. The cuts of my bangs pricked my knuckles. Cameron turned and asked me if I was going to be okay. I found enough breath in my lungs to tell him that I would be okay, which was a lie. He turned back around and continued to move with the line.

A gasp caught my ear. Turning, I looked out the open entryway and saw my mother standing in the middle of the road. Next to her, I watched my Uncle Dan put his hands back in his pockets. My mother was holding something. Her face immediately paled.

Someone behind me tapped my shoulder. "The line has moved."

I shook my mother's white face out of my mind and took a step forward.

By the time Cameron and I were in the front of the line, I noticed the portrait of Ryan and Lilly, the size of a bulletin board, perched in the corner of the room. It was the same one that she used to have on her bedroom wall, back at her mom's house. Yet this one was blown up, huge, placed beautifully in a golden frame on top of an easel.

I couldn't stop staring at it as I waited my turn to see Ryan. Lilly's green eyes were empty, just little drops of the Earth cupped in thick lines of eyeliner and black eye shadow. Ryan, sitting behind her, had his chin across her shoulder— but at least he was smiling.

God, I would never forget that smile.

Something haunting shot up my back. My body wriggled itself out of the cold spell by the time I reached the front of the line. Suddenly it was just me standing there, and it was my turn to see him.

It was an open casket. I wasn't expecting that.

How was it appropriate to have an open casket for a young boy who had shot himself in the face?

As I inched closer and closer, I heard a voice from behind my shoulder. "Baby, it's okay." My mother was somewhere behind me. "Just tell him you're here, baby. You can do it." She broke in half during her second statement. I could hear it in her voice as she tried her best to hold it together. Anyone who could hear my mother was now battling their own smothered cries.

I looked into the coffin and gasped. That wasn't Ryan lying atop a bed of white silk.

There was something horrific about the structure of his face. The fact that his nose was not perfectly lined up with his eyebrows, the kind of symmetry I'd learned by looking at his face closely for the last five years, meant that his features had shifted when he died. The color of the skin surrounding his eyes and nose...it appeared blue in some places, jaundiced in others. The glossy surface of his forehead was disturbing: abnormally glassy. It was almost transparent.

Why Ryan's viewing was an open casket, I had no idea, but I pitied the attendant who had to fix what was left of his face. It was apparent that the professionals pored themselves into restoring the youth and innocence of this young boy. It was obvious that they did what they could. They'd salvaged what they could, and yet the *thing* lying before me was the best they could do?

Where was the real Ryan?

My fingers clenched. "Mommy?"

"Abigail, just step away."

"But..." and then I reached out and touched him.

Oh.

The pale, jaundiced skin there sank a bit. Immediately, I pulled back. I hadn't expected that, either.

An employee of the funeral home approached me. He asked if I could finish my condolences so that others could see him.

My eyes burst with water. That wasn't enough time for me to sit down and talk to Ryan, talk to him about everything, everything that happened between us, everything I remembered that perhaps he didn't. There was just so much that I wanted him to know before I said my goodbyes. Clawing my fingers around the edge of his coffin, my fingertips cradled against the soft silk encompassing his body. I glanced at his face. Again, I couldn't believe it was an open casket.

Finally, I pushed myself away from his coffin. In a cold breath, I whispered down to his freakishly quiescent body, "I miss you so much." Then I turned and walked away.

That's when I saw her.

Lilly was sitting on a bench near the front door. She was wearing black pants and a sparkly pink shirt, something that I knew Linda had bought her just for this occasion. Her hands were folded in her lap. As soon as her eyes met mine, the corners of her mouth turned up. That was a relief. She stood as I approached her. "Let's go back here." She nodded towards Norma, who was smiling and cheery, grabbing at anyone's hands when they entered the funeral home. "I can't be around her any longer." I didn't know what she meant by that.

"Okay." I followed her to a separate room, one off to the side, away from the traffic in and out of the viewing room. We both sat down on another soft bench.

Other students followed us. Cameron and Scott sat across from us. Both of them were sobbing. Moments later, Adam filed into the green room and sat a few seats away from Lilly and me.

By then, she was trembling so much that I reached over and held her hand. I didn't let it go. More and more friends of Ryan's summoned themselves to be in the same room as we were. Jace came, too; even Bradley snuck into the room and sat with us. Everyone, the closest of friends or not, became a brand new family; everyone was crying. The cacophony of our collective sobs filled my veins with solidified salt. My heart burned as the sodium brushed the gaping holes in my chest.

Was someone supposed to say something, or were we going to spend the rest of the evening listen to one another cry?

Suddenly, in a room adjacent to ours, there was a loud *boom*. Like something being dropped on the floor. Lilly looked up, a Kleenex held to her nose. "What the..."

My Aunt Paula rushed out from a hallway, looking for something, and then her eyes met mine. She ran right for me. I looked up, horrified, "What's wrong?"

She was out of breath. "Your sister just passed out."

"What? Why?"

"She saw him."

My teeth clenched. "I don't know *what* is in that coffin, but that's not *him*."

Lilly choked in her tissue. "Abigail, *Jesus*."

My Aunt Paula sprinted away. A few seconds later, my mother ran into the room. We could literally smell the smoke floating from her body, she was that fresh from finishing a cigarette outside. I didn't even give her time to speak. I pointed up at the doorway, "She's in there," and she rushed away, in the same manner my Aunt Paula entered the room.

Lilly shrieked and jiggled my hand in hers. "You're squeezing."

"Oh." I pushed the anger out of my fist. It wasn't right of me to inflict my rage on Lilly.

A few minutes passed. I saw my mother escorting my pale, ugly-faced sister from the room nearby. My mother looked up at me, "Are you ready?"

I actually laughed. "Are you *serious* right now?"

She sighed. "Okay." My mother hurried her efforts to basically carry Diana back outside to the car.

It was around that time that Lilly's entire body went into convulsions. At first, I thought she was having trouble controlling all of her emotional tremors. But it continued, affecting her entire body, and she was making strange noises. Thinking she was having a seizure, I reached out with both hands and grabbed her face; I wanted to make sure she wasn't trying to swallow her own tongue. Her eyes were clenched shut, and she was uttering Ryan's name under her breath like some sort of supernatural incantation.

Finally, after I managed to tone down her emotional collapse, after everyone around us stared and watched and wondered, Lilly was able to free herself from her own horrible world.

She sighed aloud. "Oh, God."

"It's okay now," I told her. My hand went back to clasp hers—its rightful place, where it had been the entire evening. Nearby, Jace had stood up, prepared to help me ease Lilly out of her memories. After he saw the two of us sink back into the bench, he sat back down.

Lilly's fingers wormed into mine. She somehow managed to laugh: her first in days. She shook her hand, the one I held. "People are going to think we're dating."

I managed to laugh, as well. "Well, let them think what they want."

She smiled. *First laughter, now smiling?* "I bet Ryan thinks we look like dorks."

Her smile was contagious as it bled into my own face. "I bet he'd want to watch."

She laughed so loud that a bubble of snot popped under her nose. Someone near us snickered at my comment. Lilly dipped her face into the bend of my neck, "Abigail, he is watching."

My eyes moved up. His casket was now closed.

Did I question her use of the present tense? Or did I bring up the obvious fact that Ryan was too dead to even see us?

I didn't do either one. Instead, I drew her hand into my lap and whispered, "I'm here."

Something brushed my ear. A breath or a laugh, it felt like a kiss from a butterfly. "I know. I know."

Fifteen

Immediately following Ryan's viewing, not a second after I slithered out of the car and approached my bedroom door, my mother asked me to meet her in her bedroom.

I expected to spend the next half hour listening to her try her best to bring me back up to a safe place, to a place where I could forget what the rubbery-skinned, pale thing looked like in the casket back at the funeral home. As I stepped into her bedroom, she ordered me to close the door. Cautious, I stepped back until my spine shoved the door into the frame. My mother held something, a few pieces of folder paper, in her lap.

When she unfolded the items, I noticed two dreary faces printed on the sheets of paper. The faces were mine and Lilly's. Each piece of paper offered a different photo. Before I even saw the rest of the photograph, without seeing anything else but the severely heavy eyeliner ringing our eyes or the arm warmers stretched up and down our arms, I knew exactly what my mother was holding.

She began, cradling tears in her eyes, "Your Uncle Dan gave these to me."

So that was why she gasped at the funeral home.

In every photo, Lilly and I were pressing knives against our chests, wrists, necks, and the centers of our foreheads. We weren't wielding a standard steak knife or butter knife from the silverware drawer. Back in April, one of the weekends that Lilly spent the night with me, we snuck into my mother's bedroom and found Patrick's collection of knives. They were dangerously sharp, fired with vines and symbols all down the blades, and the handles were polished and complemented with golden threading and ivy leaves. Some may have been ivory.

We only sent the photos to one person, a classmate whom I dated briefly after Christmas break. It wasn't our smartest decision; that classmate was also the Gunners Valley School principal's stepson. No wonder my Uncle Dan obtained the photos. He was the district's counselor.

My mother didn't have many words for me that evening. She commanded me to apologize to Patrick when he got home, for stealing his knives. She asked to see the bellies of my forearms, which I showed her reluctantly. There were only a few new cuts there since the last time she checked. Her eyes usually skimmed over those marks, looking for something more promising, like a bloody wedge severed directly above my vein.

After that, she told me she would ground me, but then she sighed. Her head dropped against her chest. "I can't do that to you. Please, just… Don't do this anymore. Stop doing this to me. Please, Abigail."

I stepped out of her bedroom before I suffered more from watching my own mother sob.

The next day, while my mother was holding my hand and guiding me through Morgantown Mall, offering me anything and everything that I wanted for my 14th birthday, I couldn't shake the thought of watching a coffin slip down into the ground and hearing fingernails scratching the contraption from the inside. None of the kids were allowed to attend Ryan's funeral at Norma's request, including Kimmie and Lilly, so we could only imagine what it was like. Kimmie was respectful of her aunt's wishes and remained distant and quiet; Lilly, however, was vicious and kept writing *I hate you* on her assignments. It was the first time that I knew she wasn't writing about me or Laney.

My mother did what she could to try to distract me from the obvious: while I celebrated my birthday, Ryan was being laid to rest in the plot of land directly across from his parents' house.

There were moments when I stopped moving—stopped thinking, stopped breathing, just *stopped*—and wondered if, at that instant, Norma was reciting some sort of eulogy for her late son, while I was reaching for my second hot bun at the Texas Roadhouse for my birthday dinner, or some other mundane activity. That happened a lot. My mother eventually caught on when my body slipped into a state of catatonia, eyes doubling in size, a salty film practically foaming against my lids, but never sliding down the sides of my pale face.

During my fits of shock, my mother shook my hand or brushed back a piece of my hair. The only moment of clarity I experienced that entire day was when my mother picked out a t-shirt from Hot Topic that was strikingly blue with a cartoon-style rib cage and a heart dangling in the center. She handed it to me and said something like, "This heart isn't broken," and I smiled.

That night I sat in my bedroom with two Hot Topic shopping bags sandwiching my cold body. I listened to the new Yellowcard CD on repeat, a gift my sister picked up for me at F.Y.E. while my mother and I were treating ourselves to pretzels from Auntie Ann's. Every time I closed my eyes, I saw myself lying in a bed of red silk. The sounds of gravel and dirt surrounded me. Even the smells were strange, aromas similar to rotting fruit and orange clay mud leftover from a hillside construction site, and I had to open my eyes to remind myself that I was *there*.

I didn't sleep much that night. I expected that.

The rest of the school year came and went in an agonizingly slow, dizzying haze.

Our 8th grade year didn't end right. Everyone anticipated that.

At the 8th grade graduation ceremony, classmates were handed awards in regards to the end of the year 8th grade trip to Charleston. Audrey and I received the Worst Driver awards, since she and I were the only ones to get banned from driving on the Go-Kart track. We literally lasted one lap, and that was because I full-throttled my way to the front of the line—only to T-bone Audrey as she veered out of control. The Go-Karts suffered severe damage. My legs were bruised, and Audrey had a little cut on her arm. While the rest of our class waited in line for the Go-Karts, Audrey and I played laser tag with another class from a different school, and we managed to give the Red Team a victory every single round.

The worst part of the trip was when I was catatonic in my hotel bed, my suitemates unable to motivate me to move. One of the chaperones had to climb in bed with me and sing me back to life. She was my homeroom teacher, Mrs. Simmons. She held me, massaged my back, wiped away my tears, and refused to leave until I smiled. I will never forget that.

Mrs. Simmons must have called my mother after that happened, because every time the class went somewhere, my mother called the business to check up on me. I was so numb that I didn't even feel embarrassed when she called me at the bowling alley. Over the sound system, the shoe attendant said, "Abigail Kavanagh, please come to the front desk." I solemnly walked up, retrieved the phone, told her I was okay, and hung up.

All parents were given schedules before the trip outlining where the class would be, but my mother seemed to be the only parent who actually studied the list. She knew the phone numbers to every establishment in downtown Charleston after that.

Lilly didn't go on the 8th grade trip. I would have called her to check up on her, had she not hissed, "Don't call me," before we parted ways after school the week before.

The graduation ceremony ended with the junior high choir singing songs from the spring concert lineup, including the 8th grade graduation song of choice. There was a short moment of silence right before the last song, which was a Motown Medley put together by Mr. Banks himself. I sat at the piano, sheet music ready, microphone dangling in front of me. Nearby, classmate and friend Samuel Smith held a good-sized acoustic guitar in his lap. He stared over at me and mouthed, "What's going on?"

I mouthed back, "I have no idea."

We should have started the medley by then.

Right before Mr. Banks cued us to begin, Lilly dedicated her solo to Ryan, saying into the microphone, "This last song is for you." It caused the entire crowd, class included, to feel the weight of her loss as she sang. Everyone looking at her, she swallowed hard and readied herself. Her hair looked strange; it was an odd yellow-gray color at the time. Linda had made her dye away the black and red soon after Ryan died. Linda also made her get rid of all of her clothes from Hot Topic. Lilly's wardrobe was now bubbly and bright, and everything came from either Aéropostale or American Eagle.

Slowly, as Lilly approached the solo microphone, the tempo dwindled. I quickly shifted my electric piano from 144 (jazz punch) to 256 (strings).

Then she started singing, flawlessly, effortlessly, letting the words slip from her lips like Chinese silk. "People say, I'm the life of the party, 'cause I tell a joke or two. Although I might be laughin', loud and hearty, deep inside I'm blue. So take a good look at my face. You'll see my smile looks out of place. If you look closer, it's easy to trace the tracks of my tears." She blinked back tears. We all saw it. But she never once cried as she sang.

Her fists clenched at her sides, and she cried out, "I need you, need you."

It didn't make sense, how someone who was as skinny and frail as her could possess a voice heavy enough to break steel.

Chills crippled my body as I listened to her sing, and I nearly skipped over keys my eyes were so flooded with tears. It was a confusing cry; I wasn't sure if I was crying out of happiness, or sorrow.

Next to me, Samuel bit down on his bottom lip and pushed all of his emotion into his guitar. I was close enough to him to see that he was crying, too. In between strums, he flashed me a worried expression. I knew he was concerned that I was going to tell someone I saw him crying. I tried to smile. I tried to tell him with facial expressions that his secret was safe with me; then we both returned to our instruments.

The best part of the song was fast approaching. I readied the climax of the song by flashing into horrible posture, placing my lips directly on the micro-phone, fingertips still holding out the chord and ready to move at the sound of the choir's finger snaps. Lilly pushed both of her arms behind her, clasping her hands together at the small of her back. While she sang from the depths of her little lungs, I pounded away at the keyboard in unison with her staccato singing. Samuel closed his eyes, lifted his knees one at a time, up and down, and Mr. Banks nodded in rhythm.

We all played together, sang together; the choir was one with Lilly.

She screamed out, "My smile is my makeup, I wear since my breakup with you. Baby, take a good look at my face. You see my smile looks out of place. Yeah, just look closer, it's easy to trace, the tracks of my tears. Baby, baby, baby, baby—"

The crowd erupted in applause before the song was even finished.

As Lilly stepped back from the microphone, the small crowd in front of us stood. The rush of their bodies lifting in the air, the snapping sounds of palms smacking against each other... The applause was enough for Lilly to see, right then, that everything would be okay.

The audience looked like it was glittering. Turning off the electric piano, staring out into the adults watching their children graduate from middle school, I determined that the glitter was in fact everyone's tears as they applauded Lilly for both her performance and for her ability to make it through.

She turned to look at me. She smiled, mouthed something like, "You played well," and then disappeared back into the mouth of the junior high choir.

The applause continued far after we finished our performance. When Mr. Banks dismissed the students, adults formed a line to congratulate Lilly on her solo.

Even as I graduated from 8th grade and officially became the dreadful label of high school freshman, even though the celebration was pretty much perfect and all of us seemed like a tight-knit happy family, those types of moments don't last forever. I knew that. Everyone knew that.

Not long after school let out, I had to attend my sister's graduation from high school. It wasn't until my mother and I walked hand in hand into the commons area that I realized why she wanted to hold my hand in the first place. A banner was draped across the top level of the platform: a sheet of white covered in blue and red handprints, signatures, and small blocks of words written in Sharpie. Something covered every single inch of its surface.

The banner's largest message: *We Will Miss You*

The entire student body signed the banner, all 130 students. It was the first time in years that the high school all came together.

I stood in front of the banner until my eyes filled with dust. It wasn't my intention to read every single note, every single memento that a classmate of Ryan's wrote in his honor. Instead, I traced the shapes of classmates' hands, and I compared them to the pages of handprints I had traced back in one of my first journals, the one hiding underneath my bed that I had dedicated solely to Ryan, many years earlier. Nobody had quite the hand shape that he had. His hands were small, perhaps smaller than mine, with thin, frail fingers and knuckles that always appeared bone white underneath his skin.

Eventually, my mother tugged at my arm. "Abigail, honey, let's go."

"Okay."

My mother made me sit close to her in the high school auditorium. A haze washed over my eyes, a puddle of iridescent colors that was far too thick to look through.

I didn't mentally attend my sister's graduation. Physically, perhaps, but my mind was elsewhere. I was elsewhere. Shortly after Ryan passed away, my therapist upped the dosage of my medicine yet again. The side effects were terrifying, but I was willing to accept the numbness, at least for a little while. I needed to feel numb for the next few days if I wanted to get through it all.

While my sister approached the graduation podium, gleaming and beautiful, her usual glittery self and all things pink, I sat like a balloon in the audience, swaying with the sough of applause, back and forth. My mother continued pushing me away, only for me to come right back. She did this for at least two hours.

Rumors churned again after the community saw me in the audience. A lot of people asked my mother why she still let me wear black clothing with skulls and crossbones and blood. My mother always responded, "If I don't let her rebel in clothes, where will she go next?" Stream Ridge compared my mother's parenting skills to Linda's parenting skills, so it seemed the community was confused that Lilly was forced to shed her dark exterior while I was able to keep mine. The reason the rumors started up again was because people believed that I was doing drugs. They couldn't determine why else I was suddenly so frail. It was almost as if they had forgotten that I had just lost a friend to suicide a few weeks before.

For days, I waited for the phone to ring. I was hopeful that Lilly would eventually call me and ask me to purge, so that she could catch everything, mold it together, fix it, hand it back to me, and make everything better. It was her turn to take my waste and turn it into something beautiful, the same exact thing I had done for her the day Ryan died.

After a few days, I grew impatient.

Then a week went by.

Then a month.

Eventually, I gave in and called her. She answered in a feigned exhausted voice. "Hello?"

"I need to talk about him," I said.

She made a noise, like smacking her lips together. "Abigail, no, I'm done talking about him."

I wasn't letting her get away. "I need to tell you something." At that point, I wanted to tell Lilly everything—the morphine, the knives, our late night conversations long before she was ever involved, the fact that the boy never slept—because I needed someone else to know, someone else to feel guilty for harboring such details.

I could pretty much see the look on Lilly's face as I said it. Eyes falling back, eyebrows jerking, the look of total disbelief spreading across her face. She sniffed hard. "I don't care, Abigail. I don't want to talk about this right now. God, can I go one day without someone asking me about him?"

My heart doubled in size, I was so angry. "Well, no, you can't. You can't just step out of the picture at your own convenience." I bit my bottom lip. "Lilly. *I need to talk about him.*"

Slowly, the pressure draped across my shoulders lightened. It was a beautiful thing, physically feeling the weight of her control lift from my body.

She breathed out through her nose with so much force that she could have knocked me over. "I want to spend this summer alone. I don't want to see you or Laney or anyone. Okay? You don't understand. You never will. So just leave me alone." Lilly didn't even say goodbye before she hung up. I listened to the two clicks, followed by at least five or six beeps, before I, too, disconnected the call.

I threw the cordless phone across the room. My sister heard it from her bedroom, on the opposite side of the house. She came running to find me huddled over on my floor, holding my legs against my chest, screaming until veins exploded in my throat.

Diana was never a caring big sister. Yet as I continued to scream and cry out and imagine the various ways I could kill Lilly with my own two hands, my sister knelt down and pulled me hard into her chest. At one point, she left and came back with a glass of water to mend the sand in my throat.

Her long fingernails gently scraped my scalp. She smelled like an angel. The singer that she was, she rocked me back and forth and sang to me one of my favorite songs, "Only Hope," from the movie *A Walk to Remember*. In the midst of my kerfuffle, I begged her not to tell any of her friends that I was crying so hard like a baby. She replied, in a high, soft voice, "You're my little sister. I just want you to be okay."

Now that I needed a friend in Lilly, now that she was at a point in her life where she could wake up without thinking about taking her own life, she was suddenly too busy to be there for me? Ryan had passed away almost a month earlier. I was there for her for weeks.

It was finally a sufficient time after for me to spill my guts, to talk her ear off about how *I* felt, but it wasn't expedient for her. What about Laney? When would she be given a time to mourn?

I felt as if Laney and I went from thirteen to thirty in a matter of days. We put on adult faces, walking around with this aura of knowledge that we could listen to anyone about anything and still have enough courage to face life head-on. It wouldn't have been fair of me to call Laney and ask her if I could talk to her about Ryan, when she may not have been given a moment of closure, either.

That was all I wanted. I wanted closure.

The only person who could give me that was too preoccupied with her own so-called hard, misunderstood life to lend a helping hand to the girl who had saved her over and over and over again.

My sister held me out in front of her so I had to look at her. She was so beautiful. "Abigail, do you want to talk to me about anything?"

As much as I wanted to talk to her, to someone, about what was going on in my warped little head, I didn't want to waste it on my sister. So I shook my head and softly said, "No, thanks." She told me that she loved me again before she exited my bedroom.

Glancing over, I saw the back of the cordless phone on one side of my bed. The phone itself was somewhere near my dresser. I would have to explain to Patrick later why the phone was missing its back. Right then, however, I crawled into bed and stared out my open window. I stared for days.

I spent the first half of the summer cleaning out my MSN Messenger folders so that a_nightmares_fear@msn.com never existed, including archived conversations between me and Ryan as far back as 2001. Nothing was more difficult than telling MSN Messenger that I was sure that I wanted to delete all of those files.

Shortly after that, I slipped in bed and felt as if I would never leave. Audrey visited on occasion, but she didn't do much other than beg me to play Digimon World on PlayStation so she could watch me, something we did many years earlier. During my best mornings, I had enough strength to tell her to go away; when I was too weak to fight back, she would hook up the PlayStation, hand me the controller, and tell me to play. I only played for a few minutes—never longer than an hour—but it was enough for her to fall asleep on the bed next to me. I slept next to her every time.

On her last visit, she threatened to never see me again if I didn't get out of bed. She also ordered me to call all of my friends and make sure they were okay, too. In her archaic, wise voice, she said to me, "You're not the only one sad, okay?" and closed my bedroom door.

My friends and family misunderstood the new heaviness that weighed me down. I wasn't incapacitated in my own self-despair because I missed Ryan. Frankly, that was the sort of feeling that lay deep underneath my skin, like a years-old splinter: something that would always be there, and only bother me when I remembered. I refused to leave my bedroom because I hated myself. I hated myself for not telling someone else about his morphine addiction and the knives underneath his pillows, as if sharing those two facts with someone else could have somehow saved him from himself.

A part of me was absolutely sure that the spontaneous, lethally impulsive behavior he demonstrated shortly before taking his own life was a direct side effect of the medicine.

The fact that nobody else, not even Kimmie or Lilly, mentioned morphine, knives, or insomnia was a haunting thing when the pieces came together, and I learned that I was perhaps the only person who knew.

Instead of telling anyone why I felt so damn sad, I did as Audrey said and picked up the phone.

First, I called Scott. He didn't offer me anything more than the last time we spoke on the phone, but at least he wasn't lying when he said Jace was getting better. I asked him if it would be inappropriate for me to call Jace. Instead of answering me, Scott told me to hang on, and before I knew it, he was attaching me to a three-way call with Jace. He didn't sound like the Jace I'd met at the football game a year before, but at least he laughed at Scott's jokes, and he asked me if I wanted to go to the first Stream Ridge Fair with him and Scott in a few days. I said yes.

A part of me believed it to be a date. The sound of Jace's voice when he told me goodbye made me believe it, too.

After calling Laney and crying for a few seconds, we promised each other to stay friends and to not let his death affect that. I knew we made that promise because Lilly couldn't promise the same.

Finally, I called Lilly. I was shocked when she actually answered the phone. "Hello?"

I tried not to frown. "Hey, what's up?"

"Not much. You?"

I should have told her the truth, that I was rotting from the inside, that I was losing my hair, that I couldn't eat or sleep or think, that I just needed her to be there the same way that I was there for her. "Same."

There was a lot of air time. She sniffed a few times, and I took large sips of coffee so it was impossible for her not to hear me. In between moments of complete silence, I thought about how she spent her summer. Lilly had friends, but Laney and I were her closest; so without us, what did she even do? Linda probably took her shopping a lot. Maybe she and Bradley got closer with Ryan's passing. Maybe she was finally catching up on having a decent relationship with her older brother.

I opened my mouth to ask her if she was going to the Stream Ridge Fair.

Lilly started before I could. "Abigail, I am okay now."

Coffee caught in my throat. I coughed until the walls of my esophagus cleared. "Uhh, erm, sorry. What?"

She repeated herself down to the finest of articulation. "Abigail, I am okay now."

I drew circles in the beige carpet. I was sitting at the computer desk, but not in the computer chair. "Well, that's good. That's really good."

"I'm glad you were there. I could not have made it through it all without you."

Those were her exact words. That was her metanoia.

I didn't say anything at first. My ears were still in disbelief that Lilly was admitting something like that to me. She wasn't the kind of person anymore to hand out compliments, to show any form of gratitude, to acknowledge that she was not alone. My grip on the cordless phone tightened. Erasing my carpet circles with the heels of my feet, I started drawing other things. Three stick figures, a heart between each of them, a line bisecting one of those hearts, and blood. Everywhere, blood.

My hand swallowed the shortest stick figure. Me. I covered it with my palm and bit down hard on my bottom lip. "Me, too."

"Hey, did you want to come over this weekend and spend the night?"

I erased her stick figure, leaving just Ryan in my carpet's skin. "Maybe next time. I have some things I need to do with my mother, like clean the house and stuff."

Lilly sighed. "Oh, well, that's okay. Yeah, next time."

"I'll see you at the fair?"

"Yeah, sure."

I just couldn't bring myself to tell her that I didn't want to stay with her.

The weekend before school started, I met Scott and Jace at the Stream Ridge Fair. Both of them appeared different, in a lighter, more shallow shell than I recalled, but I also noted their more positive features, like how Jace's face was complemented with a pale glow, a film of oil just thin enough that it cast a light across his soft face; and Scott's feathered hair was uncontrollable in the wind skirting all of the mechanical rides. Every time he righted his hair, he cried out, "Goddamnit, son of a bitch! God, wind, get the fuck out of here!"

We walked around the Field of Dreams, each taking note of certain areas, exact places, where a fourth person should have joined us: in line for the Round Up, swapping corn dogs for popcorn, smacking friends with inflatable animals and running away.

In between conversations, we could hear Lilly singing from the entertainment stage near the front of the grass lot. She was booked as one of three performers for the weekend. My eyes found her every few minutes, her slender, tall body stepping left or left, blonde hair cut right below her tiny ears, skin tanned, green eyes stealing all of the summer light—it was almost like I was seeing a new person there, a new girl wearing brand-name clothes in pinks and blues, white sneakers, and plain hair.

The black was gone. Her darkness wasn't coming back.

As the three of us walked in front of the stage, I momentarily looked over my shoulder. Lilly saw me in the growing crowd of lawn chairs and flannel shirts. She held the microphone up, a gesture to say hello, and then she dropped back in her lyrics, eyes focused on those there to see her, knowing that now was her time of recovery: nobody else's, her time to show the community that betrayed her that she was okay. She belted out, "I need you. I need you."

It came as no surprise that "Tracks of My Tears" was in her lineup that evening. It was the song that suited her most.

I went home that night realizing that I may have been one of the last to move on.

The reality was sickening. It was heavy, too, almost too much for my frail arms to carry. But I dropped my Blink-182 CD in my player, and I listened to "I Miss You" over and over again.

"Don't waste your time on me you're already the voice inside my head." I hated how right that was.

Before I started high school, before Scott and Jace began their junior year without one of their closest friends, we had to do it. We had to move on. We had to stop searching the most profound recesses of our brains. We had to stop swimming through years upon years of memories for even the smallest fragment of evidence—for answers. That was the most difficult, horrifically beautiful part about moving on. We closed the book without ever knowing the ending.

We would spend the rest of our lives not knowing *why*.

It happened without us knowing, and maybe that was how it should have been.

It was like one day, Ryan suddenly stopped walking alongside us. We used to be a group, a family, a mold for one another. If we were separated, air pockets and holes were exposed.

We turned as one, and asked him in one voice if he was coming along. We asked if we needed to stop so he could take a break, but he waved us off, smiling the entire time, and reassured us. "Go on, I'll catch up." Believing him, we turned and kept going.

It took us a long time to keep going, to not look back, and to never stop.

After that, sometimes I dared to look over my shoulder. A different part of him was there, far off in the distance. Blurred and out of focus, but still there. Most days, I saw him as I did on the bus ride the day before he died, with his orange-topped black hair, yesterday's heavy eyeliner, and unlaced combat boots. The better days, I could reach out and grab a young boy wearing a blue t-shirt decorated with white wolves and Chinese calligraphy, and he was wiping his nose on the top of my hand, licking at the crusted corners of his mouth, all just like I remembered.

The best day was when I turned to see him, and he was not there.

Then I felt something next to me. Without looking, I knew he was there, just like he said.

That was how we moved on. That was the only way we could live after losing him. That didn't mean we missed him any less.

Sixteen

On the first anniversary of Ryan's passing, Stream Ridge High School bought a golden plaque in his honor and placed it on his locker, the only way a school itself could keep his memory alive. The plaque read "In Loving Memory, Ryan Matthew Mills, 1988-2004." The students glorified this plaque on May 11th, 2005. By the end of the school day, his locker was covered in notes from those who missed him and magazine cut-outs of phrases and images some thought he might have liked.

In between classes, groups of three or four stood in front of Ryan's locker, respecting the fact that the padlock would never be opened. They took turns reading aloud their mementos before taping them up with the others. Some even prayed.

Scott and Jace stood there a lot longer than most. Lilly, meanwhile, navigated the halls as empty as a corpse. I monitored her, watching like a hawk. That was how I knew she never once stopped at the locker. She never wrote a letter. She wouldn't dare lower herself to that kind of publicity.

When the class of 2006 graduated, Jace approached the podium and recited a poem that he and Cameron wrote in honor of Ryan. Parts of the poem were taken from some pieces Ryan himself wrote, years earlier. Two porcelain pillars stood next to him as he chanted the poem, with Ryan's full name in gold on each. The poem, "Carousel," gripped the entire audience.

As I stood with the high school choir on the risers, I quickly searched the crowd for Lilly. She was sitting with the school's spring band, clutching her flute with a ravenous desperation, her arms trembling, her shoulders jerking back as she cried out and crumbled in front of the entire community.

The high school principal asked for a moment of silence.

That was when we heard at least fifty people crying. It was awful.

The hardest part of that graduation was seeing Mrs. Livingston waiting in the commons area, with a single red rose in her hand. She was one of the 8th grade homeroom teachers for Gunners Valley School, and every year, she asked that 8th grade class to fill out a personal form, a series of questions like, "Who is your best friend?" and "What is your favorite subject?" She sealed those forms for four years and gave them back to the 8th graders when they graduated high school, a test to see just how much had changed since their original entries.

Mrs. Livingston carried a single red rose for Ryan. In her other hand, she held his sealed form. Norma accepted her son's form with an embrace. She left Stream Ridge High School that evening and never went back.

By the time my class graduated in 2008, Ryan was nothing more than a friend we honored and remembered at least once a year. We knew better than to give him any more time than that. Had we succumbed to the profoundness of our hunger for answers, we wouldn't have made it.

I eventually buried my questions and my desperation for closure shortly after I graduated high school. There was no point in me still clinging to the idea that Lilly would set aside a few minutes to listen to me gush about what I knew that she didn't, about her late boyfriend. I wasn't able to know what closure tasted like. I never knew; she never let me. After all, she went to a different college for nursing, while I pursued a degree in English. She flunked out twice and moved to one of the Carolinas.

Last I heard, she was divorcing her first husband and moving back to West Virginia to live with Linda.

I would never know if Lilly knew about the morphine. I would never know if she knew about the five knives underneath Ryan's pillow.

As for Scott, Jace, and Cameron, they began their lives after high school at different colleges. Scott and Cameron went to Fairmont State University, and Jace to Shepherd University. For years they occupied one another's weekends with old-school video games and craft beer. Jace spoiled them with his Betty Crocker touch of homemade chocolate chip cookie balls and pizza from scratch. I occasionally claimed the couch as my own while the three of them traded turns duking it out on *Joust*.

For years the four of us shared stories, some of our most shameful memories, and the worst kind of feelings. Not once did any of us mention Ryan. We left it at that.

There was one thing that we all noticed. Without having to say a single word, we were aware of the strange happening that repeated itself since Ryan passed away. Every year after his death, on May 11th, it rained in Stream Ridge, West Virginia. It did this for ten years.

The first few times we believed the sunny showers to be coincidence, an anomaly of sorts—but after the fourth year, we couldn't find any more excuses. We couldn't deny it.

The tenth year, in 2014, I waited at my bedroom window for some sort of shower, a rain or a dew. A few days shy of turning 24, I sat in the window sill with a fox plushie clutched in my hands, like a child waiting for something. My husband, Mathieu, asked me every few minutes if I wanted to come to the living room to watch television with him. I kept turning him away with silence. As he approached the door, he pulled me with his voice alone, saying, "I love you. So much."

My words trembled. "I love you, too, honey. I'm okay. I will be okay."

Mathieu eventually left and came back with a cup of coffee. In his coal-colored eyes, the almond shapes softened underneath his dark eyebrows, I saw in him that he couldn't understand why I waited for so long. He didn't know why I was upset when I didn't see a single drop fall from the Alabama sky. He healed me with a kiss and told me to come out when I was better.

When I didn't see any rain that day, I emailed Kimmie and asked her if it was raining in West Virginia.

As disappointed as me, she told me no.

That was when we knew.

Acknowledgements

Moon River has seen its fair share of drafts. It is a novel that required four years of personal research, careful reflection, and a journey back into the mind of a child. I did not travel that road alone, and for that, I must thank the following individuals:

My husband, who listened to me purge my memories and carried me the last four years while I sobbed and whined and drank far too much coffee (and sometimes alcohol).

Kassandra Broadwater, who without her guidance and warm motivation, I never would have continued with this painful, yet beautiful journey. She answered all of my questions, and she never once doubted me. *Moon River* would be nothing without her, and that is why I wrote it for her and her family.

My mother and my father, who always supported me in my dream to become a writer.

Jane Pearson and Sarah Gardiner, who lovingly took *Moon River* under their wings and gave it necessary and critical reviews. Sometimes even with witty commentary fueled with an evening's glass of red wine (here's looking at you, Pear).

The Sapp family, who gave me a childhood filled with the wild and comfort of the Appalachia.

And to the team from Jan-Carol Publishing, who decided to give *Moon River* a chance.

Thank you.

About the Author

Born and raised in the heart of the Appalachia, Amber spent her childhood growing up on gravel roads and playing Pokémon Red on her Game Boy Color. At the age of 10, she discovered her fascination with creative writing and turned a 1-page homework assignment into a 35-page document for her 5th grade teacher. Less than a year later, she wrote her very first book about a female basketball player with leukemia. She is determined to never share it with anyone.

After graduating Magna Cum Laude from West Virginia University in 2012 with a bachelor's degree in English literature and a concentration in creative writing, Amber moved to northern Alabama to marry her husband after meeting him in a Dragon Ball Z chat room. She is currently employed as a senior technical writer and Scrum Master for a software company. In her free time, she enjoys playing League of Legends and discovering dive bars with her girlfriends. You may contact her on Twitter and Instagram (@amberdtran) or visit her website at amberdtran.com.

www.ingramcontent.com/pod-product-compliance
Lightning Source LLC
Chambersburg PA
CBHW030116260626
47156CB00008B/2684